VICIOUS PUNKS

DOLLS AND DOUCHEBAGS PART TWO

MADELINE FAY

"They say all good boys go to heaven but bad boys bring heaven to you."
~Julia Michaels~
Here's to everyone finding themselves and healing.
You're a true Queen.

TRIGGER WARNING

PROLOGUE

Payne

"Hold still, you stupid cunt," I sneer down at Lorrie as she flops around on the table like a fish out of water.

Worthless whore can't tolerate her cocaine anymore, just a spaced out junkie who will do anything for the next hit. I should just kill her, a bullet right through the skull, but then again she is good at spreading her legs with a smile on her face and a needle in her arm. Obedient. Loyal. Those are the only things I ask for, people to be squeezed tightly in my fist. My fist bangs on the table near Lorrie's hip, startling her enough that she stops sliding her hands up and down her body that's pumped full of drugs. She shoots up into a sitting position with a screech leaving her gaping mouth. Fucking powder slides off her stomach and on top of the table underneath her, disappearing through the cracks of the floor. So much money goes in and out of the club with drugs, but to waste it like that makes my eyes haze over until all I'm seeing is red.

The rock music shuts off abruptly, my club members looking over from their lounging positions around the bar. I grab Lorrie's halter top, that's stuck to her sweat slicked skin, to bring her closer to my face until her trembling chin is almost touching my beard.

"I'm this close to making an example out of you." I grab her cheeks, squeezing until her wide eyes focus on me, terror shining through them. "You remember what happened to Tillie, don't you? How you gloated for weeks after she was fucked within an inch of her life, left bleeding on the basement floor. Why don't we see if you can scream higher than she did." My spit flies into her reddening face; the harder I squeeze, the more labored her breathing becomes.

She shakes her head in my grip, her puckered lips trying to move, but I've had enough with how worthless she is. At least the other cunt, Tillie, looked me in the eyes, yearning to be broken. I was just the man to place her right under my boot to control. I should have taken more from her, made her remember who's in charge, just like I did with her mother. Women, all good for only one thing. I become more enraged the longer I think about that slut running away from me. Roughly grabbing Lorrie off the table, I push the sobbing mess away from me in disgust. She crashes into a chair on unsteady feet, the legs of it breaking under her weight and leaving her on the floor, pleading up at me.

"I'm sorry! I'm sorry, Payne!" she screeches through pathetic sobs, disgusting me further and making my club brothers laugh at her expense.

The music starts back up, the sound of fucking and

drunken laughter resumes as if nothing happened. They know their place, who's the leader, and when to turn a blind eye. Liquor spills, drugs are passed around, and there's enough pussy to last all night, no matter how used. My boots stomp across the worn wood floors, passing two of my members fucking a sweetbutt at the same time on the pool table. Her moans are high from pleasure, but it's not the kind of sound I like to hear anymore. It's unsatisfying, I want to hear her scream in pain instead. I want...no... I *need* Tillie begging for her life, on her knees, as my hands cause her unbelievable suffering.

"Nix! Where the hell is Cruz?" I bellow, fed up after everyone looks at me with blank stares.

Cruz has earned my respect over the years, killing and getting rid of bodies without questioning me. It's unnerving how he stares at me as if at any minute he'll stab me in the back, and not give a fuck, as he burns the rest of the club to the ground. I try to keep an eye on him at all times because something about him doesn't sit right with me, like he's lacking any emotions with that empty gaze of his. Although he doesn't question my shit like my little brother used to. Since Rig disappeared, Cruz stepped up and paved a way to show that he earned his spot. I did promise Tillie to him, but that cunt is mine and only mine to have. She deserves everything she gets and what is coming for her, thinking she can escape me. You can never leave hell once you've been burned by the flames.

"He's in the basement again," Nix says in a bored tone, leaning against the bar with a beer in his hand as he watches the debauchery taking place.

Without another word, I walk past the high table tops and approach the basement door that holds a lot of memories for me and spilled blood. The door creaks on its hinges as it opens. I descend the wooden stairs, my boots stomping down each step to announce my approach. I'm not surprised he's down here without any lights on. I've caught him sitting down here enough times in the dark.

"Jesus fuck, Cruz," I grind out through my teeth, once I flip the lights on and see him clearly.

He's sitting in a chair looking up at the rafters that hold rusty chains that have been well used over the years, his head tipped back as he smiles at the ceiling. His hair is slicked back, greasier than usual, and he has dark circles under his eyes. But it's the crazed smile that has me scratching my beard, eyeing him warily. His obsession with the girl started when I took him in as a kid, he followed her around with a need to watch her every move. I remember seeing the empty look in his eyes that day I found him in an alleyway. Not once showing fear for the big, scary biker in front of him, and it made my decision easy. I molded him into the man he is today, he'll do as I say until one day he doesn't. A man's control snaps suddenly and without warning, but I think Cruz never really had control over his urges. It's only a matter of time but I'll be the first to pull the trigger until then. He has his uses, getting the job done without caring who he has to kill.

"You know, Payne, I find it funny how secrets can reveal themselves over time. Something buried so deep can rise to the surface, even a missing body can be found eventually." He chuckles to himself, his icy blue eyes suddenly connecting with mine.

My head pounds in sync with the blood rushing through my body as my anger controls me, making my nose bleed from the excessive cocaine use. I let it soak into my beard, watching how Cruz's eyes follow the trail of blood with a hungry gaze. I crack my neck side to side to relieve the tension there and walk behind his chair while fixing my cut, he stares straight ahead once more. He doesn't fear me standing behind his back. I've seen death, caused it plenty of times, and seen the grim reaper claim a soul. For Cruz, I think even death doesn't want to linger around him.

"What are you going on about, boy?" I ask casually, picking up tools randomly on the workbench, and notice something misplaced near the knives.

A tan piece of fabric with a design rests against the table wrapped in a napkin, with jagged edges and its color a discolored brown. Not the most messed up thing I've seen, but to see the cut up piece of flesh laying there like a delicately wrapped gift... really takes the icing on the cake.

"You recognize that tattoo?" he asks with a smile in his voice, ignoring my question.

My secrets go to the grave with me. Only myself and Rig know my deepest secret, the one that could ruin me, but he's gone, so there's only me left. I peer closer at the raised design, seeing the club's Demon Jokers symbol with small red roses surrounding it and the edge of wings cut off from the rest. Yeah, I recognize it.

Doris.

She's been around the club for a long time, a sweet-butt, but never an old lady. The club took Doris in long before Lorrie even showed up. Lorrie doesn't even know who Tillie's real mom is, but I placed her in that role of motherhood so no one could ever question it. As if you could even call Lorrie a mom. I internally scoff at that. She hates Tillie because of the attention I give her. Not even the other Demon Jokers dare to bring up who Tillie's real mother is, the ones who have been riding since I became President keep their traps shut. It's in the past, where it belongs. It does something to me if anyone dares question me, makes me pull the trigger faster than they can blink. It would make sense that Cruz doesn't know because no one utters a word behind my back.

"Your methods don't surprise me anymore, Cruz. What did she do?" I slam my fist on the table at the thought of her double crossing me.

If she's betrayed me, I'll lock her up where the sun doesn't shine and make her wish for death. It doesn't matter that she's kept my bed warm over the years, she's just another warm cunt to sink into.

"I found your traitor and she had a lot to say. I left a nice little present on your bed for you." He chuckles in delight, the chair creaking as he climbs to his feet to walk towards the stairs and glances over his shoulder just before he reaches the door. "She said that Tillie was hiding with her mom but I find it funny that Lorrie seems to be walking around daughterless. Don't you? But don't worry, I'm going to find her and she won't be going anywhere once I have her in my grasp. Finders keepers right, Payne?" He smirks and climbs the stairs without a backward glance.

My breathing is labored as uncontrollable fury consumes me. The door shuts behind him and not a moment too soon as I swipe my arm across the bench of torture devices, sending them flying.

After all I've done for that kid and this is how he repays me? Thinking he can take something that is right-fully mine, no matter what I've promised him. He should know by now that lies come out of my mouth in smoke.

He knows my secret, that small thread of information he just hung over my head tells me that Cruz is now a threat. I won't be having anyone taking my position as President, not until I'm ready to hand it over. I'm not going to be knocking at death's door early because of Cruz stabbing me in the back.

I'll just have to get to him first, let him find that ungrateful cunt and maybe I'll let him go a few rounds with her before I kill him, too. Making my decision, a smile spreads across my lips as I head back upstairs and to the main part of the compound. Nix is still in the same spot, leaning against the bar while watching two whores get face fucked on the pool table. He catches my eye as I give him a head nod to follow me from across the room.

"Get the fuck out of my way before I'm having someone dig your grave. Ever been buried alive?" I ask the drunk prospect, whose name I can't recall or care to remember, but he's blocking the hallway that leads towards my office and bedroom. I watch him in disgust as his dilated eyes widen and he stumbles away, mumbling excuses under his breath like a little bitch.

I'm grinding my teeth by the time I swing my door open and instantly take a step back at the rancid stench that hits my nostrils. I've been wondering why Doris has been avoiding me, I guess I know the reason. That fucking cocksucker cut her up until she's almost unrecognizable and left her on my Goddamn king mattress. I honestly thought the useless woman was avoiding me because she knew I was planning to give Tillie to Cruz. The whore doesn't know that Tillie would always be under my boot, no matter who thinks she belongs to them. I own this compound, the people I feed and continue feeding until they want for nothing...They signed their lives away to me right when they chose this path. Once a Demon Jokers, always a Demon Jokers. Patch in and patch out by death.

"Damn, Payne. At least clean up after yourself," Nix suggests with a gag, wrinkling his nose at the sight of Doris spread eagle on my bed.

I should feel something. I've known the whore for a very long time, she's warmed my bed a lot over the years, but I couldn't care less to be honest. She wasn't always a Demon Joker, jumping from club to club until she landed here just like all the whores before her. There was one she stayed with for a long while...what was that club's name? Devils? Some Charter based out in Los Angeles... Rig did some business with their president years ago. Come to think of it, he's the one that brought Doris back home with him. A shame really she's dead, she knew what I liked in bed, but I have just the person in mind to warm it whether she wants to or not.

"Cruz has a way of getting a message across, does he not?" I nod to the twisted way Cruz stripped pieces of her skin until she only resembled a juicy slab of meat. I mean fuck, the kid even took out her eyeballs.

"He's stepping out of line, boss. Should we just kill him before he gets any ideas?" Nix picks at his nails with his knife in a nervous gesture and looks at me with a raised eyebrow in question before quickly shifting his gaze away.

"Not yet. If anyone can find her, it's him. He wants her badly enough and he's the only person I know who won't sleep until she's his completely. I want you to keep an eye on him and let me know what's going on." I hold eye contact with him until he swallows hard and glances away.

"Yeah, I'll contact you if anything comes up." Nix spins

around to leave but before he's halfway down the hallway, he glances over his shoulder at me. "A dangerous game you're playing, Payne. You should have left Cruz on the streets because even I know he won't hesitate to kill you if you try to stop him from getting Tillie." With that, he enters back into the bar and disappears into the sound of drunken laughter echoing through the music, along with pussies being fucked roughly.

My rage explodes once I'm completely alone.

My boot connects with the door over and over until it's hanging off its hinges and blood is dripping from my nose again, mixing with the cocaine from earlier. Looking at Doris with disgust, I head back into the main compound to fuck some pussy, willing or not, snort another hit of pure white powder, and all while wondering who I can trust within my walls. No one can know my secret. I'll kill anyone who tries to take over my club, to expose my lies. Anyone.

I need to go back to the beginning because the only person who would know where Diana is hiding is Rig. Impossible to ask him since he's gone, but that doesn't mean he didn't leave any hints behind as to where that cunt is. I could let Cruz find her first, but something tells me he's gunning for my spot, my legacy. And once he has her, there's no stopping him from doing whatever he wants.

My club won't think I'm fit to be president anymore if I can't handle my own daughter. Cruz will prove that to them. My time is running thin and that makes me a desperate man.

I'll do anything to stay in power. Anything.

CHAPTER 1

Tillie

I don't know how long I lay on the cold garage floor, staring at the small dent in the red toolbox and willing myself to cry, but nothing ever happens. I've shed so many tears throughout the years that now, even when I try my hardest to cry, nothing ever spills.

"I-I can't go through that door," I croak out, leaning heavily against Doris as she stumbles under my weight and grips the doorknob tightly to keep us both from falling, before she turns her head to look at me.

"You're not free yet, girl, but for now...you walk through that door with your head held high, no matter how much you want to look down. Don't. I don't care if you have to crawl your way out of here, but don't give them this power. They took enough away from you already," Doris grounds out through her teeth, wiping a trail of blood away from my hairline. She

grasps my hand that is thrown over her shoulder into a death grip.

My breathing is shallow, my ribs protesting with each breath, and the pain between my sticky thighs, that makes my legs buckle, is a reminder of what just happened.

"I don't know if I can survive out there. What if I fall and can never get back up? Even those who look like they are sleeping peacefully are trapped in a nightmare. Will I ever really escape my living nightmares, even if I'm far away from this place?"

Doris glances at me for what feels like a long time, until she slowly shakes her head.

"You may be in a nightmare now but that's the thing about living a dream, you can make it anything you want. It will take some time, a lot of obstacles along the way that will be painful, but one day you won't hurt as much as you do now. It will always stay with you, but it won't feel like you can't breathe." She swings open the door without waiting for me to respond and grabs my chin with her free hand, so I don't glance down as we shuffle through the sea of club members.

The memory repeats in my head, rewinding again and again as I lay there shivering. I'm breathing now, aren't I? My chest rises up and down slowly as my pulse stops racing the more I reflect on my thoughts. Doris was right, I lived a life of hell, but I escaped to where the Demon Jokers can't reach me. I have a feeling Logan, Nicky, Dalton, and Tey are more than what they appear to be. Toxic power that makes anyone kneel at their feet with just a snap of their fingers while radiating fear and danger.

It's something I know better than most, I've been around it most of my life. The only difference is the four assholes have some standards, not to kill without a reason.

I've only been here a short while, but I watch and listen even when it seems like I'm not. I don't think those four could ever stab each other in the back. They live by a code, even if they are major assholes who think they can force anyone to do their bidding. Being around Logan and having him pounding away inside of me like he's going to die tomorrow, I already know that man has control issues, needs it to survive. He'd stop at nothing to protect those he cares about. That's something I've never seen before. Payne would have plunged a knife through your back as you walked away. I know what Logan did tonight and why. Doesn't mean I'm not going to stay here all night and think about my mouth stuffed with cocks without my consent, even if I liked the way they stared down at me, controlling my movements. I swear I saw affection in Tey's eyes as he said the crazy shit that comes out of his mouth. I've had much worse in my life, tonight was just the cherry on top, and it's time that I showed them that I'm not as weak as I look.

With that in mind, I heave myself into a sitting position, off the epoxy floor and wince as I finally stand on my feet. Glancing down my body, my knees are red from being forced to the ground, and my feet are bleeding. When did that happen? My brow wrinkles, trying to remember when that could have taken place. My mind goes through the whole night. The guys kidnapping me, shoving me mostly naked into the car blindfolded, and leaving me stranded in the middle of the car lot as the cops came blaring down the road. It was the glass window I had to break, the adrenaline made me feel nothing at the time. The anger I was holding onto fueled me to keep going, but now that I'm alone...it fucking hurts like a bitch. Tiny pieces of glass are stuck in my feet, digging in deeper as I start limping into the house.

Ugh, just that they keep occupying my mind, over and over again, is pissing me off. Who the fuck tattoos their cock? That had to hurt and just makes Nicky as crazy as the rest of them. That asshole, the look he gave me when he lifted his gun and I thought he was going to kill me then and there. His facial expression was completely blank, but his eyes...those emerald eyes told a different story. A thousand words can be held in one glance and even if I thought he was going to pull the trigger on me, I should have known there's more than meets the eye with Nicky. Doesn't mean I trust him. Hell, he shoved his tattooed cock down my throat. Doesn't matter if I got extremely wet between my legs, or that I wanted to keep sucking him, it was the way he thought he had the right to do it, as if he knew that I liked it.

Well, fuck them!

I hold my head high as I walk on quiet, sore feet through the house towards the second floor, leaving a trail of bloody footprints behind. I look both ways in case one of those asses are hiding in the dark somewhere. Why does that make my heart race? Why do I feel an excited thrill creeping down my spine? Why am I like this? You'd figure I'd put a ten foot pole between me and men, but for some reason I crave to be touched by my guys, needing the passion only they seem to be able to give me. I just want to feel, to be held, and maybe one day, cherished. A girl can dream. I really need to stop thinking of them as mine, I don't want them! Nope. I have to keep telling myself that until it sticks.

But I have to remember this is just a game to them. I'm a nobody who shouldn't be in their house, an intruder who can't be trusted in their eyes. My bedroom door is open when I get to it, it's quiet and dark, two things I hate the most. I peek my head around the corner hesitantly, seeing it empty as I tippy-toe quickly towards the bathroom with a grimace as pain pulses through my feet.

I wonder where they went? Is it just Logan in the house or did he leave with the others? I'm not looking for any of them but I do like to be prepared; I wasn't tonight. I'm still on edge wondering if the cops will be showing up at the door any moment to drag me away. My eyes burn with the need for revenge, to put them in their place. If I'm stuck here until I can figure out how to get rid of the blackmail Nicky has on me, I might as well try to drive them crazy and make them wish they never met me.

Sweet revenge will be mine

A little too loud chuckle leaves my mouth, but cuts off as I turn on the bathroom light to take in my reflection. My hair is a mess, sticking up in every angle as if I just rolled out of bed after a rough night of passionate fuckery. I can't help snorting at that. My eyes have dark circles under them, and it's no wonder given the sun starting to peek through my white bedroom curtains. I glare at my underwear, swearing from this moment on I'll be wearing granny panties, and a sports bra to suck in the girls. I hate how I look, my figure and face. I've tried over the years to hide my body in baggy clothes, but Payne demanded that I show more skin to keep his club members happy. Taking in my body, I can't help the twisted snarl that edges on my lips. I really do take after Diana, the curvy hips and smooth tan skin that draws in the eye, no blemishes in sight. It's what caused me all this pain to begin with. I sometimes think about taking tweezers to my face and just plucking away to leave me with scars until I'm unrecognizable. People won't want to look me in the eye if my scars are hideous, it makes them uncomfortable. The tattoos cover most of my scars, no one hardly notices unless they are looking close enough. Does anyone ever really look long enough to see the real me? No. They don't.

Pinching my eyes closed, I take a deep breath and slowly let it out just before I open the drawers to search for tweezers for a completely different reason. Finding some, I hop onto the counter exhausted. Grinding my teeth together, I bring my leg up to cross it over my other one to see the condition my feet are in. Shards of glass poke out of my skin, making me cringe at the thought of wearing shoes, but ignoring the pain gets easy over time.

"This is those fuckers' fault. Stupid, small dick assholes," I mumble that lie to make myself feel better and hold my breath as I hover the tweezers over the glass hesitantly.

I'm so used to pain that this should be nothing, but I'm so frustrated. I'm sick of having open wounds and torn skin without my consent. Biting my lip, I pull the first piece out and drop the glass into the sink. It makes a clinking sound that has me flinch at the noise. I watch blood slowly go down the drain with my brows furrowed. I'm scared because the moment the sharp edges of the tweezers dug in and pulled out the tiny piece of glass... I felt relieved. Not relief because it's no longer attached to me, but at the feeling it gave me. It hurts, makes my heart pound, and helps me focus clearly so I can pull the rest out.

What is this feeling? I only get this way when I'm racing on the street, the engine rumbling under me, or when a certain douchebag drags his cock-- That thought cuts off faster than it can fully form.

When did I suddenly start liking the pain?

I stare at my bleeding foot, setting aside the tweezers, and slowly bring my hand to the arch of my foot. Pressing down on the cut flesh, I hiss out a breath and squeeze my eyes shut at the throb it brings. My mind clears completely, like I'm waking up from a long dream, nothing else but throbbing pain to occupy my time.

"Why does it feel so good?" I whisper to myself as soon as the last piece of glass is out and tip my head back to rest against the mirror with a thud.

"It feels good because it's something you're used to and all you know." Logan's voice is a deep, smooth rumble, not even startling me because he seems to keep showing up in places when I'm at my weakest.

Slowly blinking my eyes open, I release my foot and side-eye him as he leans against the doorframe with his arms crossed over his chest. With a sigh, I imagine repeatedly bashing his disgustingly beautiful face into the mirror, but restrain myself. He's stronger than me, that's for sure, but he's never met a woman like me.

"What now? Come to gloat? I'm not going anywhere," I sneer, turning my face away from his direction, so I don't have to see his beautiful smirk that hides all the ugliness behind it.

All lies.

He doesn't know this but he does make me weak all over, inside and out. My heart races whenever he's near, my stomach flutters with damn butterflies when he's around, and my fingers itch to trace the sharp angles of his face. Even after all he's done to me, I can't help but be drawn to him. It's ridiculous. I've hated men for a long time, never trusting anyone to protect me. I think of our moment in the shower, glancing quickly at the glass door and away before he notices. He's the first guy who's ever given me a glimpse of heaven, I don't even care that he's tainted the memory with him trying to prove a point. I already know who I am. What he doesn't know is that I'll always be grateful to him that he made me feel alive.

I'll never tell him that though.

Doesn't matter how much I wish everything was different. I'd love to have a man like him at my back, to stop anyone from hurting me. To see Tey threaten anyone who dares try to touch me with that scary ass knife of his. The protective glare Nicky gives to anyone but his friends, as if he'll kill for them. Dalton... I want his passion, the way he looks at an object he needs, can't I be looked at that way?

When is it my turn?

So lost in my miserable thoughts, I almost forgot Logan was still in the bathroom with me until he's suddenly at my side. Gripping my chin with his thumb and index finger, he turns my face towards him while I try to resist. I don't want to look into his honey eyes, to see the distrust and heat that sets me on fire.

"No, you aren't going anywhere until I'm done with you." His grip tightens as I try to release his hold, but freeze when he tangles his fingers into my hair, tipping my head back until I'm left with no choice but to look up at him. "I'll leave you alone for now, if you admit it."

My body buzzes, I can't look away from his stare and I try to remember it was only a few hours ago he held me down on my knees. The mind and body are like warped twisted lovers, a push and pull that never stops. It wants one thing and needs the other. It's almost like having a fever, the delusion that holds control over you until you're strong enough to wake up.

Glaring at him, he just raises an eyebrow as he waits for me to answer him. I refuse to give him what he wants, after I've already given him enough in the last twenty-four hours.

"You know nothing about me, so stop acting like you do. You and I are nothing alike." I harden my jaw at that, the words more true than I wished they were.

"You're right. We do come from two different worlds. I'm at the top and you're way at the bottom, but we all have our demons, don't we?" His eyes flicker between mine, looking for something before a slow smile tips his plump lips.

Without warning, he shoves me back until my head bangs against the mirror behind me and causes me to hiss in pain. He doesn't wait for me to recover, his strong tan fingers press on tiny pieces of glass on the pad of my foot, watching my expression the whole time. I suck in a breath, feeling his hand smooth over the spot, ignoring the blood smearing over our skin.

"You like this, don't you? This is where we clash, baby girl. I like giving the torment so you can feel what I'm feeling inside, and you... you like receiving it to escape from here." He taps my temple and drops my foot, turning on the faucet to wash his hands.

He acts like he didn't just suck my soul out and eat it with just a few words. He doesn't say anything else as he dries his hands on a towel and reaches under the sink to retrieve a first aid kit. Not speaking and shocking me to no end, he grasps the tweezers off the counter and starts pulling out the glass in my foot. I watch him silently, my fingers twitching with the desire to run them through his soft looking wavy brown hair. He keeps peeking up at me under his lashes, his shoulders hunched as he concentrates on his work with skilled fingers. Before I know it, he's done gathering all the glass out of both my feet, and for some reason the pain mixed in with the feel of his strong capable hands calms something inside of me. The strange feeling held me still like a lake on an early morning. Standing up straight, he drops the worlds smallest torture object in the sink and cages me between his arms as he leans close. His nose skims mine, staring at me without blinking and my breath pants through the air at the closed space between us. I stare at his lips, knowing how much pleasure they can cause and craving it. Our lips almost touching, he starts talking, breaking the illusion I was lost in.

"You can deny it, but you like getting punished. The rush of what can possibly happen next... I can smell the desperation." He breathes deeply through his nose and nips my bottom lip before pulling away.

Left in a daze, he smirks cruelly down at me with satisfaction and it takes me a second to register what he said.

"I'll kill you, Logan," I threaten, sick of his games and me falling for it over and over again.

"Oh, baby girl, you can try, but most don't get far. I'm watching. Better get ready for school...sister," he whispers with a wickedly handsome smile. His hand skimming down my cheek just before he turns away and fucking swaggers out of the bathroom.

Fucking sister, my ass. The things we did weren't so brotherly of him.

I'm going to burn him, burn him so good that he'll have something to remember me by once I'm done. I just have to find his weakness first... what he values most out of everything.

Glancing down, I open the first aid kit with my brow

wrinkled as I think of what I know about him. He gives his father this cold look, almost like he despises him, but he still does as he says. I still need to figure out who exactly this family is, what kind of power they hold. Maybe I'll get on Franco's side, learn enough to blackmail them back. It's not like I can go to each of his best friends and gather information... unless...

My eyes widen as I place the last band aid on the heel of my foot, frozen when the thought crosses my mind. It's crazy. I can't possibly get away with it. I glance at the bathroom door that leads to his room. His three best friends are like family to him.

What if I turn them against each other? Make them fight over something that could tear them apart? The one thing a man can't help but let it lead him around. It's his cock or his heart. I'm pretty good at both, after all, Doris taught me best.

I bite my lip to hold in the evil laughter that wants to come spilling out of my mouth, and hop off the counter to hurry to my room before I start giggling manically at the crazy thoughts processing through my brain. Staring out the windows with the sun rising over the valley, I stand there with my heart racing as a slow smile graces my face.

Could I really do this?

Yes. I fucking can, I have nothing else to lose.

CHAPTER 2

Tey

Smoke drifts in front of my face as I grin lazily up at the ceiling, blocking out the noises from downstairs. A typical Thursday morning in the hood, living in a foster home with multiple people never gives you a moment of peace. It's six in the morning, and already I can hear Mickey's purple, custom Monte Carlo bumping down the block with his music blaring. I should have stayed at Logan's last night, but the need to shove my cock into my sugar plum was too strong. What I wouldn't give to watch her bleed for just me. My knife slicing through her delicate golden skin as she takes every pierced inch of my hard cock. I bet she would like it, too.

"Tey! Is that weed I'm smelling?" Belva yells in a slur through my door, making me roll my eyes.

I'll never understand why she comes up here to nag at me through the door and asks that question every day. My supply of weed is strong, only the best, so yeah you're going to fucking smell it. With a long sigh, I sit up on the side of my bed and search at my feet for my cologne. Finding it under the bed, I spray it a few times and take one more drag, with billows of smoke clouding my room, before tossing my joint out the open window.

"You better not be smoking in my house, you little shit." She bangs on the door, rattling the handle as she tries to come in.

"Sorry, Auntie Belva, I can't hear you. Gotta go!" I bellow back at her, chuckling in amusement as she curses on the other side.

She really gets on my fucking nerves, always insisting that I call her Auntie Belva, even though she's just my foster *mom*. I think the old bitch gets her jollies off by bossing around a younger stud such as myself. She's currently demanding that I open the door, but I'm kind of busy looking around for my unicorn. Can't forget the little guy. Running my hand through my hair, I swing my gaze around until the rainbow colored tail catches my attention from under one of the pillows.

My unicorn's been through a lot with me. Foster home after foster home, fifteen in total since my mom overdosed, and dad was already out of the picture, as far as I can remember. Prison, maybe? Who knows? Ever since my prostitute of a mother died, nothing has been mine. Precious items stolen or lost after a new move and now this small stuffed animal is all I've got left. I'll fucking carry it everywhere, never out of sight because it's all I have left. A little girl named Madison gave it to me as I watched her get adopted, climbing into her new family car and leaving me standing on the front porch of another foster home once again alone. No one ever wanted the quiet, crazy blue eyed little boy who stared into your soul until you had no choice but to look away first. I'll cut anyone into tiny pieces, and feed them to the birds at the park if they try to take my unicorn away from me.

Since my doorway is currently being blocked by a raging alcoholic, I decide the bedroom window is the best exit. I'm too tired to deal with Belva's shit this morning, or the miserable looks of the rest of the foster kids staring at the TV downstairs. I have less than half a year left here before I can leave and get out of the system, but I told myself I'd stick it out until after high school. It's the least I can do for the kids by keeping an eye out for them and making sure there's food on the table, since Belva has an obsession with the liquor store down the street. But just for today, I need to get out without worrying about someone else... just today.

I shove my boots on, sliding my precious knife in next to my right ankle and my cigarette pack in my mouth, as I smoothly jump out the first story window. Once outside, I grab my knife from my boot and spin the blade on my fingertips to give my hands something to do. Belva's house isn't in the best neighborhood, houses line close together down the street, falling apart after years of neglect. Brown lawns are littered with junk and gang members sit outside on their stoops or on the couches placed in their front yard to watch who comes up and down the street. The good thing is everyone knows not to mess with the blond haired angel who won't hesitate to kill you. I'm kind of a celebrity around these parts it would seem. Every gang knows who I run with, my reputation.

I'm from the streets myself, born into a hard life, and I've earned respect from others by keeping my mouth shut... while causing the fear of Tey into them. I chuckle to myself, thinking about that one time the cartel sent one of their minions to get the drop on me, but it just ended badly for the other guy. Always remember to check a person for any extra weapons on their body, or you'll end up with a knife up the ass. Literally.

Good times.

I think Dom, the new leader of the fucking cartel gang, La Demonio, on the east side coast got the message when I sent their little friend back in a body bag. He's messing with the wrong people, a history he shouldn't repeat like his pops did. If it wasn't for the missing money and timing, I'd believe our little Latina that she's innocent in all this. Too bad she might be working for Dom, or spying for her Demon Jokers. There's always someone trying to claim power and you have to take out the one who's at the top first. Maybe it's time we took a trip to the east side and had a little talk with Dom. Just have to control Logan while we visit since Dom's father is the one who murdered Helen. At least Jin, Nicky's father stepped in and helped Franco get his revenge. The police department was doing jackshit to help their own officer. I wonder if Jin saw it as an opportunity to go under the radar and help a rookie cop, who was going places, up the ladder on his side. A bond formed and here we are years later.

I'm really glad Nicky hasn't turned out like Jin. That fucker is manipulative and colder than a dead fish. Just thinking about Nicky brings a smirk to my face. He's an idiot, but my idiot. He's real good at hiding his feelings but not from me. He wants things he shouldn't because deep down Nicky is just like me. He wants to take and take until he can't breathe anymore, choking on that last breath as he puts one foot in front of the other, and he tries to hide behind with the cold expression he likes to wear. It was the way he was gazing down at Tillie as she sucked his tattooed cock into her pretty little mouth that told me his needs. He could glare all he wanted, but I saw a lot more that he tried hiding. The way his cock twitched as soon as her luscious lips touched the tip of him, his eyes squeezing tight for a split second, and his shirt molding to his abs as he sucked in a breath when she glared right back up at him. That image has been on repeat in my mind since the crack of dawn. The moment I got home, my zipper was down and cock out in my hand with the image of Tillie between Nicky and I. Lately, I've noticed more and more how Nicky looks at me when he thinks I'm not looking. I purposely play with my lip ring when I catch him staring at my mouth like he wants to bite it. Maybe he'll want to play games with me and Tillie?

"Young man, you better be hurrying to school," a familiar voice calls behind me, making me smirk at the strong tone she uses even though she's seventy years old and only half my height.

"Of course, Miss Rita. You know I'm all about those good grades and school spirit." She cackles from her porch, setting down her Coca-Cola and fanning herself with a piece of paper as she gazes at me through her thick glasses.

I don't think she can see well because I highly doubt that she'd be talking to me. One look at me and most can tell there's something not right with me, a loose screw. It could be my eyes, I've been told that it looks like I'm gazing right past the layer of skin and into a person's soul. My hair is a dead giveaway when I'm roaming late at night around the block, the Gods really cursed me with bright as fuck blond hair. It's hard to hide blood in these locks after a night of killing, but I usually pretend it's not here as I smile and wave to anyone walking past me. I do try casually to blend in with the shadows as much as possible, black clothes, silent boots, but anyone who really looks at me closely can see the dark side of me that has you stepping back. I'm not talking about my black nail polish or the eyeliner I put on to make my blue eyes pop to scare the shit out of you. I'm talking about the way I walk, watching everyone around me without ever taking my gaze off anyone for a split second.

"You're a troublemaker, boy. Those who try, succeed in life. Don't want the law to come knocking at your door now, do you?" She squints at me, adjusting her glasses, and misses me sliding my knife back into my boot.

If it was anyone else, I wouldn't hesitate to come back later at night and smother them with their pillow, but not Miss Rita. She's a blind, old bat that seems to really care what happens around her and she looks after the kids in the neighborhood. I've caught her a handful of times beating little shit drug dealers off my street with just a slipper as they tried to sell to the kids. Not on my turf, I don't want the foster kids to end up like me. They deserve a better life, where they aren't broken. Just when I'm about to reply, the loud noise of an engine approaches from behind me but I don't bother turning around because I'd recognize that sound anywhere.

"Don't worry, Miss. Tey is going to school right now. I'll make sure of it," Nicky's throaty voice rumbles, his slight accent peeking through, but he'll deny it.

I personally think it's hot how deep his voice gets when he starts speaking Japanese. It always makes me want to grab him by the back of his neck and have his lips slide against mine, so I can feel the rumble of his voice instead of hearing it. Turning around, Nicky is staring straight ahead and pretending like he didn't go out of his way to come pick me up when I never asked him to. He's always tight lipped, his shoulders straight in that white button down long sleeved shirt, and black ironed pants sculpted to his thighs.

Why does he do this to me?

I've tried my hardest over the last couple of years to give him space until he's ready to admit he wants me, but it's been like pulling teeth. I'd rather pull teeth than wait around for him to come to terms that it's okay to like your best friend. Feelings can deepen. I wonder if my sweet sugar pie can convince him to let go. Tillie doesn't know it yet, but she's one of us. I've seen enough fucked up stuff to last me a lifetime that I can recognize it in someone else. It's how I decide if someone lives or dies.

"You boys be good, no causing any trouble!" Miss Rita shoos me away with a wave of her hand before leaning back in her chair to look up and down the street.

"Always." I grin widely and open the door to the green Camaro, smoothly sliding in with ease onto the leather seats.

Nicky punches on the gas, the tires screeching down the street within seconds and that tells me enough that he's itching to race soon. We all have our hardships, a home that we wish we didn't have, so we find an escape any way we can, just to feel like we belong somewhere. Mine just happens to be addictions. Currently, it's weed and a little hand in gambling, but it might just be changing for my Tillie. She's already mine. If we have to kill her, I'll claim that shit so even when she's dead I can tell everyone that I had her last breath. She can't leave that easily, there's no escaping me.

"What did you do?" Nicky asks, turning his head

slightly to glance at me with his brow raised as he looks me up and down with suspicion.

"I don't know what you're talking about." I bite my bottom lip, playing with the piercing there and catch him looking before quickly glancing away... as if I wouldn't notice.

"You were practically skipping down the street and smiling like the joker. And what have I told you about calling me? I'll come pick you up, but instead you make me stalk your ass." His voice is authoritative as he glances out the front windshield, looking lost in thought as he shakes his head and slides his fingers through his shoulder length hair.

I don't like when he gets that faraway look. Usually, it means something happened at home, but I'm not going to pry. I'll let him talk when he's ready to, he'll close up like a clam if I try digging it out of him. We've been there before and it took months for him to stop giving me the cold shoulder. Sometimes I wonder if he's made of marble and how I can chip away at it when his father just keeps hardening him.

"How was it?" I ask, gazing out the window to see the highway signs pass as we head to Logan's house to pick up my plaything.

"How was what?" He questions in confusion, his almond shaped, emerald eyes meeting mine when I glance over with a smirk.

"My ass. How was it from behind?" I chuckle as the car swerves off the road for a second before he straightens the wheel.

He clears his throat a few times, shuffling in his seat as he glances over at me a few times with a faint blush staining his cheeks. Well, shit. I think I embarrassed him.

That never happens. I decide to take mercy on him by changing the subject.

"How is the research goin-" I choke on my own spit as he starts talking at the same time.

"It was a good view," he says so quietly under his breath that I don't think I was supposed to catch it. He quickly whips his head around to look at me and his lips twitch before he glances back at the road, putting a little more pressure on the gas. "What were you saying?" he asks casually, and I decide to roll with it before he closes himself off from me again.

Maybe those feelings he locks up so tight might be ready to come out soon. I'm going to paint him and Tillie with my favorite color soon. Red. Bright red. I can hardly wait, it makes my fingers twitch with the need.

"How is your research going with Tillie's background and the list of people Franco gave you?" I ask, pulling a joint out from behind my ear that was hidden by my hair and playing with it as I try to make up my mind if I should smoke again.

I need a smoke. The sexual tension is getting to me lately. I'm only seconds away from saying fuck it and slamming my lips against his. We finally pull onto Logan's street, making my leg bounce in excitement. It's only been a couple of hours, but I'm excited to see how she's handling everything. Has she made a run for it yet? God. I hope she runs, I bet she's a sprinter. I love a good game of cat and mouse.

"Nothing is coming up. It's like she's not in the system. She has a school record that showed me absolutely nothing. She kept her nose down and got good grades, enough to pass, but nothing stands out." Nicky's lip curls in frustration, his sharp jawline hardening as he grinds his teeth.

He doesn't like how he can't dig up her past because everyone has a past that they try hiding. Something isn't right. He should have been able to find something on her. His hacking skills are good enough that he could probably hack into the Pentagon... he might have already done that once as a test drive, but then again I was probably drunk off my ass at the time. The drunk phrase is a little blurry.

"What about the others? Anything? It's about the Demon Jokers, right?" I ask, taking a deep breath before putting the joint back behind my ear for an emergency.

He parks the car in Logan's driveway and cuts the engine before slapping his hand against the steering wheel repeatedly. I just sit back and wait until he's done. Sometimes when you bottle all that rage up, it explodes at random times that you can't control it. That's why I never keep it under lock and key, I let my crazy show.

"Yes. I found some stuff that I need to let Logan know, before telling Franco." Nicky finally calms down, tying his black hair back away from his face, and opening the door to get out.

Franco may be the boss around here, but Logan is where our loyalty lies. Franco is slowly losing it. Ever since Helen died he's just become a broken man and he won't ever find that piece he lost with Diana. He can try as hard as he wants, but it's impossible. I'm observant that way.

"Fuck it. Let's go find Logan, but I need to find my bae first. I want to play for a few minutes." I smile wickedly, watching his eyes widening, pupils dilating.

I bet he's picturing his cock slipping past her lips again. It was a sight to remember that's for sure, and that girl can suck like no other even when she pretends to hate it. Patting my pocket to make sure my unicorn is there, I get out of the car and practically run into the house without knocking. We are past that point of pretending I'm not in Logan's house all the time, I have a key. They can't keep me out.

"I'm going to get Logan. Dalton should be here any minute," Nicky says, walking away with his hands in his pants pockets and climbing the stairs on long limbs as I stroll behind him slowly.

I'm about to follow him up the stairs to Tillie's room, but something catches my attention out of the corner of my eye. Glancing into the living room, I spot movement and see in the mirror above the fireplace a reflection that's up to no good. In the mirror, it shows Tillie sneaking down the hallway that leads to the master bedroom and Franco's office. Now, what could she be up to? On silent feet, I follow after her until I'm only a few feet away from her as she pauses outside of Franco and Diana's bedroom. She should really be careful, anyone could sneak up on her.

I'm about to ask her what she's up to but a breathless moan stops me. I step closer until my black t-shirt is almost skimming her back and peek over her shoulder through the cracked door.

Well, well. It looks like Dalton isn't the only one who likes to watch people, but then again, she isn't gripping her breasts in pleasure or slipping her fingers into her panties. I don't blame her. Watching your parent get fucked from behind could scar you for life. I wouldn't know, but I'm betting it does some damage. I glance down at Tillie and it looks like she's barely breathing as she stares straight ahead but her fingers are trembling by her sides. I follow her gaze and catch sight of Franco staring right at her, not breaking eye contact as he fucks her mom who won't shut the fuck up as she moans like a pig.

It's almost like Tillie isn't even really here when I look down at her. Her gaze is locked on Franco with wide eyes as if she can't stop staring, even though she wants to look away. The blood drains from her face and I swear she's muttering the word no in quick hard breaths. Slipping my hand around her waist, she jumps in my grip as I slide my hand over the skin between her shirt and jeans. She glances up at me over her shoulder with dark brown eyes, wide and distant looking. I've been there before. Sometimes you see something that reminds you of the past and it traps you in a memory you wish you didn't have. Reaching around her with my other hand, I glance away from her and lock eyes with Franco who hasn't paused the whole time. I don't like how he's looking at her. She's not his.

Mine. My plaything.

I slam the door so hard that it rattles against the frame and I'm roughly dragging her away down the hall before she can blink. My emotions come out that I try desperately to keep contained in a locked box. Anger isn't something I experience a lot... that could be because I'm always absorbed in my addictions. I currently feel like my heart is going to explode out of my chest.

Fucking Franco.

Why was he staring at her like he was imagining fucking her instead of his *wife?* I wonder if it would upset Logan if I twisted my knife into his father's gut and watched everything spill out until he took his last breath.

"Let the fuck go, Tey!" Tillie seems to unfreeze and starts struggling against me as I make her walk in front of me with my arm still around her waist.

I lift her off her feet to carry her to the living room as she resists me, making my cock hard as her bouncy ass keeps rubbing back and forth right on the front of my jeans. Dalton chooses that moment to walk through the front door, looking down at his scabbed over knuckles in annoyance. He quickly glances up as Tillie starts cussing me out, a smile slowly coming over his face. He leans against the living room wall, his eyes sweeping up and down Tillie's body. She's completely oblivious as to how much her struggling in my arms turns me on, and the show she's putting on for Dalton. It's a nice side effect, being angry and horny. Just makes me more blood thirsty, an overwhelming urge to fuck her senseless. I hunch my shoulders, bending over her so that she can't miss how hard I am. She stops suddenly, her panting breath loud, and her hair a mess, blocking her view of Dalton in front of her. I tighten my arm around her stomach and whisper into the shell of her ear.

"Keep struggling, hellcat. Give me an excuse to bend you over the couch and fuck your tight ass. I bet Dalton would enjoy it too, he does have the perfect view." She sucks in a sharp breath and quickly whips her head back to look up, but in the process smacks her skull into my nose.

"Fuckkkk!" I groan into her ear, feeling the blood starting to drip from my nose and land on her white Adidas t-shirt.

She slips out of my arms and spins around to glare up at me with an annoyed scowl. Before I can lunge at her and ask her to make me bleed more, she surprises me by doing the unexpected. I thought she'd come at me swinging because she's scrappy like that. Instead, she steps closer until her feet touch my boots and reaches her hand up to pinch the bridge of my nose to stop the bleeding.

I freeze, gazing down at her in wonder with my hands fisted at my sides. I'd like nothing more than to grab her hips and bring her curvy body against mine. I watch my blood trail down her wrist, over her veins that are pounding fast, and have to look up slowly at Dalton to have him get her away from me before I lose it.

"Little bitch, are you that desperate to suck Tey's cock? I know you missed the chance last night but I'm more than ready to have you on your knees in front of me again," Dalton drawls out, grinning the whole time. His smile widening as she looks over her shoulder with narrowed eyes.

She doesn't realize but her fingers tighten on my nose, causing a shock of pain to travel through my body. I can't contain the pleasurable shiver down my spine as I smile widely at her, not giving a damn if blood stains my teeth. You figure I'd rather be stabbing people left and right because I, well, like to watch their eyes go empty, for them to feel what I do inside. But that's not the case with Tillie... I'm starting to like our little spy. I mean, I still want to see her bleed, but only for me.

"That's the last time you'll ever force me to my knees." She actually growls at Dalton and turns back towards me with a frown as she looks up at me to see how tight she's pinching my nose.

She releases me quickly as the blood stops flowing and spins on her heels to leave the room, shoving past Dalton to knock her shoulder against his. I like it when she's angry, you can tell she's trying to hide all that pent up rage behind a mask, pretending to be calm when in reality she's anything but. No one fools me when it comes to any kind of pain, including anger. She stomps up the stairs, muttering under her breath, and doesn't even notice Nicky and Logan coming down the steps in front of her. She pulls her shirt away from her chest, cursing under her breath at the blood staining the white material, and whips it over her head without slowing her angry stride.

"What is wrong with you now? Why is there bloo-" Logan starts to say but is cut off when she throws her shirt in his stunned face and rushes up the rest of the stairs until it's just the four of us.

Nicky pauses on the steps, looking at where she disappeared to with a wrinkled brow. I wonder if he's just noticing the scars that litter her body. Most of the puckered scars are covered with tattoos but in the right lighting, they stand out against her caramel skin. I noticed them last night in the garage as I stood back and watched. Nicky shakes his head and carries on down the stairs with an annoyed Logan, who clenches her shirt in his fists. Nicky leans against the mantle as usual, he's looking down at the top of his hands before fisting them at his sides with his jaw locked in place. Nicky's hands are also littered with small scars from years of having a cane whacked there for lessons in obedience and pain tolerance.

"She keeps giving that sass and all it makes me want to do is shove my cock in her mouth to shut her up," Dalton says with a groan, biting his knuckle as his eyes shift towards the stairs like he might just go do that.

"Focus. You can play later. While she's changing, Nicky, tell us what you found." Logan smacks the back of Dalton's head as he passes him and sits on the back of the couch, finishing buttoning his cuff links while huffing under his breath in annoyance.

I don't know why he and Nicky insist on dressing in

button downs and slacks, but I guess it works for them. Coming from rich families sets a high standard that society expects, dressing the part that screams of wealth since money flows right into their bank accounts. I usually just say fuck it and wear black, that way it matches my soul.

"Nothing on Tillie came up, she's almost like a ghost. No parents on the registration. Doesn't even state who her mother is, it could be a possibility that she isn't Diana's daughter. Maybe she was sent here to trick us into believing that her dead daughter came back from the grave." Nicky pauses to clear his throat, strumming his fingers on the mantle, lost in thought before he shakes his head. "As for the other two Franco told me to research, it showed up right away in the system. A long background, dating back to the late seventies." Nicky looks to me and nods his head towards the hallway leading to Franco's office, telling me without words to be the lookout, but what he doesn't know is Franco is otherwise busy at the moment.

That son of a bitch.

Now I'm angry again at that reminder.

I walk to the entrance of the living room to get a clear view of the hallway, plotting all kinds of ways I can kill Franco but still listening to Nicky at the same time. I ignore the weird look Dalton is giving me, I'll explain in a little bit and see if anyone wants to join me in getting rid of the body.

"The first name I searched for was the Demon Jokers President, Payne Lorzen. Born in nineteen sixty-three, Las Vegas, Nevada. Started dipping his hands into armed robbery and stealing vehicles at a young age. This guy has a record a mile long for abuse, rape, stealing, breaking and entering, illegal weaponery, but most went under the table because he was never charged. Spent a few years in prison but was released after a short time and his father passed away not long after. He took over the spot as Prez and the rest is history," Nicky states casually, it's not something we haven't seen or heard before.

"Interesting. Dalton, did you talk to your old man?" Logan crosses his arms with his dark brow raised as Dalton rolls his eyes and tugs on his cut to straighten it while cracking his neck.

"Yeah, he had a few words to say, but it was more than enough," Dalton says slowly, giving me a pleading glance to help him out with his pretty boy looks, but nope.

He's on his own with this one. It's way too early to get Logan mad and for once it's not me. He narrows his violet eyes at me and sighs before gazing at Logan with a grimace. I'm thinking I need a better spot for the shitshow that's about to happen. Wish I had some popcorn. I move back to my comfy position on the living room floor and lay down with my arms behind my head. Fuck being the lookout for Franco, he's fucking his wife at the moment.

"He said that no good, fucking dickless asshole is a waste of space and he wouldn't let his daughter near him if he had one. Or a sweetbutt or his granny who's dead." Dalton bites his lip and straightens to his full height when Logan stands from the couch with clenched fists.

"That's all he said? He didn't give you a reason?" Logan grinds out through his teeth, looking like he's about to start choking Dalton if he doesn't give him an answer.

"Nope," Dalton replies back, popping the p just to annoy Logan.

"And what about the other name Franco told you to look up, Nicky?" I ask lazily from my spot on the floor to distract them before one of them explodes into a match of yelling that won't stop until someone is bleeding.

I personally just want as much information as I can get about Tillie. It's like my stalker mode has been activated and I'm addicted enough that it's almost unhealthy.

"Regan Lorzen aka Rig. Vice President of the Demon Jokers and brother to Payne. Same background but no sexual assault on his record. Seems the brothers started out young getting into trouble with the law, anything Payne went down for... Rig was right there with him. But nothing is showing up on his record or accounts for a few years now. It's like he just disappeared one day," Nicky's voice trails off as he glances towards the stairs and pushes off the mantle quickly as if he's going to bolt over the furniture at whatever he sees.

I sit up and see Tillie standing behind Logan and Dalton looking like she's seen a ghost. Her big brown eyes have a distant gaze to them as she stares at Nicky with her bottom lip slightly trembling, until she bites down hard on it to stop herself from showing any kind of weakness. I like that about her, too.

The guys stop talking and turn to glance at her in the archway. She's changed into a white sundress with small sunflowers woven into the fabric, it fits her like a glove and stands out against her smooth tan skin. It's the dress Nicky picked out by himself for her when we were at the mall.

"That's all you found out about Rig?" She makes her way around the guys and comes to stand in front of Nicky with, dare I say, a glimmer of hope in her gaze.

Who is this Rig to her?

I'll kill him.

"What's it to you? Are you his old lady and missing

being passed between the two brothers? I guess once a whore, always a whor-" Nicky sneers down at her but never expected her to slap him across the face.

"You shut the fuck up, Nicky. You have no idea. Absolutely no idea what you're talking about," Tillie whispers, staring him in the eye, not noticing how still he became the moment she whipped her hand across his cheek.

I'd kill anyone who would even dare think about laying their hands on my friends, but I think I'm going to watch from a distance and see how this plays out. I lean back on my elbows with my ankles crossed to watch the show that could only end up in fireworks. Nicky's hand lashes out, grabbing her wrist and roughly pulling her against his chest.

Her lips part in shock at the unexpected move as she stares up at him with huge brown eyes. Her body is plastered to his from the tip of their shoes to their chests pressed tightly together. Just the sight has my imagination running wild, the things we could do to her between us. The things I'd do to Nicky as she watched and was denied pleasure until I was ready to give it. I adjust my jeans, which are starting to feel uncomfortably tight.

"You ever touch me like that again and I'll bury you so deep that no one will ever remember you existed in the first place," Nicky whispers dangerously down at her, his face stone cold.

"Jesus," Dalton whispers behind me.

Yeah, no one touches Nicky without his permission. Years of abuse by his father will do that to someone, make them fear the touch of another person that they resort to violence.

"Maybe that's what I want," Tillie says so quietly back to him that I almost missed it but Nicky hears it loud and clear as his jaw twitches, probably grinding his teeth again.

"That's enough!" Logan demands and moves around the furniture to pull my honey bear away from Nicky, just as Franco makes an appearance in the archway.

Dressed from head to toe in his uniform with his badge a shiny reminder of the mockery. His Chief uniform, a dark navy blue suit and his briefcase under his arm give him an air of power, as if no one can touch him.

"What's enough? And that's no way to touch your stepsister, Logan," Franco commands, nodding his head towards the grip Logan has on Tillie's wrist, but no one sees what I do.

I don't like the way he's staring at her, how he's not looking away from Tillie as she stares down at the ground with her body slightly trembling. He clears his throat and glances away from her, but catches my eye as I don't blink, meeting his gaze that screams I'll make sure he's in the ground at an early age.

"You should all get to school. Logan, come to the warehouse after school. Make sure someone is watching her." Franco addresses Logan without looking her way again, not daring to stare at what's mine because he knows I'm watching.

I'm a loose cannon and he knows it.

With that, he leaves the room and the heels of his shoes echo until he goes through the garage door.

"Your dad is really a cop? You weren't lying?" Tillie mumbles, her face twisting like she just swallowed something nasty as she stares with wide eyes full of shock.

CHAPTER 3

Franco

"Helen," I whisper with longing, her touch warm underneath my hand as it strokes down her spine and back up to slide through her long, silky brown hair.

"No, Franco. It's me, D-" She trails off with a long, drawn out moan.

Her voice is different, not so soft and quiet. I stroke deep inside of her, making love to my beautiful wife. Her hair is shorter, just below her shoulders... Helen always wore her curls long and wavy because she knew how much I loved to slide my fingers through it. Her beauty knows no bounds, her smooth Italian skin that makes her light brown eyes shine and show every vulnerable emotion that crosses her face. The sun to calm my storm, my everything.

Something isn't right. This is wrong. Her smiling face blurs around the edges when she turns her head to the side. Flashing blue and red lights reflect off her skin as her dull eyes stare off into the distance, not blinking. Gone. My heart speeds up and sweat drips down my naked back as my pace slows until I'm barely moving and having to shake my head to clear the image.

"Franco, what's wrong?" Diana asks breathlessly, getting to her knees, trying to look over her shoulder at me.

Pain slithers into my heart every day. It hurts so much that I feel colder and colder inside, until I'm numb and lost. My memories of the past blend together with the present. Never being able to get the last image of her out of my head.

"Did I say you can move? Get back down on all fours." My voice comes out harsh and drained of emotions.

I watch her swallow hard, a drip of sweat rolling down her temple from her fake blonde hair, her dark brown eyes wide as she slowly lowers back down onto her hands with her back arched.

The tattoo at the base of her spine holds my attention, the design of a joker surrounded by thorned roses. It reminds me of the day I had to watch my wife die - what felt like a thousand times - through a surveillance video. The symbol of the tattoo visible on her murderer's forearm, a gang stamp on his skin. That day, my hope died, my future turning in a different direction when the Chief pulled me into his office to stop me from looking into something that would get the rest of my family killed. I was pulled off the case and watched it get put into the evidence room, where it would just collect dust. I knew becoming a cop would be a dangerous job, but going undercover as a rookie came with a price I never saw coming. I knew who her murderer was, but could do nothing about it. It all came back to the cartel gang on the east side and I was ready to go in guns blazing, to take down their leader for putting a hit on my wife. I was willing to die to be with my Helen again, but I never made it that far.

I drive aimlessly around for an hour, feeling the pressure of the semi-automatic gun on my passenger seat. Logan is in the back in his carseat, sleeping peacefully with a bag of goldfish clenched in his tiny fist. I pull the car over, place my head against the steering wheel, and feel my world fall apart around me. My own son doesn't fully understand what's happened to his mom, but he knows she won't be coming back.

What kind of father am I to just let his mother's killer keep walking around freely? Not when he could be taken down, so he can't harm anyone ever again. For once the law isn't on my side, so I have to take it into my own hands. But what if I don't make it out of this alive? What will happen to my boy? Will I become a monster just like them?

My choice stared right in front of me, the drug house I was watching for six months straight, where Alejandro has his cocaine made down in the basement. I was about to take him down, and had most of the evidence that we needed, but that was before he sent one of his men after me. He destroyed me without causing any physical harm to my body, and I am about to return the favor. Making my decision, I glance at my boy one more time in the rearview mirror and then open the door while grabbing my revolver from the passenger seat.

It is raining, and within seconds I'm soaked to the bone, but I couldn't care less. Revenge is fueling me, making it easier, step by step, as I walk across the wet grass that silenced my black boots when I got closer to the house. I'm a man on a mission, to carry it through no matter the outcome, but I don't make it that far. Just before I make it to his front steps, a hand comes over my mouth and I am being dragged to the side of the house. Shoved up against the peeling paint, I blink rapidly against the rain, making it difficult to see. Fighting instincts come over me, but as I try to swing my fist at his face, he blocks me and holds his forearm over my windpipe to restrict my breathing. With his face so close, I take in his pale skin, tall form, and almond shaped brown eyes that are laughing at me.

"Franco Russo, Los Angeles cop, a father, and now a widower... Do you think this is a good idea storming into the lion's den? Don't you seek full vengeance, and climbing to the top without dying?" he asks me, releasing the pressure on my throat and stepping back.

He looks like the devil dressed in a business suit, just waiting for me to sign a contract that will forever leave me soulless.

"Who are you?" I croak out.

"My name is Jin and I'm going to make sure you have your revenge, Franco. You and I are going to help each other."

Years later and I think Jin is still the devil in disguise, but he kept his word as he watched me cut off Alejandro's head, my dead wife's killer's blood staining my fingers. It was only the beginning. I left his boy alone, Dom, who now runs the cartel, but I don't give a shit as long as he stays on his side of town.

"Franco, please. Deeper," Diana groans out loudly from under me, panting like a bitch in heat.

I thought marrying a woman who was completely the opposite of my Helen would make her disappear from my memories. So that she doesn't haunt my every waking moment, but she's still here. She's everywhere. I feel myself starting to go soft, the thought of my dead wife always does that. Movement by the door catches my attention and my hips jerk deep into Diana at the sight that greets me. Dark brown hair, expressive big eyes and it's almost like Helen is standing right there in the doorway. Blinking rapidly, the vision of her is gone and replaced with Diana's daughter, Tillie. She looks frozen in the doorway, not knowing what to do with herself, but she hasn't glanced away.

There's something about her, a lost hope, no way out but a warmth you can't help be drawn to. Without breaking eye contact, I pound into Diana harder, rattling the bedframe and wishing she wasn't the one under me. To feel that smooth, warm caramel skin under my fingertips, her big perky breasts bouncing at every thrust of my cock into her tight cunt. My breathing picks up, feeling myself coming closer to the edge and seconds away from coating her mother's cunt with ropes of cum. I notice movement over Tillie's shoulder and see the burning hatred of icy blue eyes staring back at me just before the door suddenly jerks closed with a slam. Diana doesn't even notice as she screams out in pleasure, but the image of Tillie's big brown eyes staring at me helps send me over the edge.

Breathing heavily and collapsing onto my side, I lay there staring up at the ceiling as Diana cuddles into me. What kind of man am I? Suddenly craving a woman who reminds me of my dead wife because she radiates a warmth that a moth seeks. I'm that moth. I can fix her, that damaged piece which no doubt comes from spending time with the Demon Jokers. I was looking for a replacement who was the exact opposite of my late wife, but I'm starting to wonder if I chose wrong.

"Let me up. I have to get ready for work." I'm already pushing Diana away from me as I get out of bed with a quiet groan.

I'm beginning to wonder just how far a man like myself will go before enough is too much.

What more could I break that isn't already broken. You can't put back together a shattered man, unless he's willing to help pick up the pieces. There isn't hope for me, I'm already a lost cause.

CHAPTER 4

Tillie

"No, he's not a cop. He's the Chief of the Los Angeles precinct," Dalton states simply with an eye roll, staring at me with his all too knowing violet eyes.

I have a hard time looking at his cut, the way the leather molds to his broad shoulders, and the smell of engine oil makes it hard to breathe, but holding his gaze helps center me. Flashbacks and triggers are close but far in between at the same time. I'll be fine one minute and the next I'm stuck, back in that cold, dark basement. It could be a smell, the way people crowd close to me, a certain word, and all of a sudden I'm there, in the dark, feeling my flesh scrap against the concrete floor...one of the Demon Jokers breathing heavily over me as he ruts into me bone dry. I like to think most days I'm okay, that I can survive anything thrown at me, but I feel like a ticking time bomb. I hate to show any sign of weakness in front of anyone, so I put a smile on my face and keep walking forward even when I stumble.

So, yeah, the leather cut he's wearing hasn't triggered me. Maybe it's because of the patch embedded into the black leather, the devil sprouting bat-like wings from its spine. It's completely different from the cuts of the Demon Jokers, and Dalton won't ever know this but the smell of engine oil actually brings back good memories for me with Uncle Rig in the shop. That reminds me. I'm fucking pissed off. It's already getting old, them looking into my past and finding small snippets that I'd rather move on from, but the mention of Uncle Rig is like a noose around my neck. I can't let that go. It gives me something to focus on instead of what I saw this morning with Franco - nope. Not going there. I can't. It's not much different from the club, Lorrie used to fuck Payne in front of me all the time. As if she had something to prove, and I had to sit there in a room full of bikers, pretending it didn't bother me. What makes my stomach twist now is how Franco was staring at me. It's the same look men get in their eyes when I dance on stage. Greed and lust.

Focus, Tillie, take your anger out on something else.

My gaze collides with Logan's over my shoulder as I glance around, all the emotions of the last few days are bubbling up and he's one of the people who keeps it going. How dare Logan keep my own shit from me and share it with the rest of the guys?! It's none of their business!

"You motherfuckers tricked me! I've been thinking the police were going to show up to take me away any second because of you numb nuts. I didn't know one was sleeping in the same house!" My tone comes out strained as I yell at Logan, who just calmly stands there staring at me and shrugs.

"It's not my problem. Maybe you shouldn't show up at a stranger's house in the middle of the night? Then again, you're probably just pretending since you came here for a reason, isn't that right? Have you always been this pathetic?" Logan's gaze roams me up and down with his upper lip curled, his honey eyes raking over my sundress with a look of disgust. "Why are you wearing a dress? Go change, you're showing too much skin and I don't feel like killing anyone today, at least not until noon," he commands without bothering to look me in the eyes, as if he just dismissed me and it just pisses me off even more.

Before I can fully turn around to punch his smug face, Nicky reaches out and stops me. His hand over my wrist has enough pressure to tell me he's not letting go until I calm down. I glance back up at him, about to tell him to get his hands off me, but he's not even looking at me. He's glaring at Logan over my shoulder and hisses under his breath while dragging me closer to his body.

"The dress stays on," he tells Logan with so much authority behind his voice that it makes me shudder, but not in fear.

What is it about the sound of a male's voice going lower in pitch and deadly quiet, barely a whisper, that makes you want to throw your underwear at them? I'll never understand it and it's very new to me.

"I'm not an object. You can't tell me what to do." I grind my teeth and feel my pulse pounding hard in my neck.

Nicky quickly cuts his gaze towards me and he actually huffs under his breath like I'm a disobedient child.

"How are your knees, little bitch? Still sore? I bet that

garage floor was cold," Dalton drawls out in that deep voice of his in a rumble as I turn towards him.

He pushes off the wall from his lounging position, coming towards me on the silent feet of a predator. Why are they so freaking quiet when they move around? Graceful almost, but deadly. I hate the way their shoulders shift and muscles ripple under their clothes each time they move, just to prove how strong they are, and stupid me can't stop staring. I hate the natural way they swagger with confidence because it's kind of sexy and I don't want to be attracted to that. Makes me want to grab the nearest object and beat them with it until they are limping instead.

"You know, when someone feels really cold, it means they are just at the brink of death. Just before your soul leaves your body, that's when you finally become warm. Should we test that on you?" I feel a small ounce of victory when Dalton stumbles over his own feet and nearly trips over Tey who is cracking up on the floor.

"I knew there was a reason I liked you. Whenever you're ready to start popping out my kids, sweetheart, just give me the go ahead." Tey winks at me, chuckling as he stands and stretches like a cat from a long nap.

"Unbelievable," I whisper under my breath and glance back at Nicky, ready to ask him the one question I'm dreading.

It makes it hard to swallow because it feels like a golf ball is stuck in my throat.

"Rig. You found nothing on him in the last two years? No trace of his whereabouts?" I stare up at Nicky with a hopeful expression, maybe give me answers I've been longing for and to give me a reason to dream again.

"Why would I tell you anything? Maybe if you start

telling the truth of why you're here, I might just give you that information. Seems like he's someone important to you. Are you his old lady?" Nicky tilts his head to the side and strokes his chin just before his facial expression evens out into a blank mask. "Thank you for giving me that. Another piece to dangle over your head if you step out of line," he whispers, his voice menacing and gravelly.

My heart drops down to my feet in devastation. I shouldn't have expected anything less of him. I shove myself away from him only to collide with Dalton who wraps his arms around me from behind, tightly, like you would with a teddy bear.

"She's no one's old lady!" Dalton growls at Nicky and bends his head down to place his cheek against mine, his whispered words vibrating along my skin. "Little bitch, you can ride me- I mean on the back of my bike on the way to school." Dalton's raspy chuckle against my skin feels oddly good, sending pleasurable shivers down my spine.

"I'm good. I don't think you know how to handle that *bike* of yours," I sass back, unable to help myself, the need to cause trouble pulsing through me.

A taste of freedom can do that, makes you rebel and I don't plan on stopping anytime soon. A man can place me on my knees but he can't keep me there. They want to play a game... I can play too.

"Enough. Who's on babysitting duty after school? Tey and I will be at the warehouse doing business." Logan's eyes cut to me real quick before glancing between Dalton and Nicky with a raised brown eyebrow.

"I can't. I have church tonight. A small supply ship-ment went missing last night," Dalton grumbles as he tips his head back to glare at the ceiling, his fists clenching at his sides in clear frustration.

I would feel bad for him if I didn't know what he meant. I wonder what kind of dealings his club is involved in. It's always drugs. At least, that was what Payne had the club running, and human trafficking he dipped his hands in from time to time. God knows what else.

"Guess that leaves you, Nicky," Logan announces with an evil smirk, twirling his keys around his finger before tossing them in the air and catching them again.

"Are you sure that's a good idea?" Tey questions, his brow furrowed as he stares at Nicky as if he can read his mind.

That makes me wonder if I should be worried if Tey is concerned.

"It's fine." Nicky's deep voice dips lower just as he glances down at me. "You can follow orders like a good girl, right?" He doesn't wait for me to reply, clearly thinking I'll follow whatever commands he barks at me just before he storms out of the house, slamming the front door behind him.

"Good girl, my ass," I mutter to myself in a quiet tone, glaring at the front door as if I can see through it, and hoping he can feel my annoyance.

My breath catches in the back of my throat when I'm suddenly spun around and tossed over a firm, strong shoulder upside down with my sundress over my hips. I brace my palm against Dalton's lower muscular back, clenching his cut in my fists as I feel the blood rush to my head.

"You'll be a good girl or that little video of you stealing the Ferrari might just go viral all over the internet. The Chief of Police can lock you up until your club comes to collect you," Dalton threatens, the smirk can be heard in his voice.

He smacks my ass unexpectedly, hard enough with the flat of his palm to make me gasp at the sting, his warning clear. My skin pulses on the surface where he slapped and oddly enough, I like the way it makes me squirm at the thought of him doing it again.

They don't bluff.

With a throbbing, sore buttcheek, and my plan to turn them against each other flushing down the toilet, he strides out of the room with his hand on my thigh to hold me in place. He walks out the front door with a whistle towards his bike, my ass exposed to the early morning sky.

"Keep an eye on her, Dalton. Don't know what kind of trouble she can get into before school even starts." Logan skims his fingers down the back of my thigh as he walks towards his car.

"Please get into trouble. I can't wait to punish you again. Be a bad girl, sweetcheeks." Tey crosses his fingers and grabs my thong between my ass cheeks until it's tight enough, before letting it snap back into place.

I'm going to murder him and bathe in his blood. My buttcrack hurts now.

Dalton lets go of me without warning, making me squeal as I slide down his body and land my already sore ass on the concrete driveway with a thud. I blow my hair out of my face and glare up at him from my sitting position. He just crosses his arms with a smirk, making his biceps bulge and strain against his white tee under his cut.

"Getting comfortable down there, aren't you?" he says with that annoying smirk that brings out a dimple. He turns around towards his Harley as he chuckles, swinging his long legs over the seat with ease.

I hold back a frustrated scream and take a deep breath before climbing to my feet. He just watches me with that stupid cocky smile as I walk towards him while dusting off my dress and plaster a smile on my face. His eyes drop to my lips before flashing back up to meet my gaze, just as I reach his motorcycle. He doesn't know that I was partially born to ride, he only knows I'm pretty handy with stealing a car. I'm not surprised one bit that the beat up Ferrari isn't in the driveway, already taken care of. I think I'll keep my secrets close to my chest until I need to use them for my revenge. I'll catch them all by surprise.

"Get on, little bitch." His smirk widens as the guys pull out of the driveway and it's just the two of us.

Placing my hand on his broad shoulders, I swing my leg over the seat behind him and plaster my body against his back with my thighs molded to his. My arms wrap around his waist, playing with the hem of his t-shirt and feeling his abs ripple under my fingers. A man can't resist the heat a woman can bring, the comfort of a body. That's what Doris told me at least. Give them what they want, let them think they have all the power, and then crush them. With my dress hiked up to my hips, he has to feel the warmth I'm radiating because almost as if he can't control himself, he reaches back to slide his calloused hand up and down my thigh.

The engine rumbles underneath us, the familiar feeling giving me a spark of excitement and makes me miss my crotch rocket. I wonder if anyone has found it in the desert yet and if they are scrambling? I hope I never find out.

"Hold on. You might want to tighten your grip, don't want you falling off. Although this one time, we chained up a guy, for trying to kill Logan, to the back of my bike and I drove for an hour straight. He was almost unrecognizable by the time I stopped. Are you into that type of stuff? That's what we do with anyone that crosses us," he shouts over his shoulder at me in a threatening tone. Trying to scare me, but the thing is I've seen that happen before.

The club wasn't allowed to touch me without Payne's consent. There were plenty of times I was groped, shoved to my knees in hidden corners, but I wasn't raped again. Didn't mean someone didn't try. Cruz had a way of giving a warning that I was his property without even having to say a word. So I know what a man looks like from being dragged behind a motorcycle on asphalt. The skin peeled away like an orange, leaving the insides to spill out. Twisted limbs, missing body parts, and so much blood that you could drown in it. Nothing will ever surprise me again, but the fear will always be there, lurking around the corner, just waiting to snatch me up. I feel bile rise up my throat and my fingers clench his white shirt as I place my forehead against his back.

"You know... with me being on the back of your bike, does that mean I'm your old lady now? I didn't know you felt this way," I mutter just loud enough into the fabric of his shirt for him to hear me, sarcasm thick enough to cut through with a knife.

"Shut the fuck up for the rest of the ride." His voice is full of disdain and he cuts off any reply I was dying to give by revving the engine, and speeding down the street at a neck breaking pace.

Well, fine then. Not like I wanted to talk to him anyways, but this did give me an insight into his mind. From what I gathered already, he has commitment issues. First, with the teacher and the display he gave me the first day we met, anyone could have walked in. Now, the two little words *old lady* makes his entire body go rigid and stiff.

Maybe I'm going about this all wrong with him. I should try smothering him to death with affection, attach myself to his side because if there's one thing I know, it's when you've never been shown any love and you finally have some... you crave it more than anything else in the world. He's going to run, but I'm going to give him what he secretly wants, have him on my side then make him pay.

I might just be my father's daughter after all.

My thoughts are dark and twisted. It's what scares me the most, and keeps me up at night.

He parks his motorcycle next to Logan and Nicky's cars, shutting off the engine, and starts to stand but I cling to him like a spider monkey. My hands glide over his shirt, feeling the ridges and curves of his eight pack, and to be honest with myself I'm impressed. He freezes and quickly whips his head around to glance over his shoulder at me. I smile sweetly at him and hum under my breath in anticipation.

"God, you're so big all over." I stare into his violet eyes and lick my lips slowly which draws his gaze right there like I wanted it to.

I move closer, pressing my breasts against his bicep and letting my lips barely touch his earlobe as I whisper in my most husky voice. "Think of me when you're with that teacher. Just remember who knows how to make it good for you." I'm off the bike and walking fast across the school parking lot before he can stop me as he sits there frozen staring after me.

Score one for Tillie. Zero for Dalton.

I can't help the small laugh that escapes me and I know he hears me because he starts swearing. Looking over my shoulder as I reach the double doors, I see him stomping across the lot with his gaze narrowed on me. It speaks of payback.

I went too far! Oh shit. Oh shit!

Swinging the door open quickly, I practically run into the school and start shoving people out of my way in the crowded hall as I look around frantically for an escape route. I shouldn't have said that. Shouldn't have teased him like that so early in the morning. God knows what he's going to do to me in public.

Shit. Shit. Shit.

"Little bitch!" Dalton roars, causing everyone to stop and stare as he heads towards me like an angry bull, ignoring the students that quickly jump out of his way.

A pair of familiar glasses catch my attention at the end of the hallway as he places his books in his locker. I'm thankful Evan is nerdy enough for me to pick him out in a sea of bodies. He's even wearing a different Star Trek shirt. My very first friend and I'm already using him as a safety net. I'm a horrible person.

"Evan!" I bellow, waving my arm around like a limp noodle, no doubt looking like a loon as I pick up my pace to reach his side before Dalton catches me.

Evan looks up at his name being shouted, his brows wrinkled in confusion, like he's wondering who the hell would be shouting his name when everyone seems to ignore him. I watch him adjust his black framed glasses just as his gaze collides with mine. His eyes widen as he glances over my shoulder and he quickly starts stuffing the rest of his books in his locker in panic, grabbing his book bag off the floor to swing over his shoulders with jerky movements, his hands are trembling. He better not ditch me! I'm going to need back up to face my big, bad scary biker. Wait...He's not mine!

Get your head out of your ass, Tillie, and stick to the plan, don't let them dig their way past the barrier you've taken years to build. I nod at myself, at my thoughts, and focus on my partner in crime.

"Evan, wait up!" I say breathlessly when I finally reach his side, panicking as I glance behind me to see Dalton staring, but his attention is otherwise occupied at the moment. Mrs. Sullivan comes prowling out of her classroom like the predator she is and steps in front of Dalton in red fuck me heels. As if it's not obvious enough, she starts stroking his bicep with her red fingernails and blocks his path. He doesn't even bother looking down at her, his gaze is firmly locked on mine promising retaliation.

"Dalton, if I could have a moment of your time. I'd like to go over something from that deep discussion yesterday," Mrs. Sullivan mutters, in what I think is an attempt at a raspy voice, instead it sounds like nails on a chalkboard. Too whiney and breathless.

Evan grabs my elbow, swinging his gaze left and right, like he might get attacked on a battlefield any second, but snatches it away like he was burned as Dalton tries to step around Mrs. Sullivan. He gives Evan a hard glare that speaks of death.

"Dalton!" The hoe of a teacher actually stomps her foot, her grip unyielding on his arm so he has no choice but to follow her into her classroom.

I can't seem to stop glaring right back at him, my left eye twitching at the way she tries to control him. I don't like her hands on him. No one deserves to be handled or touched without consent first. It is completely noticeable that he doesn't want to go with her. Why isn't he stopping Mrs. Sullivan? Is he going to fuck that twat?! That alone has me stepping towards him just as he reaches the classroom doorway, but Evan stops me.

"Are you nuts? Let's get the hell out of here before he decides to kill us!" Evan's voice goes high pitched, like he's going through puberty, as he shoves me along with his shoulder bumping against mine so he's not touching me with his hands.

I almost regret wearing the sundress with the noodle straps that leaves my shoulders bare, I feel completely out in the open like my shield of armor is gone. My scars and tattoos on display. Why did I think it was a good idea to do this? I stood in front of the mirror after changing into the dress and thought it was fine to start doing normal things I've never been able to do. I've only made myself a target because now people are staring at me. It's either with hate, burning jealousy, or lust sweeping up and down my body. I wish I could hunch my shoulders, let my hair fall in front of my face to hide, but that's not who I am anymore.

"You better be going to class, little bitch!" Dalton shouts, his voice echoing around the hall as people turn to stare at me, just before he disappears inside her classroom.

I don't like that fucking teacher. Just because she's going through a midlife crisis and is getting old, doesn't mean she gets to prey on anyone younger than her. A predator who shouldn't be around kids. She makes me want to bash her head into her dry erase board, repeatedly. My cheeks turn red at the attention of people staring at me, but I hold my head high as Evan and I start walking towards our class after a few seconds of just standing there.

"He wasn't going to kill you. Probably just me. Or at least do something to make me wish I was dead," I mumble, crossing my arms over my chest as we dodge out of the way of students rushing to class before the bell rings.

I hate the way my breathing picks up without my control every time I'm in a crowded place. The way I can't have eyes in the back of my head, or how I constantly have to have my guard up. One day I hope that my heart won't race, and my palms won't grow clammy, when a stranger stands too close to me. Even with my new friend, I feel like I can't relax, that my body is a tight string ready to snap.

"If you weren't one of the coolest chicks ever, I would probably be hightailing it out of here before one of those four douchebags eats me alive for just talking to you." He snorts at his own joke, gripping the straps of his leather bag as he walks nervously beside me.

I'm not so sure that he will stick around. I don't want him to get into harm's way either. I really hope the guys leave him alone and don't do anything just because he talks to me. Hell, they threw a fit and told on me to Franco just because I was in another guy's car. My life has been threatened enough times.

"I'm hardly cool. I'm probably the most boring person you'll ever meet. What class are you heading to?" I change the subject, not knowing if he's going to ask me anything personal.

I can't answer anything he would be curious about.

Why I have so many tattoos. How I came to know the guys after only just starting here. Nothing about my past can be brought up. I'll make sure I protect the innocent, even from myself.

"AP chemistry. Do you, um...want to meet for lunch? I mean you don't have to but if you want to uh... you know, hang out?" he asks slowly, like it's forbidden to even ask me and he nearly trips over his Converse sneakers as he fumbles with his words.

"I'd like that. You can give me all the deets about who's who around here too. This is my class, I'll look for you in the cafeteria!" I wait in the doorway with my arms crossed in amusement as he shuffles on his feet, looking nervous.

"For sure! I'll put some flashcards together on topics we can talk about..." Evan trails off and stares at me in horror, his cheeks a bright red.

"I totally love flashcards," I chuckle as he quickly nods his head and spins on his heels, walking with his head down as he mutters to himself.

I watch him make his way down the hallway as kids walk into him as if he's not really there. I glance at their faces, remembering them for sometime later, and slowly make my way into my classroom, noticing seats already filling up.

If I'm going to come out on the other side unscathed, I have to gather as much information as possible.

Biting my lip to stop laughing at the ridiculousness of high school drama when my whole life has been a soap opera. I scan the rows of seats to find an empty chair. I spot one in the back left corner with no other desks behind it, so I don't have to worry about anyone sneaking up on me. Old habits die hard. My eyes connect with a girl in the front row, her glare makes me stop for a second to figure out what her problem is, but then it clicks. It's the stuck up bitch who thought I needed a refresher yesterday by dumping her drink all over me. Real classy.

Paris.

The chick who follows Logan around like a dog after a bone. That bone would be his penis. It's not hers... I don't know where that possessive thought came from. I make my way through the desks, glaring at Paris as I pass her and give her the bird. She sticks her leg out at the last second, trying to trip me but I expected something like that from her, so I just skip over her outstretched leg and calmly walk towards the last desk.

"Stupid cunt," she mutters under her breath and leans towards her friend to the right, whispering in her ear as she flips her hair while staring at me the whole time.

"Logan likes my cunt," I respond back, for only her to hear, and I'm enjoying the way her face turns a blotchy red.

What are we? In second grade? If she ever saw half the stuff I've seen, she'd be admitted to a mental hospital and wouldn't be trying as hard to gain attention from everyone. I can stomach a lot now, after years of practice, but she wouldn't make it one day in my shoes.

The moment I sit down, I know I've made a mistake by not checking the seat first. Something squishy is under my ass, instantly soaking through my dress and making me shiver at the disgusting feeling. I hiss out a breath as I slide out of the seat and twist to look down at the clear, slimy jelly-like substance covering my butt.

With a curled lip, I leisurely glance up to see Paris holding up something in her hands with a satisfied grin on her smug face. My eyes zoom in on the lubrication packets being held up for everyone to see.

"Figured a whore like yourself would need some help with that used pussy," Paris sneers, her expression satisfied as if she won whatever game she's trying to play.

I ignore the laughter from the other students as I calmly walk towards her with my facial expression blank, so she can't guess what I'm thinking. I stare down at her without saying anything for a long minute until I slam my palms on her desk and lean forward just inches from her face which has her slightly drawing back from me with uncertainty in her gaze.

"I appreciate the gesture, but I don't need any lube to get wet. I can understand for a dried up bitch like yourself needing the help, that would explain why you carry them around." My lips curl in a smirk and I straighten to walk out of the classroom like I don't have a care in the world, even though everyone is staring at my white dress that's decorated with globs of lube on my ass.

The final bell rings loudly as I stomp down the halls in anger, muttering to myself and almost colliding with a teacher turning the corner. He steps out of my way, looking like he was about to say something but must have seen something on my face that has his jaw snapping closed because he lets me pass without a word. Maybe the tube was a sign not to get comfortable in front of others by wearing this damn dress. I head towards the gym at the last second, instead of going to the bathroom to try to get the jelly off, arguing with myself the whole way, knowing I have a pair of shorts and shirt in the locker room.

This is why I hate trying to blend in because no matter how hard I try to be invisible, someone is going to notice the broken girl and make her into a target. I think people can see right through me, smell me coming a mile away... maybe that's why the world is so cruel to me.

My wedge heels echo along the quiet hallway as I make my way to the other side of the building where the gym is. The thought of running out the front doors of the school without looking back is tempting, but I know I wouldn't make it far because Nicky seems like the type of man to make good on his promises of blackmail. I'd run out of the little money I have left in no time and would be caught within a few hours. Who knows with the way Nicky can hack into computers, he can probably get into any camera feed.

He can trace my steps easily, bringing me back kicking and screaming.

Rounding the corner of the empty gym, I jog across the wood floors and reach for the girls locker room door around the corner from the bleachers. It looks like gym class isn't scheduled at this hour. That's one good thing about today, enough students have seen my humiliation since school started this morning. I need a break before I completely lose it. There's nothing wrong with wanting to find a quiet place and let your mind wander, to recharge before facing the outside world again.

I have to pause with my hand on the door handle when I hear muffled male voices on the other side. I double check the sign to make sure it's the girls locker room, confirming it is. I debate what to do. Wondering If I should come back later. What if someone is getting their freak on in there? Maybe it's a hookup area everyone knows about since this class period is free.

"Get. Chicken butt. Ah! Get off me. Off me, asshats!" A girl shouts in repeated words, her voice high pitched and panicked somewhere inside the locker room.

My decision is made at the fear I can hear in her tone. I swing the door open so quickly that it bangs against the wall, enough to catch the attention of the three jocks surrounding the girl from gym class yesterday. The one who threw a book at Paris.

Her almond shaped green eyes meet mine, the hysteria clear in her gaze as the biggest one of the jocks crowds in front of her with his hand on her hip under her shirt. The other two are holding her arms in a grip tight enough to bruise, pinning her in place against the lockers.

"Hey, asshats, I don't think she wants you touching her." My tone comes out bored as I lean against the frame of the door with my arms crossed, so as to appear like the whole situation is no big deal.

I'm stalling. I glance around to see what I can use to beat them over the head with, but there's only a book on the ground. Looks like I don't have many options and I'm not about to leave her with these guys.

I slowly slip off my wedged heels as tweedle dee and tweedle dumb release her, looking at the one who seems to be in charge. They don't seem to know what to do with little ole me showing up and ruining their plans. I think it's the jocks from yesterday, the big one with red hair looks familiar.

"It's none of your business, new girl. Although I can be with you in just a second, after I'm finished with tourettes over here. Nicola owes me, but it's not like she doesn't want it. No one wants you anyways." Red leers down at her and twitches his gaze over to me. I feel disgusted with his brown eyes sliding over my body as if he has a right to think he can have me.

"You wish. Little penis. Little," Nicola snarls like a rabid dog, her eyelids blinking rapidly, and that just makes me want to become her friend even more.

She's cool. Her attitude is basically her sticking her

finger up at the universe, not caring about standard society rules. She's wearing black skinny jeans with colorful suspenders, and a black t-shirt with a giant purple butterfly that takes up half the shirt. It really goes with the butterfly clip she has in her hair, but it's kind of ruined by the way her hair is sticking up in every direction.

"Shut up, stupid bitch. I'm going to teach you a lesson. You're not as protected as you think." He slams her roughly against the locker, grabbing her short black hair in his fist to stop her from moving.

"Gary, man. I don't know about this. What if he finds out-" Looks like one of them has brains as his eyes shift behind me in a nervous gesture, as if whoever he's scared of might show up.

I wonder who he is talking about? I can't help the chuckle that escapes past my lips, which makes them pause to stare at me like I've lost my mind. Maybe I have.

"Really? Gary? That's your name? I'm going to give you five seconds to release Nicola or I'll make sure you all regret thinking you can lay hands on an unwilling female." I stare coldly into Gary's eyes without blinking, meaning every word.

Nicola fidgets, shaking her head viciously and as if she has no control over her limbs. She reaches out to dive her elbow back into Gary's stomach and twists his nipples through his jersey as he releases her. He hisses out in pain and I take that as my cue to step in. Without hesitating, I grab my wedges and chuck them hard at Gary's two minions. It catches the one closest to me right between his eyes. He stumbles back a step into the lockers as he groans in discomfort and holds his hands over his face, right over the shoe print it left on his forehead. Nicola screeches like a wild animal and slams her knee up into Gary's balls. He drops to his knees with a girly high pitched scream, his face turning pale then a plum color as the pain registers. The other jock trips over his buddy on the floor as he tries to reach for me, you can tell he's not the most graceful on the football field.

"Move. Peep corn! Move!" Nicola shouts, confusing me with what she's trying to say in her panic.

She slips out from between Gary and the lockers, reaching for my hand to drag me out of the locker room, but she smacks my outstretched palm away just as I reach for her. "Sorry. Can't help it." She grimaces and grabs for my wrist this time, leading the way out back towards the gym.

I hear shuffling behind me and am suddenly yanked back by my long hair, my arm slipping out of Nicola's grip just as she steps through the locker room doorway. She spins around in alarm, horror washing over her face just before the door slams closed just like a gunshot going off.

"You're going to pay for that. You might not have been my first choice, but you'll do. Jesus. It's a good thing you have a fantastic ass because it's hard to look at you with so many ugly scars on your body. A shame really, but it still gets the job done." Gary tightens his hand in my hair, twisting so that I'm hunched over and bent forward at the waist as he starts limping away from the door with me held in a grip that's impossible to escape.

He drags me farther into the locker room with his two friends following, both of them eerily silent besides their heavy breathing. Gary lets go of me, shoving me towards his friends who grab either side of my arms to hold me in place. I refuse to glance away, I meet Gary's gaze head on as he stands in front of me with a leering smirk that sends a shiver of horror down my spine. I won't let him know how truly scared I am. My mask will be firmly in place, no matter what, I can't go back to who I used to be.

"Larry. Stan. Hold her still while I teach her a lesson on who runs this school," he orders and glares when a snort escapes me at their names.

Just like the three stooges.

My head whips to the side at the unexpected blow, the back of his hand cutting my lip. Breathing hard, my head hangs between my shoulders as I stare at the floor. Lip throbbing, my blood trails hotly down my chin and drips onto the tiled floor one drop at a time in little bright red splats.

"You're a nobody. Nothing in this place, whore." Gary brings my head up by my hair, his voice sounding far away.

I can hardly see his blurry face in front of me as my body starts to tremble, the only noise I can hear is my breathing, even though I know he's talking. I'm not really here anymore. I'm transported into a time and place from the past, a memory that I try to bury deep into the back of my mind. No matter how fast I run, how much I hold back...I can't escape.

"Dad. Have you seen Uncle Rig?" I ask timidly, wishing I didn't have to confront my father, but I haven't seen Uncle Rig for days. It's not like him to not check in on me.

Dad turns his head away from Nix, setting his beer down on the bar top, and glances at me with a smile that seems not quite right.

Deranged. Twisted.

"Sometimes I forget for a while that you're alive, but then I see your face and wish you were never born." Dad delivers that blow, making me stumble back in shock at the cruelty.

I always knew that he didn't like me as a daughter. I'm a disappointment, all because I wasn't born a male, but I never knew how deep that hate ran until now.

Lorrie laughs from her position on Dad's lap, kissing up his neck as she stares at me with a nasty smirk, like she knows a secret I don't.

"Wha-what have I ever done to make you hate me so much?" *I croak out, staring up at my dad, looking for an ounce of love that I desperately crave.*

I'm always starving, feeling like a shallow body just waiting for someone to love me until I'm completely full.

"Absolutely nothing. I despise you, what you stand for." *He laughs loudly, the sound echoing back as the Demon Jokers members join him in his sickening display of hatred.*

I always pretended what went on around me was never really there, the drugs, the fucking... it never existed in my mind because I had an escape with Uncle Rig and Cruz. The only people who make me feel like a somebody. Someone important to them.

"I'm sorry," *I whisper, feeling my eyes fill up with tears, and the need to run makes my body tremble.*

"Pathetic," *Dad says with a mocking smile as he stares at me.* "Rig isn't coming back, he didn't even want to be around you. You're nothing, Tillie, and never will be," *he taunts, like a slap to the face and I search his eyes for the lie, but I find nothing.*

"You're wrong!" *I cry out and don't see the fist coming towards my cheek until it is too late.*

Sprawled out on the worn wood floor, I brace myself on my hands with my legs curled under me as I choke on my sobs, my mouth pooling with blood. I can't breathe, can't gasp or draw in a breath as I watch my blood soak into the wood under my palms. A hand grasps my hair, pulling hard at the strands to make me look up at him, my neck strains at an awkward angle.

"Do you know why I was named Payne?" He crouches over my huddled position, waiting for my answer, but I don't have one. "Because I'm known for causing pain, everyone earns my fist as I bring them close to heaven. This is all you'll ever feel until you draw in your last breath, but even that I'll own. Your lessons start now, Tillie. Take her to the basement." He shoves me away, nods his head to Nix who reaches for me and starts dragging me across the room towards the basement stairs.

"You'll know your place."

Those are Dad's last words to me before Payne enters my life, destroying everything beautiful I once held close to my heart.

It was only pain.

CHAPTER 5

Dalton

"Don't be like this, Dalton. I can make it feel good, I promise." Mrs. Sullivan runs her fingernail down my chest, trying to play the game of seduction, but I've already seen someone who matches my tastes and darker needs.

"Really, Mrs. Sullivan, I'm more into hot, tight pussy, not the loose ones." I shrug my shoulders, glancing at the door impatiently.

Her gasp of outrage has me looking back at her, taking in her tight clothes that are inappropriate for school. The way she styled her red hair in curled disarray, right down to her bright cherry red lipstick, it all screamed attention to me. When she first came onto me, I thought fuck it. An older chick wants to ride my cock because she's desperate to feel heaven. I'm not one to brag or anything, but my dick is legendary around these parts. Big enough to make you question your sanity, but by the end of the night you'll be screaming my name. I mean, I'm not going to pass up free pussy that throws itself at me. Anything to get my dick wet... Now I have my sights on one pussy that's not going to give it up easily.

I keep picturing her staring into my eyes, her chocolate gaze not breaking eye contact as she took control and focused my teacher on my cock. The thought alone makes me groan out loud, and makes the cougar in front of me reach for my zipper in excitement. Maybe if I let her jerk me off, my thoughts won't stray to the little bitch. The way her lips stretched wide around my girth, her tongue flickering over me, that almost brought me to my knees. She can put on the act all she wants, but that girl can't help but love a focused hand. I may have brought her to her knees easily with a little blackmail, but I almost didn't go through with it until I saw her furious gaze directed at me. I felt the way she wanted me, but hated it at the same time. Her breathing was heavy, pulse pounding on her neck, and eyes wide, but not in fear.

Rapture.

Eagerness.

Sometimes when I feel like I'm missing something, just beyond my reach, I find another way to fill that void. Usually my method is with my pants around my ankles and my cock deep in any pussy it can find.

"Let me take care of you and then you can take care of me." Mrs. Sullivan's whiney voice draws me out of my musing, her actions greedy as she reaches for my belt buckle.

She gasps in shock as I slap her hand away, and walk around her without bothering to answer her. The final bell rings as I open the classroom door and I know I'll have to catch Tillie after her class is done, which just sucks ass. She's going to pay for her little game this morning, getting me hard to the point it hurts and then running away from me. I'm still hard, maybe I should rub one out again before heading to class. It's a lost cause though, I'll be hard again in seconds just thinking about her.

"Dalton!" Mrs. Sullivan shrieks, but clears her throat as she realizes how loud she's being and tries to change her tune, talking to me like I'm being unreasonable. "You can't walk away from me, I'm the authority figure around here. If it's that girl from yesterday, she can't do anything for you! I'll make sure she gets transferred out of here before you can-" She was smirking, but it quickly slipped away as I shove her beside the door with my hand wrapped around her throat, grasping enough to drive my point home.

"Know your place, woman. I don't take kindly to anyone going after what's mine. We aren't anything. A quick fuck to get your jollies off and make yourself feel young again. Am I wrong?" Her eyes are wide as she claws at my hand, her face a bright red tone that matches her lipstick. "Don't mess with me. You won't like the outcome." I stare hard into her eyes, making sure she understands that I won't hesitate to make sure her body is never found before I release her.

She falls to the ground, drawing in deep ragged breaths, loud enough that I almost missed the sound of the ding on my phone going off. Stepping over her legs and walking out the door without looking back, I pull my cell phone out and see a video in my messenger

Pressing play, my steps slow as it becomes clear what I'm watching. Shit. I'm hoping that Nicky's phone has magically stopped working and he doesn't find out about this. He really liked that dress on her, the stoic faced bastard can't hide shit from me. He can keep his features all emotionless, but I like watching people. I may be a kinky fucker but it has its advantages at times when it doesn't involve my cock. Nicky couldn't keep his eyes off her this morning, watching her stand there in the dress he picked out just for her. He can deny it all he wants, but she's caught his attention.

I really liked how it clung to the curve of her ass, I could get behind that. Literally. It's a shame now that it's covered in thick coats of something clear and wet looking... is that lube? Whoever took the video better pray that it doesn't reach Nicky. I send a quick text to Logan, he'll hunt down who took the video and make sure it's taken down. Maybe the school needs a reminder of who runs this fucking ship. We live harsh lives so when we see something we want... we don't wait around to claim it because tomorrow you might have lost that chance as you're lowered six feet under. No regrets and no hesitations. Besides, I'm kind of taking it personally that someone dared to think they could mess with our plaything. That's my job to make her life miserable.

This whole thing reeks of Paris. She thinks she can do anything without consequences. We gave the word to mess with Tillie, but not without asking for permission first. That's just how it goes.

Now, where could the little bitch have gone after that show of embarrassment? She wouldn't dare leave the school without one of us. I pause in the middle of the hall at a thought and quickly turn around, heading towards the gym. She has gym class near the end of the day and I only know this because I went over her schedule, but not in a stalker way. Okay, maybe a little stalkerish, but I'm curious about her too much. I wonder if Logan can transfer us so that at least one of us is in all her classes to keep an eye on her. My dad doesn't like the sound of her appearing out of the blue at a time when everything in the club business goes to hell with missing shipments. It's not a coincidence. I take the stairs down to the basketball court and cross the gym with my head down. I'm so lost in thought about tonight's church meeting and having to tighten security around the compound that I didn't see her until she's pounding on my chest.

"Help. Help! Help her. Pencil dicks! Shit. Shit!" Nicola hits my pecs repeatedly in her panic, pausing to flick my nose then starts hitting me again as her head tics to the side without her control.

I grasp her shoulders to push her away so I can look her in the eyes, about to tell her to calm the fuck down but the look on her face stops me. Her hair is a mess, messier than usual. Her shirt ripped on her shoulder, hanging off like someone grabbed her.

"Who did this to you?" I bend my head down to make sure she's only focused on me, asking in my most calm voice to help her get her words out, but I'm seething inside.

Someone is going to die today.

"Not me! Asshats! Save. Little penis. Save her!" She pushes me away, flailing her arms around while her head tics to the right side with her eyelashes fluttering, and she points towards the girls' locker room.

Something in my gut tightens, not having a good feeling and everything is telling me I know who's on the other side of that door.

"Go get Logan. Don't tell anyone. Especially Nicky or Tey. Second floor, class 202 and hurry the hell up!" She nods her head fast and takes off running towards the stairwell.

"Fuck." I don't waste time breaking into a run with my boots pounding on the gym's wooden floor. Swinging open the girls' locker room door as quietly as I can, the thoughts of murder running through my head.

The moment I'm inside, male laughter reaches my ears and I walk on quiet feet past lockers, deeper into the room towards the showers. Peeking my head around the corner, I see those fucking jock losers on the football team holding someone down on the tiled floor.

"See. What did I tell you guys? She wants it, she's not even putting up a fight," Gary, captain of the football team, says on top of the girl who isn't moving.

I look down at my knuckles, seeing them still shredded to shit from last week's match, but it's worth it even if I can't fight this weekend. I debate which one to take out first as I sneak up behind them quietly. Two other guys are holding her down by her arms, but it comes to me easily who should get beat to death first. Gary leans back from on top of the girl, giving me a view which I swear causes a film of red to cover my eyes as rage sets in and locks my muscles up tighter than a bow. Seeing the sunflower dress wrapped around her waist, and her straps torn at her shoulders, I hear this distant echo, a roar that bounces off the walls and that's when I realize, it's me.

I rip Gary off her by the back of his collar, sending him flying into the lockers with a bang, and roll my eyes as he passes out so easily. Larry and Stan stare up at me with their mouths gaping open, and turn to look at each other in fear as they release Tillie.

"I-I... it wasn't-t my idea-a, man!" Larry backs away

from Tillie with his hands held up, but I hardly notice as I stare down at Tillie who isn't moving.

Her head is turned to the side, her chest heaving, and her eyes wide open, but it's like she's not even here. The trail of blood on her face sends me over the edge. Larry screams like a little girl and pushes Stan down to the ground as he tries to escape.

"I don't think so," I growl at Larry, stepping in his path and punching him in the face just once.

He drops to the ground, knocked out cold, and I turn my murderous gaze toward Stan who wets his pants when our eyes meet. He crawls backwards on his hands, whimpering as he crowds against the wall.

"Dalton. I'll handle this," Logan announces from behind me in a deep, angry voice that promises pain.

Lots of pain.

I glance over my shoulder, seeing him standing there with his gaze narrowed on Stan with death in his eyes. I notice the handkerchief in his fist, knowing that blood is about to be spilled. He doesn't look away from Stan, stepping over Larry, and nodding his head at me without having to say a word. I take a deep breath and turn towards Tillie who still hasn't moved even though she's not trapped under their hands anymore.

I approach slowly until my boots are right in front of her face but she doesn't even blink or acknowledge me. Crouching down, I hesitate for a second but shake it off, as I reach out and grasp the hem of her dress, bringing it back down to cover her thighs. I flick my gaze up to see if she's about to knock me dead on my ass for touching her, to see that murderous gaze like the other night, but her eyes are wide and staring at nothing... still unblinking. Her mouth is moving fast but I can't hear what she's saying. Placing my hands under her knees and one under her shoulder blades, I scoop her up until she's against my chest. Her head falls onto my shoulder like she's exhausted, her whole body trembling in what I can only guess is shock. I quickly stand up, clenching her tighter to my chest, and can finally hear what she's muttering over and over under her breath. The noise of pounding flesh and whimpering echoes behind me, but my complete focus is on the girl in my arms who is lost in her own world.

"Not again. Not again. Not again." Her trembling lips form the words, her voice a soft mumble, and her gaze distant.

"Little bitch," I whisper down at her, waiting for her to reply, but she just curls in on herself in my arms as if she wants to bury herself under my skin. "Tillie. I need you to snap out of it. If you show your weakness, they'll eat you alive." I grumble into her ear, wondering how I'm going to snap her out of it.

Her chest rises and falls rapidly against mine, her skin flushed warm under my fingertips and her hand suddenly grabs a fist full of my cut to pull me closer.

"Can't. Breathe," she gasps, her panicked eyes finally meeting mine as she looks up and clenches my cut with a death grip.

"Hold on. Just take a deep breath, okay?" I grunt out as I pull her up higher in my arms and as fast as I can, I get her the hell out of here before anyone can see us.

Busting through the locker room doors like a man on a mission, I suddenly stop walking under the basketball hoop when I hear the bell for classes to be dismissed ring out. Just great. The sound of the halls filling up with students, some heading towards the gym, like a stampede of horses. I look down at Tillie real quick and notice she's still stuck in a panic attack. I can't let anyone see us like this, me helping her and her not being able to walk on her own two feet to stick up for herself.

Glancing around, I notice the gym equipment room to my right and book it for the open door, just as I hear sneakers squeaking over the wooden gym floors. Kicking the door ajar with my foot as we enter, the door slams shut and it's just me and Tillie. Spying a stack of blue mats under the small window that only allows a little bit of light, I walk over to them and sit down with her cuddled in my arms. I don't think I could even get her fingers to let go of my cut if I tried. She's holding on for dear life.

It takes a lot of trust to show someone your weak spot, to lay yourself out there naked for all to see, and pray they won't take advantage of you. That's what she's doing. She may not realize it, but I just became her anchor. I'll give her this one moment to pull herself back together then give her hell again when she's ready. I won't kick a man down when his back is turned, unable to fight back, and it's the same thing right now. On the other side of the door, I can hear the shuffle of feet and laughter, but the loudest sound is her breathing that hasn't calmed down.

"Hey," I whisper softly in a raspy voice, feeling her jump in my arms as her gaze connects with mine, as if she forgot I was here. "You need to breathe. Think of something that makes you happy, a time where you couldn't stop laughing," I suggest, letting her know that it's just the two of us here sitting in the dark where no one can see her breaking.

Her brow wrinkles as she stares up at me, her deep brown eyes look a little lost as if she can't think of one. I watch her mouth open and close a few times but she doesn't say anything.

"That's kind of sad, you know? I don't have many moments but I can pick out a few that come to mind." I tilt my head, staring at her for a long minute, wondering what kind of life she's had if she can't find a moment where she felt like she could laugh.

"Like what?" she asks on a shuddering breath, her eyes closing as she tries to calm her racing pulse.

"There was this one time I got kidnapped. One of my best memories actually," I smile, remembering it like it was just yesterday, even though it was a couple of years ago.

"You're crazy." She snorts in disbelief, her eyelids fluttering open to stare at me as if I'm well...crazy.

I shift her in my arms to hold her closer against my chest and lean back against the wall to get comfortable because I'm in no hurry to leave. Plus, this gives me a chance to get some answers out of her, if I share a little about myself.

"Only the best kind. Now shut the fuck up so I can tell my story." I glare down at her to see her biting her bottom lip and I don't like the way my chest squeezes at the way she's looking at me.

As if I'm her only hope of a small escape in her dark world. Ever since she's shown up, this lost look hasn't left her eyes. It's the kind of look you get when you think there isn't a way out, you're stuck in one place and don't know what to do. I don't want her looking at me like that. I'm not a hero and never will be.

"I come from a home filled with violence. Raised in a world of crime that just seems like any other normal day to me. I've been following in my old man's footsteps since

I was a kid, being groomed to take over for him when he's ready to step down or die on his bike. Either one. Being the next to take over comes with a price... there's always someone who wants your crown instead. A traitor, snitch, a spy in the midst of the club. I learned a lesson the day I was kidnapped." I pause, staring hard into her eyes and curling my arms harder around her to the point I know it's painful but she doesn't glance away, only curls her lip at me in annoyance.

There she is.

"What did you learn?" She glares back at me, knowing where I'm going with this, and she's gripping my shirt with both fists now as if she's going to shake me.

This is more like her. Fire brimming in her eyes, her gaze looks like she's wishing that I'd burn to ashes so she can dance in my remains. I can see her doing that.

"Never trust anyone, even those who say they are loyal to you. I learned my lesson after being buried alive for three days with only a small pipe sticking out of the ground to keep me breathing." I smile widely and that causes her to draw back from me like I'm sick in the head or something.

"Why are you smiling like that?" she asks warily.

"Because it wasn't my club brothers that found me. It was Logan, Tey, and Nicky. I didn't waste time killing those who betrayed my club. I became stronger physically and mentally because I showed them all that no one can mess with me. Revenge is best served cold and now their bodies are buried in the place they tried to keep me, to forever be frozen in the dirt." I shake my head, reliving that memory and when my eyes focus back on her, she's staring up at me in wonder, her face closer to mine.

"How? Where does that strength come from, to face

something that can leave scars?" She lets go of my shirt and grasps my face between her palms, squishing my cheeks until my lips pucker and brings me closer as she begs me to answer her.

"It's either ride or die, baby. You should know that already. Now, stop being pathetic and weak. It's not like they got very far, only a busted lip and a flash of panties. Maybe don't wear a red thong to school." I shove her hands away, hating how good they feel on my skin, soft and warm.

I need space from her to clear my head. The slap comes out of nowhere, whipping my head to the side. I slowly turn back to her, rubbing my jaw as I shift the tender spot back and forth at the sting.

"I'm going to kill you." She actually growls at me, so much venom in her gaze that it's turning me the fuck on, but then again she can breathe and it makes my cock rise to the occasion.

"You can try. I do love a good fight." I stare down at my scabbed knuckles, remembering the guy I knocked out flat on his ass just a few days ago.

"You guys are unbelievable. Not everything needs to be violent or controlled. Where is that freedom of knowing peace? Aren't you tired of fighting all the time?" She grabs my hand, sliding her delicate fingers over my cuts with her brow wrinkled, like she doesn't understand why I need to fight.

I think deep down she does know. If my hunch is right about the scars decorating her skin that she tries to cover up with tattoos, she's had to fight her way through enough battles that most people never see in their lifetime. Why does she fight herself on fully living when she can be fighting her way through those that have hurt her? I've already hurt her and when she finds a way to bring me down, I don't think I'll want to get off my knees. While she's trapped under our wings, I'm going to teach her it's okay to fight your way through people with fists.

"Fight me, little bitch. Show me what you got." I grab her wrists with one hand and slam them against the mats over her head, leaning my upper body over hers before she can blink.

"Get off of me. I mean it, Dalton. I'm tired of all this bullshit." She blinks rapidly and glances away from me to stare somewhere over my shoulder.

"Where's the fire, Tillie? Why aren't you fighting your way to the freedom that you crave so much huh?" She ignores my question and that just won't do.

I want her undivided attention centered right on me.

I quickly roll, bringing her with me as I grasp her waist with my other hand until she's sprawled out on my chest. I let go of her hands and watch as she leans up with her palms braced on my pecs, her long hair falling forward to give the illusion that it's just us and no one else on the other side of the doors.

"Tell me what you need and I'll give it to you, just this once. Fight me." I grin at her as she cocks her head in confusion to the side.

"Why?" she asks, her fingernails biting into my chest, leaving marks that she's unaware of, but I'll treasure the pain like a lifeline

"If you could do anything to those meatheads, what would it be?" I ignore her question because she can't ever know that she fascinates me.

She stares at me for a minute in silence, her gaze dropping down to my mouth and back to my eyes as she bites her lip in indecision.

"I'd make them bleed," she whispers in a gasp, like she's pulling in her first breath in a long time.

I smooth my hand along her side until I reach the hem of her dress, the pad of my thumb grazing her warm, smooth tan thigh back and forth. She stares down at me, her chest rising and falling in sync with mine. I don't break eye contact as I try to control the grin that wants to spread across my mouth. I see the fire awakening in her gaze instead of that lost look that drives me crazy.

"What else?" I ask roughly, my voice deepening.

"Make them feel how I did. Powerless," she breathes on a hiss, her teeth baring as she pushes away so she's sitting up on my lap.

"How?" I grip both of her thighs to keep her in place before loosening my grasp to run my fingers over her soft skin as I push her dress up until it's bunched at her waist, giving me the perfect view of her red thong.

"By breaking their fingers first. Making sure they can't lay them on any female ever again." She grins in delight at that thought and I swear my cock is going to burst through my zipper at the sinister smile that's spreading across her face.

"And?" I'm practically salivating for her to continue talking, desperate to just shove her panties to the side and stuff her with my big cock until she feels me climbing up her throat, but I can be a patient man.

I did say she can have anything this one time, so I'll give instead of taking.

"And I'll start by bringing a bat to at least one of their knees, so they can never play football again. Their dreams broken." She sucks in a breath as I glide my palms to the inner part of her thighs, my cut knuckle rubbing back and forth over her damp panties, right over her clit.

"Keep going," I say with a straight face even though my gravelly voice betrays me.

"Tha-that feels nice." She breathes heavily and groans in agony when I stop moving my fingers, waiting for her to keep going. "I'll, uh, make sure that they remember me. Slicing through their skin to leave my mark with my knife." Her hips shift over my lap, seeking my fingers to give her any ounce of pleasure and I'm feeling generous enough to give in to her silent demand.

"Lean back and brace yourself on my legs but don't look away from me. Keep talking. Are we clear?" Her chocolate eyes stare at me for a hot, long second before she nods and does as I say, giving me the perfect view that I can't seem to look away from.

"I'll watch the blood pool around their bodies, enjoying every second, knowing that I did that," she says in a daze, watching my fingers push her thong slowly to the side, and seeing her cunt leaking her juices down the inside of her thighs.

"Fuck. You're soaking wet. You love this, don't you? Little bitch, I'm going to make sure that your revenge happens." I promise her in a gruff voice and she flicks her gaze towards mine, which I was waiting for. Knowing she's going to ask what I mean, instead I start sliding my index and middle finger through her wet pussy, gathering her juices.

I slowly glide my fingers up and down between her pussy lips, her wet cunt soft and soaking just for me. I'm a desperate man, on a mission to hear the sound of her moans of ecstasy, something that will keep me up late at night. My eyes almost roll to the back of my head at the sound of her wet pussy, knowing how much she's getting turned on at the thought of harming others that deserve everything that's coming to them.

"I-I can't think when you're doing that." Her head rolls back as she bites her lip and that won't do at all for me.

I'd prefer to hear her scream and not giving a shit who hears.

"You want me to stop?" A grin spreads across my lips as her head whips back up to glare down at me and she shakes her head. "Then keep fucking talking, keep your eyes on me, and I'll give you what you want," I order, circling her clit slowly, coating her in her own juices that I can't wait to taste.

"Fuck, you're mean." She moans in pleasure, her hips moving in slow, tiny circles that's driving me nuts as her ass rubs all over my raging hard cock. "Once each of those fuckers are begging for mercy, I'm going to give them a show of something they can't ever have because they are beneath me." She gasps as I plunge my fingers swiftly into her pussy without warning, and then retreating, the suction sopping wet sound of her cunt driving me crazy.

"What are you going to do?" I'm curious how she will show them, but my attention is more focused on her pussy tightly gripping my fingers as I stroke inside.

I gently flick my fingers on her G spot, rubbing back and forth in a way that I know will have her screaming my name in no time for me.

"I'm going to make sure Gary is begging for forgiveness as I get fucked right in front of him. He'll see that he will never be a real man and no woman will ever want him. He'll always come in last place." She rolls her hips, riding my fingers as I pick up the pace and feel her coming close to the edge as her pussy flutters, but she needs a little push.

"I'll make it happen," I say between clenched teeth, loving how blood thirsty she is and the way she hides behind her big, innocent looking brown eyes. "Come." I rub my thumb over her clit in a fast circle as I pump my fingers into her just as fast, she gives in to my order without hesitation and the sight is seared into my brain.

Without looking away, she comes all over my fingers with a long, quiet moan and I think I like that more than her screaming. It was reserved just for my ears alone. I keep rubbing her clit, feeling her body shake on top of mine as she collapses onto my chest with a groan.

"Why do you fuckers keep messing with me and making me show you my weaknesses?" she pants into my ear with a whisper.

"Because we own you. Don't forget that. Your weakness is my gain." My voice comes out deeper than ever, aggressive.

My palm comes down on her exposed ass cheek hard, just before I'm shoving her roughly off of me. I may want to give in to my urges but I won't let her see my weakness. I seek warmth that wasn't made for someone like me and she's had plenty of warmth radiating off her. She shoves her hair out of her eyes and glares up at me as I stand up, stretching my arms over my head with a yawn. I can pretend all I want that I'm not affected by her, but my cock straining against my zipper tells a different tale of how much I want her. I'm not the only one affected, she keeps gazing down at my hard cock with hunger in her dark chocolate eyes before glancing up at me with a glare that could kill a man with one single look.

"I almost forgot for a second there," She quietly says, standing to her feet and shoving her dress back down over her hips while avoiding eye contact with me.

There she goes again, hiding and not letting me see the secrets she doesn't think I see behind her gaze. My eyes narrow on her, hating that she won't look at me. So I stand there waiting until she flicks her gaze away from the wall and glances back at my face. I stalk towards her, enjoying her eyes growing wide until I'm inches away. She doesn't say anything as I bring my hand up to her face, it hardly looks like she's breathing. I run my finger across her plump, soft bottom lip and watch her eyes flutter as she sucks in a sharp breath. I pull my hand away and she gazes up into my eyes as she licks her bottom lip, as if to savor the sensation I felt there. Her eyes dilate as she finally tastes her cum that I spread over her bottom lip, leaving behind a wet gloss that makes me want to pull her close and devour her mouth. I pull away with a deep breath and make my way towards the door without another word, before I land myself in trouble. I run a hand over my hair as I stare down at my cock, telling him to cool the fuck down. I can't walk around forever with a boner. I'll find a chick to help with my blue balls soon, someone who doesn't have big, brown eyes that are asking to be saved.

Fuck.

"What did you forget?" I was going to just walk out, leaving her alone, but it's as if I can't help myself, wanting to know what's going on inside of that head of hers.

"What a fucking asshole you are," she says angrily, and a slow grin comes over my face that she can't see as I stare down at the doorknob.

Maybe some spark inside her is trying to be lit and I can't wait to see it fully go off as I strike the match. Today was just a small appetizer and I'm a man with big appetite, we are only just getting started.

"Don't forget it for one second, little bitch. It will be your downfall if you let your guard down around us. Also, don't tell Nicky about what happened today. You aren't ready to see him let go of his control just yet," I say with a deep breath, knowing Nicky is going to go on a killing spree once he finds out that not only were jocks messing with his little sister, but his property too.

"See what?" she asks in confusion, but I'm already swinging the door open and nodding to Nicola as she straightens from the bleachers once she sees me walking out.

I don't look back, even though I want to see Tillie's angry gaze directed at me. Instead, I'm going to have to be holding back a violent Nicky who's going to be out for blood once he finds out. I hope Logan has a plan.

Fucking hell.

CHAPTER 6

Tillie

"That mother fucking cock sucker!" I mutter under my breath, pacing back and forth in the storage room, trying to decide if I should chase after him to give him a piece of my mind.

Everything keeps swirling through my head over what happened, even though I don't want to relive it. I left one place of sickening evil filled with monsters that took my innocence and made me live in fear, only to end up in the same situation. It almost happened again in that locker room because I decided to play hero when I'm anything but. Only my rape was going to be in a different place with different men. I place my hand over my racing heart, wondering how the hell I'm still standing, but I guess I owe that to Dalton. I thought while laying on the cold, dirty locker room floor, I'd open my eyes with my underwear around my ankles and more scars between my legs. Instead, I was lifted and held close in a pair of strong arms. He sheltered me in a dark room, so I could hide any weakness from prying eyes and regain my strength.

Why did he do that? I hate his 'I walk on water' attitude, that cocky smirk like he's a gift to all women, but I know better than anyone that you can hide a lot behind a facial expression. Fake it until you make it. There's more than meets the eye with these guys and damn him for making me feel, when all I want to do is hurt him as much as he hurts me. He could have left me to those jocks, but he saved me and brought me out of the past that I always seem to be stuck in. He gave me hope, a dream of revenge, to destroy anyone that tries to take pieces of me.

I kick the mat in anger and storm after him, giving chase. I'm going to beat his ass for distracting me and touching me so fucking softly. I've never had that before, and he's ruining my plans for revenge against him and his three friends by taking care of me. I throw open the door, not caring as it crashes against the wall and draws the attention of some students that are crowded on the gym floor about to start class. I only take a few steps and freeze when Nicola comes rushing towards me with clothes piled in her arms, but she stops suddenly. She jerks, her arms flinging the clothes on the ground and she kicks them towards me. I stand there with a grin as she turns and makes shooting fingers while wiggling her hips.

"Wow! Give me the drugs! Drugs!" Her cheeks turn red before she clears her throat and shuffles over to me and picks up the clothes, throwing them in my surprised face. "Cover your booty with these. Big booty!" she shouts through her cupped hands and smacks her forehead before taking a deep breath.

"Thanks. You didn't have to do that." I grin softly at her as I slip on the soft material shorts under my dress and throw the grey T-shirt on too, as I sneakily slide the ruined dress down underneath the shirt.

"Wasn't me. Logan said to cover your skanky ass." She rolls her eyes and grabs my wrist to drag me with her, but stops once to actually smack my butt in front of everyone before leaving the gym.

I can't tell if it's her tourettes that made her do that or if she just doesn't care what others think. Her way of saying go ahead and stare, fuck you all. I study her side profile, seeing her short hair is a mess and her eyeliner is smudged under her eyes.

"Are you okay?" I ask cautiously, not knowing if that was her first run in with Gary and his minions.

The thought makes me want to murder them. Nicola shouldn't have to deal with the cruel world, she's too innocent. I know by just one glance at her. But I'm curious how she knows Logan, they don't look like they run in the same crowd. Unless...no. It couldn't be, I'm thinking crazy thoughts.

"Don't worry about me. I'm sorry you walked into that. It shouldn't have been that way," she calmly says and lets go of my wrist once we are in the hallway near the windows that show the courtyard. "They were only after me because of how I am and who I am. Small penis!" She shouts that last part loud enough that people turn their heads and she smacks her forehead once against the windows.

"Hey! I think you're fucking brave and brilliant! I don't care if you were the world's biggest bitch, no one should have to go through that. No one." I glance around and notice the wide berth everyone seems to be giving us but the whispering behind their hands as they stare at Nicola pisses me off.

No one messes with my friend. Yeah, I'm claiming her, even if I have to lick her.

"You got a problem? Keep fucking walking!" My shout rings through the halls as I place my hands on my hips and glare until they look away. "Dicks," I whisper under my breath.

"You're crazy. You're going to be labeled as the girl who hangs out with the chick with tourettes. Don't leave me when you find out who my brother is." She cracks her knuckles quickly and pinches my arm, but I know she can't help it.

"I don't care who your brother is. I don't give a flying fuck what other people's opinions are. I'd be freaking honored to be your friend. Let's shine together, Nicola. We have to at some point in life." Damn my voice for catching, pent up emotion leaking through. I surprise myself and her as I side hug her because I am not a hugger at all.

What is happening to me? I used to avoid any human contact like the plague. Maybe this is me trying to move on with my life, to have something I've never had. To be accepted and loved. I clear my throat and step away from her, rubbing my arms as I try to figure who the hell I am. She looks me up and down with her green eyes that I swear look familiar before smacking the back of my head.

"Don't you know you can't go around just hugging people? Were you raised by a pack of animals?" She questions, seriously and links her arm through mine as she pulls me alongside her. I couldn't care less where we go.

Her question catches me off guard. She doesn't know that I wasn't raised by a pack of wolves, I was the meat for the pack instead.

"Do it again anytime. God knows I never get affection from home. Woop fudge fuckers!" she yells out suddenly and punches a random guy on the arm as he passes us, the bright colors of his jersey giving me a hint that he's on the football team.

She's not even sorry and that makes me like her more. She's going to be my bestie right next to Evan. She keeps walking and ignores the guy rubbing his arm as he glares after us. She leads me down another hallway and lets go of my arm as she pulls open a pair of double doors that open up into the library.

"Since I have a free period and you have study hall, let's hang out here. Don't bother to ask, I was curious and checked your schedule. I'm the office assistant," she casually says with a wave of her hand and wanders into the back of the library until she finds a table near the floor to ceiling windows as I follow after her.

"You're pretty bossy. I swear you remind me of someone." I hint at her, my hunch driving me crazy, but she just sits there smiling. There's no way they can be related because he doesn't smile.

"Just ask. Everyone always does. Bitch!" she blurts out as she clicks her tongue, loud enough to echo and hear a distant hushing in return.

I do something I never do. I start laughing so hard that my stomach hurts, tears rolling down my cheeks as I grip the table edge so I don't fall to the carpeted floor.

"Nicky is my brother, in case you were wondering," she says, confirming my suspicion.

Green eyes and high cheekbones run in their family with that cool, void facial expression. This makes it easier to be her friend because she may appear innocent but if you look past her almond shaped eyes, you can see shadows in the depth of her gaze. She's seen some shit that most never do. Also, it gives me an opportunity to get information on that douchebag brother of hers.

"Don't even think about it. Motherfucker! Fucker!" she randomly yells and continues unfrazzled, I admire her for that. "But he's my big brother. Blood." She chuckles at my expression which drops as she says that.

"Fine, but just so you know I have plans for your brother. He is on my list." I honestly tell her, not wanting it to be a surprise when she sees her brother fall to his knees in front of me.

"He probably deserves it. Just don't kill him. He's all I have." She rolls her eyes with a smirk, but I can hear the affection for that asshole in her voice.

"I'll try my best. No promises though. Can I ask you a question?" I bite my lip, leaning my upper body over the table wondering if I should sink to the floor instead because it's none of my business and God knows I'd never overshare anything about myself.

"I can see what you're about to ask and the answer is no. Gary and his asshole followers have never crossed that line until today. It's always threatening, shoving, but nothing beyond that. Most are too scared of my brother, but sometimes people have something to- eek- to prove. They think they hold the power when they clearly don't. I think with you being the center of attention to the four most dangerous guys in school... it gave them the green light to go after me." She shrugs her shoulders like it's no big deal and only a person who is used to stuff like that acts like it's just another ordinary day.

"Okay, new plan. Kill the jocks first, then I'll get my revenge on the big four." I reach across the table to fist bump her and it's sealed in a promise as she smacks her fist against mine.

We practically have our heads together as we whisper back and forth about the mission to kill the jocks. She might think I'm joking but I'm dead serious. It's one thing for myself to get hurt, to be punished for being born. It's not okay if someone messes with my second real friend. Ride or die, baby, and this chick is going for a ride until I'm breaking bones and stomping on dicks so they won't ever be able to spawn a child.

Jesus H. Christ. I've been starving for so long that I'm hungry, my need for bloodshed making my stomach cling to my spine and I don't think I'll ever be full.

"What are you two, uh, doing?" Evan pokes his head between us, startling me that I yelp as Nicola lets out a shriek and punches him in the gut so fast I almost missed it.

"I'm sorry! Forget I asked!" Evan groans in pain, clenching his stomach, and places a tray of sandwiches on the middle of the table.

I knew there was a reason I liked this kid. He speaks my language. Food.

"Sex! Dirty Sex! Gimmie," Nicola says loud enough that probably the whole library hears. She reaches for a sandwich, all cool and collected, but what has me choking back a laugh is how Evan's cheeks turn red as he avoids staring at Nicola.

"This right here is why I'm keeping you. Sit down and join our evil plotting." I wave to the empty seat next to Nicola, munching on the turkey club with a grin and completely ignoring the throb on my cut lip.

I've had worse, I think with a small shrug.

"I don't know, Tillie... he doesn't look like he would accept our evil ways. He probably wouldn't join us to get reven-" Nicola doesn't even finish that sentence before Evan slaps his hand down hard on the table.

"I'm in. What's the plan? Who, and how are we getting rid of the bodies?" His voice comes out determined as he adjusts his glasses up the bridge of his nose.

Well, okay then. I didn't see that coming from my shy, nerdy friend. I glance at Evan, looking him up and down in thought. Looks are deceiving, I should know. I never thought after all the time I spent with Cruz, he would turn out the way he did. People put on a mask and won't reveal themselves until they finally have you in their grasps with no escaping.

Seeing Evan and Nicola chatting back and forth in excitement, it's like I'm starting my own little gang. It almost feels normal, sitting here with two people who I hope I can count as friends. Makes me forget the last few hours, that we just meet every day in this spot doing absolutely nothing but talk shit. I've always been lonely, never asked anyone to take a step into my world, but here we are.

"The three jocks with a death wish, and the school's most dangerous guys. Nothing yet planned. So far setting houses on fire is off the list. Too messy to hide the evidence to make it look like an accident. Thought about taking a boat ride, but bodies can float to the top of the ocean. So it's still in the works." I tap my chin, lost in thought and feeling a little bit twitchy.

It's been days since I got my adrenaline rush, the dangerous game of racing and needing the freedom of the wind pushing at my body to keep going. Just being on Dalton's bike this morning made me miss it all the more. My poor bike.

"Honestly, I don't think you'll get the chance with the

jocks. Logan knows about it, he had blood on his hands when he threw your clothes at me, and it's only a matter of time before my brother and Tey find out. My guess, Dalton is going to help stall for as long as he can. Family means a lot to Nicky. No one messes with his family. No one," Nicola sighs, blowing a raspberry as she leans back in her chair looking at the high ceilings.

Damn it! It's my turn to fight back, to gain something I've never had. They won't take that away from me. I'll just have to beat them to it. Step one, take care of the guys first. Kill the jocks for touching me and Nicola, then I'm out of here. The thought saddens me as I stare at Evan and Nicola helping me plot death. That's true friendship even if they don't mean it, thinking it's just a game.

"Give me something here, Nicola. Anything. What your brother likes or dislikes," I plead, begging at this point because I'm coming up empty so far on what to do.

Any information would be helpful in exacting my revenge.

"Nicky keeps to himself really, he never smiles. He's serious all the time, but I can't blame him. He's been trained by my father- Wanker!" Nicola's head ticks to the side and she pokes Evan in the shoulder with both hands repeatedly, before she stops to glance between us both with a shrug. "Sorry, I've been watching Peaky Blinders. It's uncontrollable." She glances away with her jaw clenched like she's embarrassed and I can't imagine what she's feeling, but the uniqueness of her makes her a gem in a world filled with assholes.

"I, uh, like it. Don't be sorry!" Evan blurts out, rubbing the back of his neck nervously as the tip of his ears turn beet red.

"Thanks," Nicola whispers softly, clearing her throat

before looking at me all serious. "Well, Nicky is hard to read, but he enjoys being around his best friends. Having their backs. He likes reading and the quietness. Racing. Karate is kind of programmed into him, but he likes that too," Nicola says, but jumps with a squeak when my palm smacks the table as I lean over, practically in her face.

"Back the fuck up. Racing?" I ask excitedly, seconds away from shaking her as my own hands tremble.

"Yeah. Father doesn't approve. Says it's a waste of time when he could do something else that benefits the family. As a matter of fact- Big titties! Little waist," Nicola suddenly says and smacks her head as she mutters something under her breath about never listening to that song again.

"What! What is it? Tell me!" I'm hanging by a thread here, feeling like a junky.

"There's a race tonight. Nicky mentioned it in passing, he probably knows I'm going to try to sneak out again to follow him, but he hates me anywhere near places that could possibly put me in danger," she mumbles, squinting her eyes at Evan who's just been staring at her with wonder in his gaze, but I'm done listening.

A grin spreads across my face, smiling so big my teeth show and both of them draw back in their seats looking at me warily.

"What?" Nicola questions hesitantly.

"She's scaring me," Evan says, reaching out to grip Nicola's arm and she quickly glances down at his hand with her mouth popping open.

That look... has no one ever touched her before like that? With affection?

"I know what I'm doing tonight," I chuckle, it probably

sounds crazy but this is my time to shine and beat Nicky at something that will put him down a few pegs.

"I'm almost scared to ask, but what are we doing?" Nicola breaths out, reaching out to grasp Evan's arm in return in excitement.

"We're going to a race tonight." My voice comes out raspy and breathless, knowing someone has my back.

This is one step closer.

I have a fever, a sickening need to breathe in vengeance.

CHAPTER 7

Nicky

"She makes me want to murder her," I grind out through my teeth with a hiss in the computer lab as I glare at the screen.

The nagging feeling of checking the school's cameras kept bugging me. I knew she would do something like this because she's trouble. She won't listen to a word I say without giving back sass and narrowing her beautiful eyes at me.

I watch Tillie look left and right before crouching down to book it across the parking lot with my sister right by her side. My sister! How the hell do they know each other already? I was hoping to keep Nicola away from Tillie, she's only going to get my little sister into trouble. Just where do they think they are going without my permission?

"Brat," I mutter harshly in Japanese under my breath

and zoom in on the image just as she opens the passenger door to Nicola's Jaguar.

Not on my watch. I'm going to have to teach Tillie a little lesson... My chair crashes to the ground as I suddenly stand up at what I see on the computer screen.

"Nandayo!" I yell in japanese at no one, causing the girl next to me to jump in her seat and quickly scoot away.

My hand grips the computer mouse so tightly that it cracks under the pressure as I try to pause the image of that guy sneaking into the backseat of Nicola's car. At least he has the grace to look scared because yeah, I'm going to toss his body into the school dumpster where he'll melt over the weekend under the California sunshine.

Huffing under my breath and running my hand through my hair, I log off just before the nosy teacher tries to peak over my shoulder.

"Nicholas, please pick up your chair and return to your work or I'll give you detention for disturbing the class," Mr. Cass says in a haughty voice with a smirk.

"You do that. I'll personally make sure that the school board and the parents find out just what you have hiding on your computer." Sarcasm is thick in my voice and hearing him gulp nervously almost makes me smile. "It's under the top picture file, is it not?" I tilt my head, staring down at him as he stutters.

No one talks down to me. Maybe I'll send that file to the school board this weekend. I'm sure they'll wonder why one of their teachers has pictures of female students' underwear on his computer. Fucking pervert. I'd bet my left nut that he would be a potential client of my father's, and that just makes me take a step closer to him, wanting to snap his weak neck. I take a deep breath as I lean closer, down towards his short height, smelling his sweat, and enjoying the color drain from his pudgy face.

"I'd watch your back, Mr. Cass," I whisper darkly, seeing out of the corner of my eye half the class leaning forward to hear what I'm saying.

It's always like that. People turn away the moment I make eye contact but the moment that breaks, they try to draw closer because they can't help themselves. We are all drawn to the dangerous side, the forbidden. I straighten to my full height and walk past him without another word.

I pull my phone out of my dress pants the moment I'm out of the classroom, away from the prying eyes. She picks up on the second ring, answering with a groan.

"Get out of the car now or he's dead," I threaten with a promise as I hold the phone with my shoulder to unbutton my cufflinks and roll my sleeves up my forearms in case it gets messy.

"Nicky!" Nicola whines out in a plea and then starts swearing at me which has me pulling the phone away from my ear until she calms down.

"I'm feeling generous, Nicola. Aren't I letting Tillie stay in the car with you?" I say as calmly as I can once she stops yelling at me in Japanese.

"Evan is just going to hang out with us. Tillie... fucking! Cockmuncher! Tillie told me you're on babysitting duty anyways, I was going to head home with her and Evan," Nicola grumbles out and her voice sounds distant as she mutters away from the phone.

"*Just- don't touch...Oh wow! Your Tattoo is gorgeous! What's it say?*"

I wonder what the hell is going on but it comes to me as I remember Tillie has a cursive script tattooed on the right side of her ribs that starts at the edge of her side boob. All her tattoos are covered by clothes, so why is she stripping in front of another man!

"Why the fuck is her shirt off?! He better not touch her!" I roar into the phone, completely losing it as jealousy eats at me.

I hang up as Nicola screams into the phone, pleading with me, but I've heard enough. I'm already angrily dialing someone who I know loves to get rid of bodies.

"Nicholas," Tey answers smoothly in that raspy voice of his and I swear a shiver runs down my spine.

"Where are you? I'm. Going. To. Murder. Him," I snarl and Tey chuckles huskily into the phone in amusement, but that won't do. "He's touching Tillie..." I nod my head in approval as Tey starts describing how he's going to kill the fucker that's touching our plaything.

"Then I'll use a butter knife and take my time cutting off his legs, I'll make him stay alive until I'm done. I'll meet you at your car," he growls, which surprises me because he's usually laid back no matter what.

I've seen him slice a knife across another gang member without breaking a sweat, like he was having a cup of tea instead of painting with the dead guy's blood on the walls. But with Tillie... we're in trouble. Tey attaches to things that aren't good for him, and I'm worried he's going to replace his unicorn with her.

"On my way. Be there in two," I reply with a huff and hang up to jog out the front doors to reach the parking lot before classes let out for the day.

The fewer witnesses, the better.

Almost to my car, I spot Tey coming from the football field, no doubt from lighting a joint under the bleachers. He says that's the quietest place to find a moment of peace. Swinging my driver side door open, I smoothly slide onto the leather seats and start the engine. It rumbles to life, making me close my eyes, and the need to escape for a while in a race has my hands twitching on the steering wheel. I'll have to get away for a while, Lorenzo sent out a massive last minute hidden message text for anyone who wants to buy in tonight. There's a race at Santa Monica Pier where the crowd will be thick with bodies, the dark of night giving you a high that screams of danger. Jin won't be in town for the weekend so I won't have to watch Tillie while he's in the house. She'll be safe from his observing gaze and greedy hands. My sister will have someone to confide in, too, even if I don't trust our little spy.

"Where is she? Who do we have to kill?" Tey says as soon as he hops in the car, taking out his unicorn to place it on the dashboard between us, like it's joining our conversation.

Some might suggest he should be put in a mental hospital but I, well, find it adorable. He can look as crazy as he wants, it's a sexy kind of crazy with that maddening grin of his that always brings out his dimples. He paralyzes me, I always feel like my breath is trapped in my chest when he's near. Jin would rather have his son dead than one who likes men and women. I wish I could shut the voices out of my head, to be who I want to be. To grab the back of Tey's neck and kiss his plump tempting lips so slowly, savouring every second, but I'm not there yet. Something always holds me back.

"They already left. That Evan kid was in the car with Tillie and Nicola. No one with a dick goes near my little sister. I'll kill him." My teeth grind together, already planning a way to get rid of Evan's body for going near my sister and for even daring to take Tillie with him.

My property. She's in the car with another male that I don't approve of. I'm not jealous. It's impossible.

"Well, what are we waiting for? Logan wants to go to the warehouse to check some merchandise before heading to the docks. I've got some time to hide a body, although I might have to change my clothes before heading out tonight. Blood is a pain to get out, even an on the go tide stick doesn't work. What to do? What to do..." Tey nods his head and picks up his unicorn, placing it to his head like he's intently listening. "Hmm, yes. I think you're right." Tey grins wickedly and throws his arm across the space between us, his hand resting on the back of my neck.

"What is it?" I swallow roughly, holding back a groan as his finger presses on either side of my spine at my neck, staring me hard in the eyes.

"You're too tense. When was the last time you had a release?" he questions, biting his bottom lip as his blue eyes darken the longer he stares at me, he glances to my lips and slowly back to my gaze.

"Just this morning," I rasp out, wondering why he keeps torturing me like this?

I'm only so strong before I break and say fuck it to everyone who tries to hold me back.

"What were you thinking about when you came?" His voice sounds hypnotizing, I can't help but just blurt out the truth.

"You and Tillie. Taking her at the same time. Watching you take her slick pussy, sinking in deep as I told you to fuck her hard and good. Then when both of you were ready, I slid in right beside you so you and Tillie had no choice but to feel me." My cock is straining against my slacks, trying to burst through at the mental image I stroked myself to this morning.

Tey looks down with a lopsided smile and leans closer, slowly, to give me plenty of time to pull away, but I don't. I want this so bad, I can practically taste him. I can feel his hot breath between my shoulder and neck, stopping on that spot just above my collarbone. My grip on the steering wheel tightens, the sound of the leather shifting under my hands makes Tey's eyes flicker there for a second before glancing back at me. He knows how my heart races whenever he's close, his eyes always gaze at my neck where my pounding pulse betrays my wants and desires.

"I was talking about street racing, but this is much more interesting. Keep going." He bites down on my skin, holding his teeth there to keep me still.

The cool metal of his lip ring skims my neck so lightly that I barely feel it, like a whisper of a ghost. It causes a pleasurable shiver to trail down my spine, making me crave more without saying a word. I tilt my head to the side with a quiet groan, unable to resist the slight pain of his teeth digging in and the pleasure of his lips pressing against the tender flesh.

The passenger door opens, but I don't move as Tey bites down harder, breaking skin. I'm not worried though, I can smell engine grease and the woodsy cologne of the fucker interrupting my moment of intense pleasure.

"If you two fuckers are done fucking in public, we've got places to be," Dalton grumbles and reaches in to grab the back of Tey's shirt to drag him out.

"Calm your man tits, Dalt, we weren't fucking... yet," Tey says with an evil, seductive promise of what's to come, but I need to pull myself together.

I can't be caught by Jin, he always had eyes and ears everywhere. I'd be disowned or killed depending on his mood. It's hard to say no to Tey though, he drives me closer and closer to that edge of just letting go. One of these days I won't be able to hold back, no matter if it puts my life in danger.

"Where's my little bitch?" Dalton asks, leaning in the opening of the door to glance in the backseat but gazes at me with a raised brow when he notices she isn't here.

"She went to my house with Nicola... and the soon-to-be-dead kid, Evan," I mumble to him, squeezing the steering wheel just thinking about him anywhere near her.

I don't like this feeling. I don't want it, she can take it back with her when she leaves or dies by my hands.

"Fuck me sideways. Tey, you still got that chainsaw?" Dalton questions him, his violet gaze turning wild like a storm unleashing on the skies.

"Enough," Logan commands as he strolls casually up to his car on the other side of mine. "We have places to be that are more important. She'll be fine. I think the brat can handle herself," Logan says with his lips in a tight line and gives Dalton a meaningful look.

What are they hiding? And is that blood on the collar of Logan's white shirt? The fuck? He never spills a drop on himself. What has he been up to since this morning? I lean over the passenger seat to see Tey's gaze already staring with laser focus at the bloodstain. His eyes meet mine for a split second but I know that look. He'll get the information out of Logan later.

"I'm going to stop at the storage unit, to make sure all the supplies are there. Dalton, I'll call you after I'm done so you can report back to your pops at church. I'm racing later." I flash a quick grin at Logan who looks pissed as fuck but he'll get over it.

"Don't get caught. Some of the cops at the precinct aren't all on Franco's side at the moment, and I know for a fact they are talking to the FBI. Don't fuck Tillie either." He stares me down with that order but I just press my foot on the gas, letting it rumble loud enough to drown out his voice.

That's what you get for tasting the goods without telling us. I'm not jealous he already had Tillie. Not at all.

I'll keep telling myself that until I believe it.

"Five thousand, my friend, for buy in. All or nothing." Lorenzo flashes his gold teeth at me as he passes a wad of thousands over to the girls in bikinis hanging off his arms.

I don't trust him, he's a part time dealer for the west side gang, Los Muerte, that even rivals Dom's gang. They have no morals...a code to live by. They'd shoot their own members in the back without remorse. Lorenzo is sort of like the peacemaker between each gang in L.A. You want to send someone in to talk to a rival without blowing out anyones brains, you send him in. The guy knows how to talk and sneak his way out of any situation like a fucking worm. I'll give him that at least. Plus, he can put on a race at the last minute and still have the street lined up on either side with people ready for a show, ready to party with the need for an adrenaline rush.

"Have I ever come empty handed?" I arch a brow at him and reach into my leather jacket for the money, knowing it's all there as I hand it over.

He flips through the bills but stops when he notices

me still standing there staring with my arms crossed. He passes the cash over to one of the girls at his side and places his hand on my shoulder, leaning closer with his gold teeth almost blinding me. I slowly look over to the right at the unwanted touch and he quickly snatches his grip away as if I burned him. Might as well, I don't like to be touched.

"Listen, amigo, a new whip was bought in tonight. Didn't even see the driver but..." He whistles under his breath and nods his head over to something behind me.

Looking over my shoulder to scan the competition, my gaze passes over a yellow Porsche Carrera GT, not the least bit worried. A cherry red Chevy Corvette, American muscle is a beauty but still not comparable to mine. The same Audi R8 V10 is parked near the end, the same frat guy that shows up at every race thinking he can beat me, but again... I'm unbeatable. My Nissan GTR could smoke any of these losers without even trying. Only the best comes out on the other side, I never lose. Cat-back exhaust, nitrous oxide, and a tuned chip gives my car the balls to race, but it's the guy behind the wheel that makes it into first place, and that's me. My gaze shifts near the end of the line, blinded for a second by the high beams shining directly at me until my eyes adjust.

I stand taller as my eyes travel over the completely blacked out Dodge Demon with electric purple lights under the body. Sleek and blending in with the night, the all wheel drive conversion with eight hundred and forty horse power without a doubt could leave everyone else in the dust, but not me.

"I haven't lost a race before and I won't be tonight, amigo." I slap Lorenzo's shoulder a little too hard, staring him in the eyes until he looks away first and clears his throat.

"Ah, I'll see you at the finish line my friend." He throws his arms over the two hardly clothed women and walks away with them clinging to his side as he greets everyone he passes, like he's welcoming them into his home.

Eyeing the sexy as hell car one more time, and knowing Logan is going to be pissed, I walk toward my white Nissan without saying a word to anyone. Women always try to get close to me, to rub their bodies against mine but the thought of their hands on me makes me bite back a sneer of disgust. Every damn time I'm here, usually Dalton can play distraction, but I'm on my own tonight.

"Need a prize at the end of the race, baby?" A female voice purrs at my side, her Latino accent thick and raspy as I reach for my door handle.

A hand slides down the leather jacket covering my right arm, skimming over the scars on my knuckles, and tries to play coy as she slides closer until she practically tries to crawl into my skin. The overpowering smell of her perfume makes my nose burn, making me bump into my car door as she follows me, thinking I want her. She grabs my hand and places it on her hip while smiling up at me, but I don't even see her face anymore. I'm frozen, placed in a time that I'd rather not revisit because it's the time I learned what life is really about. You aren't living until you get your first taste of pain and there isn't any going back after that.

"I'm disappointed. My own son, my own blood betrays me like this!" Jin paces in front of my kneeling position, as I stare down at the floor with my head bowed. I can only see from below his knees each time he passes by.

The shiny leather shoes show my reflection as he stops in front of me. The blank look on my face gives nothing away, but if I lift my head he'll see the tears gathered at the corners, dying to escape. He places his hand on top of my hair, petting me as he clicks his tongue in disappointment.

"I thought I raised you in a house where you want for nothing, all your needs met, but I was wrong. You've been spoiled, given everything. I gave you a chance, Nicholas, to prove yourself, so you can one day take over. But you are no son of mine. Did you think you could help those useless cunts? Do you not think I have ears and eyes everywhere?" He grabs a fistful of hair at the top of my head and bends my neck back until I'm looking up at him.

His face is emotionless, a man of no thoughts, of no sympathy, no mercy. I'm starting to take after him in that respect. One day, it will all just shut off and even when I bleed, I won't feel where it's coming from.

"Did her pretty looks lure you in, thinking you could save her?" His lips curl back and he shakes my head until it feels like my brain is rattling around. "Answer me!" he shouts in my face and pushes me away in disgust.

Tears escape, leaking down my face as I sit there breathing hard on the floor with my head bowed and my shoulders hunched.

"She grabbed my hand and wouldn't let go," I whisper, admitting as tears fall faster down my cheeks, splashing onto the floor that sounds oddly loud.

I snuck into the shipping container that I saw a handful of my father's men leave, laughing as they slapped each other's backs and left the metal doors unlocked. I wasn't allowed this far back into the docks. I alway had to listen to Jin talk about the family business at the warehouse at the front when he met with his clients, but hearing words is different from actually seeing it.

I knew something was different about my father, even at a young age. Money came in easily, endless amounts on hand. His meetings always involved men who had this gleam in their eyes when they stared at me. The way they smelled of greed and evil, it was an overpowering smell of cologne to hide their toxic stench. Men who hide aren't real men, they just disguise themselves so we can't see the real them.

I went into that dark container, knowing I'd find something that makes my own father just like those men. I leave the door open a crack to see and when my eyes adjust, I can't move. Rows and rows of small cages, stacked on top of one another, filling the whole container all the way towards the back. A single aisle led between the cages and weak, dirty hands grip the metal locked doors. Some reach out in desperate hope between the bars, but not a word is spoken. I step further in, not believing my eyes as women and young girls stare back with dead eyes.

Something tugs at my sleeve, making me look slowly to my right, almost afraid of what I would find as I stand there shaking.

"Help me. Please," a girl pleads through dry, cracked lips, hardly moving her mouth as if she's too weak to talk.

She looks like she is in her mid to late teens, but it's hard to tell with her face dirty and her hair tangled around her head. She can't stand up, her body curled up in a ball, but her hand grips as if it's using all the strength she has. I can't move, frozen as I stare into her blue eyes that plead with me to save her.

"I can- can't," I whisper, trying to move away from her, to leave this place that I am sure makes hell look like paradise.

She quickly snags my hand, gripping with the rest of her strength and doesn't say anything else as she stares at me. I *stop shaking, my heart slows down to that one moment as we stare at each other. Knowing I can't do anything, but I can hold her hand because she is scared and has given up on any hope of being saved. Maybe I can be her knight in shining armor? To help her escape before anyone notices. I can help them all, one at a time, until they can see the sun again, instead of the pitch black.*

I scream as I'm suddenly ripped away, my eyes wide as they look into her blue eyes, seeing the color dim until it looks like she's not really here anymore. Kicking and swinging my legs, I cry out the further I'm dragged away from her, until I'm thrown into the office of the warehouse and that's how I start cracking at the seams. Learned that life is deceiving and hope doesn't exist.

"She held your hand? Not even a taste of pussy and you're whipped just by a simple touch. You are weak, but I'm determined to make a man out of you, even if you die before that can happen. Hold out your hands," Jin says and walks around his desk to a glass cabinet that displays canes.

He grabs a long, wooden cane and comes to stand over me without a word until I hold my hands up for him. The first wack out of the cane causes me to hiss under my breath, more tears start flowing, but after a while, as blood drips from my knuckles, the pain goes away until I am numb. I learn that I'll never be a knight in shining armor because no one can be saved, a perfect bubble pops and brings back awareness.

The sound of a deep rumble brings me out of my memories and gives me a chance to bat her away from my hand. I straighten to my full height and curl my lip in a sneer that has her smile dropping fast. The noise of an engine roaring as someone presses on the gas while in park has me looking back at the Dodge Demon car, and I swear I feel whoever is behind the steering wheel staring right at me.

"If you want to live, you'll leave now before I put a bullet in your head," I calmly say to the woman who still tries to cling to me while I stare at the blacked out windshield, as if I could somehow see through it.

She gets the hint as I look back at her without blinking, spinning on her too tall heels to run away. I climb in behind the wheel, starting the engine that rumbles to life, causing the crowd to glance in my direction.

That's right, hear me roar.

This is the only way I know how to use my voice, I'd rather sit back and observe than try to talk. When my car echoes like a clap of thunder as I rev her up, it can't help but do all the talking. It says stay the fuck away and beware because I'm going to kick everyone's ass without breaking a sweat.

Lorenzo swaggers to the center of the road as we line up on the white spray painted line one of his girls draws as she runs in her high heels in front of our bumpers. My palms slide over the steering wheel, feeling the car vibrate with life under me,and everything centers as it becomes clear. I'll win because there aren't any rules in street racing and I'm always fucking up the rules. I glance out of the corner of my eye at the Dodge Demon to my right, the person behind the wheel slides down the passenger side window just as Lorenzo pulls his gun out of the back of his pants. My eyes connect with a pair of familiar chocolate eyes and I feel the blood drain from my face.

"See you at the finish line, Nicholas. Winner takes all." Tillie blows me a kiss and sets the launch mode with a smirk as she rolls the window back up.

I glance over the Dodge, wondering if she stole it as

someone pounds on the hood of her car for good luck. The face of the stranger becomes clear as a headlight shines on her. My glare has my little sister shuffling away from the car as she grips Evan's sleeve to drag him away too. Both of them are in fucking trouble, but not as much as Tillie. Before I have the chance to get out of the car to spank her ass in front of everyone for defying my rules, Lorenzo points his gun to the night sky and fires one shot. With a whoop that's heard over the engines and squealing tires, she literally leaves me in the smoke as the tires burn rubber.

"Shit!" I grind out through my teeth and stomp on the gas to catch up before she ends up killing herself.

Following closely on the ass of the red Corvette that shifts side to side so I can't pass on the long stretch of road, I upshift a gear and whip my steering wheel to the left to move around to the front of his car before an oncoming vehicle can crash into me. Even at night, Los Angeles stays awake, parties until dawn, and the streets are kept packed as they come and go. This is why these races are so dangerous and don't have rules. You can't block off the streets, you move with the traffic even if it's in another lane heading in the opposite direction. You can die just for this thrill, but that's part of living.

Coming up on a sharp corner on Olympic Blvd heading into downtown, I curse and upshift again to catch up to Tillie, just as she's about to turn. I don't think she's going to make it, the yellow Porsche is at the back of her bumper and the light is turning red... It's almost like watching in slow motion and not being able to stop it. She turns the corner sharply, the tires skid on the asphalt and she comes within inches of sideswiping a minivan as it crosses the street on their green light. At the last second, her tires find traction and she straightens out like a pro. She takes off like a bat out of hell with the Porsche hot on her ass, and frat guy not too far behind, even though his back bumper is hanging off from hitting a fire hydrant. For some reason, it's easier to breathe, like I've been holding off the oxygen in my lungs, but seeing her execute that move injects me with a new buzz that's addicting. It's a challenge and I completely accept.

You want a race, baby? Then you got yourself a race.

Seeing no way around the corner without getting hit, I jerk the wheel and jump over the curb until I'm on the sidewalk with pedestrians jumping out of the way as water hits my windshield from the busted hydrant. I turn on the windshield wipers, almost hit a couple, and quickly look in the side mirror. The Corvette rolls and a truck crashes into him as he tries to squeeze in between cars. One down. Seeing an opening back on the street between two cars, I hop off the sidewalk grazing the underbody against the curb causing a shower of sparks. I bounce in my seat as my car settles back on the road. I'm aware of the abuse I'm putting these wheels through. A hundred and eighty grand for this thing? Petty cash anyways.

Up ahead, railroad lights start flashing and the gates start coming down, but Tillie and the Porsche go flying over the tracks just in time. Their front tires leave the asphalt for a split second before coming back down, her car jerks heavily to the right, but once again she straightens the wheel before she can lose control. Where the hell did she learn to drive like this?

The train blares, the light coming up faster the closer I get. With the Audi right next to me, everything else passes in a blur, but I can see the frightened gaze of the frat guy as he makes eye contact with me. I lay on the throttle and wonder just how much I am willing to risk to feel this alive.

Fucking everything.

The Audi pulls back, his tires squealing as he stomps on his brakes, but I just clench the wheel for dear life.

"Fuckkkkk!" I shout and start laughing, my heart racing a mile a minute.

Breaking through the crossing gate, I'm blinded by the single train light and catch air as my tires leave the tracks. My back bumper is centimeters away from the oncoming train but my foot never leaves the gas as I slam back down to the road. Swerving, I straighten the wheel and come up fast behind the Porsche. Lights of red, blue, and white flash behind me, their sirens are loud, but I can still hear their voices yelling over the PA.

"Pull over! Pull over now!" The officer shouts through his microphone.

It just causes me to grin over the irony of being chased by the cops, and an idea comes as I stare at the back of the Porsche, knowing how I'm going to get rid of them. Logan said no cops so I have to listen to him, don't I? Shifting into sixth, I keep on the gas as I fast approach the back corner of the Porsche's bumper. Slamming into him at the right angle, I whip my car to the left into oncoming traffic just as his car starts spinning out of control. He takes out two cop cars, causing them to flip. I weave between oncoming cars, ignoring the honking and flashing high beams. Seeing an opening, I swerve back into the right side of the road and come up right behind Tillie. That won't do.

"Come on, come on!" My lip curls as I try to pull up

right beside her, knowing we only have two more miles to the finish line.

Her window comes back down once I'm even with the Dodge Demon, and she's laughing as she swerves around a car and comes right back next to me with ease. She's crazy, but her face is glowing as she winks at me. She's loving this.

I can relate and catch myself at the last second, just as I start to chuckle under my breath. I'm starting to wonder if I've lost my mind, too.

Neck and neck with her, our last turn is up ahead, then back towards the finish line. No rules, no Jin, no standing so tall that my spine feels like it's going to crack in half. It's just me, the streets...and this fucking girl that's literally stealing my breath away with the power she's radiating. I squint through my window shield, seeing a sign in bright orange.

Closed road.

Glancing left and right as we get closer and closer, I spot a construction site to the right ahead, and see the chained fence locked. Speeding up, I make eye contact with Tillie and jerk my head for her to follow me. She raises a brow at me in question but nods her head firmly.

Good girl.

Shifting down a gear, my car slows and I turn the wheel hard to the right to make it at the last second with Tillie right beside me. The lock on the chain fence breaks easily as we crash through and instantly we split up. She goes to the left, to avoid the metal frame of the building under construction, as I go right. I lose sight of her, not being able to see her in the dark, but see glimpses of the purple streaks of her car lights.

"Fuck. Shit. Fucking hell," I curse on a growl as a line of orange cones get in my way.

I hit every single one of them to avoid all the metal pieces stacked on pallets around the site. Seeing an exit at the back that's going to only fit one of our cars at a time, it's either crashing into her or driving right up the pile of dirt to jump the fence. I'm sure as fuck not slowing down, so it's going to have to be her. I hear her engine rev, speeding up, and see her race towards the exit with cement all over the roof of the car as she pops out of the other side.

"Not happening. Slow down. This is my race." My heart starts pounding because she's not slowing down but speeding up.

If I could take a picture of this moment, I would. She's smiling without a care in the world, her hair whipping around her face as she sticks her head halfway out the window to yell, but I can't hear her. I shift my gaze back towards the exit that's fast approaching and glance back over to see her mouthing something at me.

"You lose." She laughs with her head thrown back and speeds up until her car is lined right next to mine, so close that I can see her brown, wide eyes in the dark.

Glancing back and forth at her then at the exit in panic, it suddenly becomes crystal clear she's not going to slow down. At the last second, I slam on my breaks and the car bumps against her tail end. Controlling the wheel, I jerk it left then right until it straightens but not without the side of my head smacking against my driver side window. She bolts through the gate and skids across the street as she turns, waving at me out the window as she takes off. Shifting gears in a white knuckle grip and stomping on the gas, I take off after her again with a sharp turn. I keep shifting until I'm right behind her, the purple light of the underbody lighting up the front of my white Nissan.

"Not today, Tillie. I own your ass," I mutter out loud and place my thumb on the nitrous button, waiting for the right moment.

She blocks me by swerving the car left and right, keeping me behind her, but I see my opening just as I spot the crowd up ahead at the finish line. Pretending to go towards her right side, she swerves that way too, but at the last second I press the button and come out from behind her left side. My body presses into the seat as I grip the wheel to remain in control even at this speed. Cars on either side of the road line up with their headlights on, acting as a runway, and I can practically taste my victory. Only a few cars from the finish point, purple lights flash out of the corner of my eye and I watch in shock as Tillie passes by me. She passes a jumping Nicola on the finish point, who's shaking Evan in excitement as she bounces around. By the time I'm slowing down and throwing the car into park, Tillie is getting out of the car. Nicola runs for her with Evan hot on her heels and hugs her while jumping around at the same time. I quickly get out of the car and slam the door, which draws the attention of Evan who was about to go in for a hug but thinks better about it as he sees my glare.

"That was fucking amazing, chica! It's about time someone smoked his ass!" Lorenzo laughs and passes a smiling Tillie her winnings.

"It was nothing, pretty easy," she replies back, grinning cheekily and tosses Evan the keys to the Dodge Demon. "She's a beauty and a dream. Here, take the money. It needs some TLC." She hands over the money still smiling, her chest heaving from all the excitement still.

So that's whose car it is. I'm going to have to look into the nerd's background because I didn't know he came from money. I'm a little shocked she handed over the cash so easily, I know she could have used it.

I walk through the crowd surrounding her, ignoring them as they part like the red sea and I grab her wrist without saying a word. She draws up closer to my back, her breasts grazing my bicep as the crowd tries to squeeze in closer to talk to her. I squeeze her wrist and walk her around to the passenger side of my car, opening the door with a nod to get in.

"You're bleeding," she says as she bites her bottom lip and reaches up to touch the cut on the side of my temple.

"Get in, Tillie." I keep my face blank so she can't get a read on my thoughts.

She sighs and gracefully gets into my Nissan, watching me the whole time as I walk around the hood and pause.

"She gets home safe or you die." Evan freezes at the threat as I point at Nicola, and quickly nods until he looks like a bobble head.

I walk around the hood to the driver side and slide into the leather seat. I whip the car around, heading away from the pier towards home so we can have a few minutes alone without any prying eyes. She doesn't say anything, but when I glance over at her, she's smiling softly and has her hand out the window playing with the wind.

"Have you always been a sore loser?" she asks ten minutes later, not being able to take the silence anymore.

That's it, she's in for it now. I was going to wait but the brat clearly doesn't understand who's in charge here. Spotting a parking garage, I quickly turn and keep driving until we hit the fourth level without many cars parked there. Sliding into a parking spot, I kill the engine and sit there for a second before getting out of the car. Walking around to the hood, I cross my arms and stare at her through the window. She stares at me with her eyebrows scrunched in confusion until I see her shoulders sag in defeat just as she gets out.

"Is this where you kill me? I would have thought it would be somewhere more, I don't know... quiet and dark." She crosses her arms and leans her hip against the hood as she lifts her brow at me.

Never before has any woman got on my last nerves like she does. So much sass, but I have a solution to that.

"Come closer." I curl my index finger at her, coaxing her closer.

"Why?" she asks slowly, dropping her hands to her sides as she sees the look on my face.

"I'm going to spank your ass until it's red and you're less of a brat. Now get over here." I point at my feet then make a swirling motion for her to turn around so I can have her bent over my knee.

It takes a lot for me to contain a smile of wicked delight as her mouth pops open and she looks from me to the hood in shock.

Why must she be so beautiful? It's unfair really, but then again life is never fair.

Closer, brat, my palm is already twitching.

CHAPTER 8

Tillie

I must have heard him wrong. He wants to... spank me? Here? Now?

What is happening? My heart was just starting to slow down from the adrenaline of the race, but it's pumping faster now.

"Wha-what?" I stutter out, my jaw hanging open. I swear I'll be catching a lot of flies in my mouth because I just witnessed a miracle...Is he teasing me? My eyes must be deceiving me, there's no way his lips are twitching as if he wants to smile.

Nicky's lips tilt at the corner, a half smile that gives me butterflies in the pit of my stomach and travels straight down to my pussy. What is it about a man with a beautiful smile? Once he starts to grin, all talking and thinking is impossible. He's not playing by the game rules, so all bets are off. He doesn't like me and I can hardly stand him half the time. If he thinks I tossed and turned all night thinking about his tattooed dick, he's wrong. Even my thoughts lie to me. I've come to terms with the fact that I'm doomed and have to remind myself every time one of them smiles at me, that I'm just another body to them. Doesn't matter if I live or die.

"I don't like to repeat myself, but I'll make it clear for you just this once. Pants down, ass up." He sits down on the hood of his Nissan, propping one foot up on the fender and pats his muscular thigh.

I've been beaten, stabbed, cut with knives all over my body... tortured for days to learn a lesson, but I've never been spanked. I call his bluff, he has nothing to gain for smacking my ass. It's not like it's going to do anything to me. I've always rebelled, even when I was being tortured. I probably won't feel a thing, it's just my butt being spanked. No big deal. I can't get a read on what he's thinking from his blank expression, his sharp jawline tightens the longer I stand still though, making me want to ignore his command even longer. He grabs my wrist before I can follow through with my plan and yanks me over his thigh. I gasp in shock as he slides down my leather pants easily before I can blink. If anyone happened to walk by, they'd see some chick with her ass in the air in only a pair of purple, lacy boyshorts and a tank top as her ass gets beat.

"Hey! What the fuck do you think you're doing?" I push against his muscular thighs with my hands, wiggling in his lap to escape, but his forearm drapes over my lower back to hold me down, locking me in place.

I blow my hair out of my face and look over my shoulder to glare at him but he's not staring at me. He places the palm of his left hand on my asscheek, staring at the difference of our skin as he runs his thumb back and forth on the curve of my ass. His pale hand against my tan skin is striking, making this more real and causing goosebumps to break out all over my skin from the feel of his calloused hand against my sensitive skin.

"Glare all you want, scream as loud as you can, swear at me with hate, but you can't deny that you like this." He raises his head and meets my gaze, his emerald eyes piercing my very soul.

Can he see me? See how dark and lonely I've been, scared to feel anything but craving the need to be wanted and touched to the depth of my soul.

"You know nothing about me. So go ahead and get it over with." I roll my eyes and turn my head away to glare at the empty parking spots.

"I know plenty but I'm going to find out more," he threatens and takes his hand away to whisper in my ear. "I can smell a pain slut miles away. Denial will get you nowhere."

"You son of a bitc-" I wiggle in his lap, cursing at him, but I stop when pain blossoms on my ass, a startled gasp leaving my mouth.

The sound of the palm of his hand spanking my asscheek echoes around the parking garage, sounding louder than it should. I lay still, my breath drawn in my chest as I feel the dull throb sting my ass. My eyes water at the pain, trying to block out the memory of the time Cruz was behind me as he carved up my back, but that fades away into the background of my mind. I exhale in shock as I feel Nicky's palm smooth over the sting, rubbing in tiny circles...comforting me. My own breathing sounds loud in the quiet parking garage as I wait to see what he'll do next.

"If you stay here with me, you'll only remember this,"

he says in a quiet tone, almost like he's talking to himself, but he definitely gives me something to remember him by.

His hand slides down to the back of my thighs, he brings his hand down hard suddenly, causing my body to jolt at the unexpected feeling. I can feel the heat where my blood gathers on that spot, no doubt turning pink. What surprises me is how good it feels when he stills his hand to skim his fingers back and forth over the spot. It's almost like he's testing me to see what I'll do.

"What is happening?" I whisper in disbelief, not looking for an answer, but he pauses as he slides his hand back up to the curve of my ass.

"Pleasure and pain go together like the sun and moon. You can't have one without the other. But I can stop if you want me to?" I can hear the smile in his voice, the soft whisper like the devil on my shoulder.

The bastard.

"No. No, keep... keep going." I hang my head, terrified of these sensations coursing through me, but I want more.

"That's what I thought. Good girl." He makes a pleased hum under his breath, causing my thighs to rub together at the vibrating sound.

He gathers my boyshorts and tugs them up between my buttcheeks, exposing more of my ass under his heated gaze. At this point, I don't care if anyone sees me or hears the sound of the moans coming out of my mouth as he brings his hand down again, five times in quick succession. Back and forth, he switches from spanking me and comforting me until my ass is burning, the blood pooled to the surface and leaves behind a pleasurable sting that has me biting my lip.

"I bet I could make you come with just this alone." He

leans down to the side of my body, grasping my chin and turning my head to look at him.

Meeting his gaze head on, his eyes are talking enough without him having to say anything. Control, power, and lust burn in his emerald eyes, turning to a dark green as he slides my panties to the side.

"If I touch you now, am I going to find you wet? Your thighs shiny with juices and sweat, dripping just for me?" His voice comes out deeper than before, hotly guttural, like it's rolling over my skin and making it's way over my entire body in a heat wave.

I can't answer him, scared of what's going to come out of my mouth. Am I going to beg him to fuck me, when I'm the one who's suppose to be doing the seduction for revenge? I stare with wide eyes into his, he doesn't blink until he slowly shakes his head and sighs in disappointment. Without warning, he runs those skilled fingers over my pussy lips slowly and dips inside to gather the juices that are currently coating my thighs. There would be no hiding it even if I wanted to, it's obvious how wet I am just from him spanking me. He lets go of me suddenly, making me almost lose my balance and fall towards the ground before I catch myself. I quickly stand up straight to confront him, wondering why he stopped.

I freeze on the spot as I stare with my mouth pooling with saliva because it suddenly becomes difficult to swallow. Nicky brings his fingers to his mouth and slips them between his parted lips, sucking my juices off and sliding them out completely clean as he stares down at me.

"Nighty night, Tillie," he whispers, that lopsided smile appearing again just as I feel a sharp pinch on the side of my neck.

Confused, I glance down to see a syringe in his left

hand and I'm confused when I glance back up to him as my world tilts. My legs collapse under me and I find myself in his arms as he carries me around to the backseat of the car.

"Do you always carry around a tranquilizer?" I mumble, my vision blurry as he lays me down on the seat, cradling my head as he uses his leather jacket to place under me as a pillow.

"You never know. Now go to sleep, you're going to need it by the time you wake up," he says and slides one finger down my cheek with a quiet chuckle.

I must have died, there's no way Nicky just laughed. Those are my last thoughts as my world turns dark.

"When she wakes up, get her ready. She wants to hide shit from us, then she's going to be more involved in what we do, so she'll have no way of escaping this life."

It sounds like Logan, but his voice comes out distant, almost like I'm dreaming and I'm wondering if I really am.

"I already found out she was born in the club so there's a connection somewhere there. Do you think she was involved in drugs disappearing on the night of the race somehow?"

That's Nicky's voice, it sounds like he's right next to me. I turn my head towards him, not being able to open my eyes which feel heavy and glued shut.

"Jesus, Nicky. How much of the tranquilizer did you give her? Enough to knock out a horse?"

Why does Logan sound so angry, the jerk better not be angry with me. I didn't do anything... wait. Did he say tranquilizer? Flashes of my memory pop up like a movie, leaving me feeling dizzy. Those fuckers. I feel like I'm floating and so physically exhausted that this must be the most sleep I've ever had. I'm drifting away again before I can give them a piece of my mind.

———

I blink my eyes open, squinting at the blinding light trying to kill me and throw my arm over my eyes with a long groan of irritation. Did I get drunk last night? This feels like the world's worst hangover in history. I take a deep breath, feeling tired still but needing to go see where the hell I am. I hear a noise that sounds like quiet typing and move my arm to turn my head towards the sound.

The first thing I see is the dark grey walls, and the light grey fabric of the comforter covering me up to my mouth. Feeling weak as a newborn kitten and foggy headed, I grip the comforter and pull it down from my face to peek around. The typing stops as I meet green eyes over the soft edge of the comforter and I can see my own eyes widening in his glasses before he takes them off, rubbing the bridge of his nose.

"Good, you're finally awake. I didn't know how much of your snoring and cuddling I could take. You practically attached yourself to me the whole time you've been knocked out," he states, looking down at me before turning back to his laptop.

"That's right! You shot me up with drugs!" I tug the blanket the rest of the way off, completely furious, and launch myself at him.

His computer slides off his lap to the side on the bed as he catches my forearms in a grip to stop me from scratching his eyes out. But luckily, I still have my teeth. Turning my head, I clamp onto his arm and hold tight as he stops moving. Reality quickly comes crashing down on me as I find myself sitting right directly over his hardening dick, covered by his grey sweats. Why is he shirtless? Still biting him, I peek out of the corner of my eye to see his eyes closed and his lips twitching before he starts laughing. A deep chuckle that vibrates through my body and makes me shudder on top of him.

"Are you seriously biting me? I would have never taken you for a biter when I shoved my cock into your mouth, but it's good to know now." He opens his eyes while his lips spread into a half smirk and his white teeth flash.

"I hate you so much right now," I mumble around his skin and release him with a groan of defeat as I hang loosely in his hands. "How many hours was I out for?" I ask and glance down at him, my hair creating a curtain around us.

"It's Wednesday, so for a couple of days. You know you talk in your sleep, by the way?" He quickly releases me and curls his arms around my back as I drop on top of his upper body with a huff.

Trapped, his muscular leg thrown over mine to stop me from struggling. I'm pinned down even though I'm on top of him. I'm going to be late for school... wait... did he say...

"Did you say it's Wednesday? I must have heard you wrong." I can't wrap my head around it, but small flashes of memories filter through my head as I lay there without moving, hearing his heartbeat under my ear.

I remember waking up a few times confused, groggy, everything fuzzy. I'm pretty sure I was fed something like soup and was carried to the bathroom like a fucking puppet but that's about it. I'm going to murder him! Did he watch me pee? Yup, it's official, Nicky is going to die slowly by my hands. I'm pretty sure he held me up in the shower and washed me. Then again, everything is a blur. I can't think clearly and I'm starting to wonder if I dreamed that Logan was here or not.

"Nope." He pops the P and skims his fingers back and forth over the skin on my lower back.

Why does it feel so breezy back there?

"Nicky," I calmly say, gathering patience and willing myself to not kill him just yet.

"Yes, Tillie?" I swear I hear a smile in his voice and grip his biceps to keep my hands busy so I don't strangle him.

"Where are my clothes?" I take a deep breath, trying to remain calm.

"You arrived hardly wearing any clothes, since I left your pants in the parking garage. I thought it made sense you only slept in underwear. Fear not, Logan dropped off some outfits for you." He slides his hand into my hair and pulls back until I have no choice but to look at him. "Women who are guests in my household don't wear clothes. Now, who is Cruz?" he asks so suddenly that I stop breathing and I swear my world stops on its axis, leaving me frozen with fear.

"How do you know about Cruz?" I croak out, feeling my hands starting to shake as I dig my nails into his shoulders.

"It could have been the time you tried choking me when you were sleeping. I would normally be jealous of you screaming another man's name, but seeing as it was a nightmare, I'll let it pass." He looks like he's going to ask more but his eyes widen as he crooks his head to the side, listening for something.

Hearing footsteps outside the door, I'm taken by surprise when he suddenly grabs my waist and drags me close to his body before I can protest. Sitting in his lap in my bra and underwear, he grabs my hips and flips me around until my head is facing his calves with my ass practically in his face.

"Bow your head and keep it down. Don't say a word, Tillie. If you want to live or not be sold. Keep your mouth shut," he calmly says, but I can hear the strain in his voice.

He picks his laptop back up and places it on the arch of my back and the top of my butt. On my hands and knees in a crouch over his lap backwards, I don't move. I'm not sure what's happening but I'll take his word on this since it's his house, and whoever is on the other side of the door even rattles Nicky.

He starts typing as if this is ordinary, his arms grazing my asscheeks and he pauses for a split second just as his bedroom door starts to open. Not saying a word, I keep my head down and peek out of the corner of my eye, as I see a man in black dress pants walk to the side of the bed.

"Father. Welcome home. I hope it was a good business trip," Nicky says respectfully and then starts typing again as I begin to mentally freak out.

I'm in my freaking underwear in front of his father, but why hasn't he said anything about it? Why isn't he yelling or trying to kick me out?

"So, this is her?" his father says, completely skipping over Nicky's greeting.

"Yes." Nicky's voice goes deeper, tighter, and I can feel him slide one hand down to the back of my thigh with a hard squeeze in warning before letting go.

"I can see what the fuss is about. She'd be perfect for next week's auction." A finger glides down the center of my back, the touch barely there but enough to make my breath pick up as I try not to vomit.

"Not for sale. I think I'm going to keep her until I'm done with her," Nicky responds in a bored tone and never once stops typing on his damn laptop.

"We'll see." His father hums in delight under his breath, his hand traveling around to my front and lightly grazes my breast.

Nicky stops typing suddenly, setting his computer to the side to caress my asscheek, while his other hand slides up my thigh to hold me still, just as I was about to flinch away from his fathers roaming fingers.

"I left a report on your desk, Jin. I mean, Father. Cocaine was stolen from the warehouse Friday. We planned on heading there with Tillie later tonight to see if she recognizes our thief. Mich caught one as a group of them made a run for it. We're waiting for Logan to go question him." Nicky presses on my lower back, making me arch my back so he has a clear view of my ass. "Now, if you'll excuse us, Father, we were just about to start her training." Nicky chuckles but it sounds fake to my ears, not like the one I heard before.

"Of course, Nicholas. If she resists, just hold her down and make her. Send her to me if you can't handle her," Jin sneers, causing goosebumps to cover my arms and I try not to shake at the scary, dark promise in his voice.

It sounds all too familiar. I'm wondering if this monster knows Payne. Two peas in a pod.

"I'm sure it won't be a problem but if it occurs, I'll keep that in mind," Nicky says and I hardly breath as I see Jin walk out the door, shutting it behind him with a quiet laugh.

My body sags, my arms collapsing under me as cold

sweat breaks out over my body. I can't seem to stop shaking like a leaf. Nicky slides out from under me and presses on my shoulder to turn me over so he can see my face.

"You did good, but the question remains: why you didn't flinch when he threatened controlling you with rape?" Nicky leans down close enough that I can see the green and gold specks in his eyes, making it easy to focus on something to stop a flashback before I'm dragged under.

"Sometimes there are worse things than being threatened, when compared to it actually happening." I subconsciously rub the scar over my shoulder and clear my throat when I notice he's watching me intently.

He lifts his arm, his hand sliding to my shoulder and around my shoulder blade while staring me in the eyes. I barely breathe, feeling trapped in his gaze and knowing he's going to feel the bumps of the scar.

"I-I, we should go." I desperately look for a distraction but his fingers glide over the raised letter C and pause.

"He did this, didn't he? Cruz." His jaw tightens as he whispers the name that gives me nightmares, looking angry on my behalf, but that doesn't make sense.

Why would he care?

"They say when the devil makes an appearance, he leaves a mark so he can always find you. Everyone knows who you belong to," I say in a raspy voice, swallowing thickly as I turn my head away from his gaze.

"There are worse things than the devil, Tillie, and you're looking at him. I said you're mine to do with as I please, so that means you're ours. No one else can have you." He places a finger under my chin to direct my gaze back to him.

"The scars on my body say differently. I've already been branded and no matter how much I cover them, they still tear through my flesh to remind me." I push at his chest and he shakes his head slowly, like I'm wrong, but I've lived it, I know better.

"You'll see. There's no escaping us, even if you're taken from our side. It will only be for a little while before we come to collect you. Now, get dressed, your clothes are on the chair. Time to see if you're a traitor. I almost hope you don't die tonight." He points to a lounge chair near the window and stands up, walking to his dresser.

I sit there stunned, watching him step out of his sweats with a pair of tight boxer briefs hugging his muscular ass. He takes his time getting ready. I'm sure I turned into a statue, by the time he turns back around dressed in a dark charcoal suit and raises a brow at me. I shake my head and slide out of bed, moving over to the chair. I hold up fishnets, a short velvet dark maroon dress, and a black leather jacket in confusion.

"You want me to wear this? Aren't we going to a ware-house?" I turn to him and see his serious expression.

"If you're going to die, you might as well look sexy." He shrugs with his arms crossed and nods his head for me to put it on.

These men confuse me. He starts off with you're a spy, we are going to murder you, but hey, let's give you plea-sure and call you our girl. With a long drawn out sigh of frustration, I slip the dress over my head, shivering at the erotic feeling of it sliding down my body. I step into the fishnets, admitting whoever picked this outfit out knew what they were doing... It looks good hugging my curves in all the right places.

Grabbing the jacket, I shrug it on and look around for

my combat boots. I turn to Nicky to ask where my boots are, but I find his gaze is roaming up and down my body as he strokes his thumb back and forth over his bottom lip. He looks up into my eyes, crooking his finger at me. I slowly walk over to him, and if I'm admitting it to myself, I add a little swing into my hips. *Seduce him*, my mind screams. Get your revenge and leave, but I'm being pulled in another direction too.

It sucks how they stare at me as if I'm wanted. Body and soul. It messes with my head.

"Turn around," he orders, spinning his finger.

I spin on my feet and face away from him, wondering what he's going to do. Why does that get my heart racing when he approaches me from behind? He slides his hands through my hair, my head tilts back at the feeling, seeking more. I could fall asleep with this slight pressure on my scalp, and I consider begging him to never stop. He starts gathering my hair and puts it in a ponytail, as if he's done this before.

"I have a little sister, remember?" he whispers in my ear at my outspoken thought and stays there for a second before drawing back. "Your shoes are downstairs, let's go." He leaves me there, feeling a little frazzled as he walks out of his bedroom.

"Don't fall for it, Tillie. It's a trick. You don't need anyone. Focus," I mutter under my breath, and quickly catch up to him just as he walks out the front door.

Does he expect me to follow him around like a lost puppy? He's not even bothering to check if I'm behind him. I slide on my boots and take my time walking to his car as he drums his fingers on the steering wheel in annoyance. That's right, fucker. You're on my time. I'm no one's dog. I slide into the passenger side and he takes off before I fully have the door closed. Soft music plays in the background as he drives us, the silence between us giving me time to think before we arrive at the warehouse.

I've seen how people like them take care of their enemies. It's always the same. People are going to die tonight. Blood will be spilled. You betray once, you don't get a second chance. It's part of the code.

Before I know it, we're arriving at a warehouse with a chain link fence surrounding the property. In the industrial part of L.A. near the run down neighborhoods, I would think this place was abandoned if I was passing by. Guess that's a way to keep people out. I bet the neighborhood knows to stay far away, knowing who owns the building. Nicky parks and gets out without saying a word. I follow after him warily, tugging down the hem of my dress as I glance around. It's extremely silent, the only sound is a light wind that kicks up the dust in the lot. I shiver, crossing my arms, and quickly walk behind Nicky as he approaches a steel door on the side of the building.

He opens it only to reveal how dark it is inside. He disappears into the building as I stand there, wondering if I should just make a break for it. I don't care if my face is plastered all over the news, I can't walk into the dark. It's just like the basement. I can't.

A hand reaches out, catching me by surprise and dragging me in by the wrist. I squeeze my eyes shut and bump into something hard as I stifle a scream. I won't make a noise, won't give Payne the satisfaction of my fear.

"Hello, sugarbutt. I know this isn't the ideal date, but I'm hoping by the end of the night we are going steady." A dark chuckle sounds next to my ear, the hard object I seem to have plastered myself to vibrates against me.

"Tey?" I ask in a shaky voice, trying to move closer to him as I grip his biceps.

"Don't tell me you're afraid of the dark? Out of everything..." He starts walking backwards, dragging me with him step by step.

"We all fear something, don't we?" My breathing picks up the farther we walk into the building, trying to focus on the person in front of me.

"I guess that's true. If anyone hurt my unicorn, I think I'd go on a murdering spree." His body shudders as if he really fears that and I shouldn't be surprised, even crazy ones like him hold something dear to his heart.

I could, for revenge, burn the stuffed animal in front of him, but even I'm not that cruel. I'd rather stab him. If someone told me I can't ever be free to live the life I want, I'd probably die. After everything I went through, to have it completely taken away from me would be like a slow death as I waste away.

"I'd probably help you on that murder spree if someone hurt your unicorn," I admit softly with a deep breath, not wanting anyone's hopes and dreams to go away because there isn't anything else to live for if it's gone.

He suddenly stops walking, making me trip over my own feet, and leans down in my face until I can only make out his electric blue eyes that make my heart skip a beat.

"You would, wouldn't you?" His teeth flash in the dark and he starts walking again without missing a beat, not glancing away from me as he leads me into the darkness.

I guess my life will always be surrounded by the dark, I can never escape that. At least I have something to hold on to, to see his captivating blue eyes stare into mine as if we're in this together.

"If you die tonight, I'll honor you by painting a beautiful picture in your blood," he says, all too seriously, his voice deepening and a hint of excitement leaking through.

He doesn't try to hide who he really is, he bares it all for the world to see. It's his way of letting everyone know just how cray cray he is.

As if we'd forget when he's reminding us every second.

Tey's crazy but, well, I kind of like that.

"Uh, thanks," I manage to choke out around a tight throat, wondering where they breed his kind of crazy.

"Anytime, pet." He laughs, the sound echoing and he stops walking so fast I bump my nose into his firm chest.

The lights turn on, blinding me as I hold my hand over my eyes so I can focus on the door in front of me as Tey steps away. Glancing over my shoulder, I see Dalton and Nicky and wonder if they've been following us the whole time on silent feet. My body shudders at the thought, knowing how deadly they can be.

"Go on, little bitch, open the door," Dalton grins, winking at me and his gaze roams over my body with an approving nod, lust shining in his violet eyes. "I knew it would look fucking hot on you." He bites his knuckle and I can only roll my eyes, looking back at the door in front of me.

A metal door with a square, frosted window makes it hard for me to approach it, but curiosity wins. As I walk up to the door and stand on my tippy-toes, I wipe at the window to see what's on the other side. Tilting my head, I'm not sure what exactly I'm seeing.

"Open it," Tey says in an excited voice from behind me, breathing down my neck and almost making me scream.

Damn him! I didn't hear him move.

Staring down at the handle, I square my shoulders and throw the door open without hesitating. If they are trying to scare me, it's not going to work. I've seen it all. Blood doesn't bother me, I could eat a hamburger with ketchup after seeing someone get cut open with blood running out of them in fountains. I was forced to watch people, who crossed the path of the Demon Jokers, get tortured for half of my childhood, and was told that I'd get used to it after a while. I guess I did.

A man sits tied up in the middle of the freezer, surrounded by clear tarp. He lifts his head and focuses right on me, mumbling something around the cloth stuffed into his mouth. It almost sounds like laughter. I glance over him, trying to figure out if I know him from somewhere. Tan skin, dark eyes, and both of his arms covered in tattoos all the way up to his neck. I get an uneasy feeling in my gut. One tattoo is inked out in black on his chest, concealing which gang he's from. I don't question how I know he's in a gang. It could be his cold eyes as he now stares at me, noticing that I haven't made a move to help him. Why does he look familiar? Has he been to the club warehouse before?

Movement to my right catches my eye and when I glance over, a clear tarp parts to reveal Logan as he casually strolls over to the gang member. Logan crouches down, clicking his tongue and shaking his head in disappointment as he rips out the gag.

"Miguel. Miguel. Miguel," Logan repeats tauntingly. He slaps Miguel's face to make him look at him, but his captive just sits there staring at me.

I step back when Miguel starts to smirk, the smile creeping me out. It's aimed right at me like he knows something I don't. It says doom. Your end. It's the same kind of smirk the Demon Jokers members had as they used my body, telling me that it can happen anytime, anywhere. My back bumps into a hard chest, making me jump before the smell of engine oil and sandalwood makes me relax my shoulders. I reach behind me blindly to latch onto any body part I can to ground myself. Lacing my fingers between whoever is behind me, I don't let go, and feel relieved when my hand is squeezed in return. That simple touch tells me I'm safe and not alone. It could be a trick but it's all I've got to survive at the moment.

"Someone's looking for you, little girl," Miguel laughs as the blood drains from my face.

"Who's looking for her?" Logan asks as he pulls out his gun from the waist of his pants, placing it on his knee.

It's a power move, letting the person know it only takes one bullet through the head to end your sorry life.

When Miguel doesn't say anything, Logan looks over and nods at one of the guys behind me. Tey starts to walk around me but stops suddenly and grabs my other hand.

"Guard this with your life," he commands seriously, as he places something in the palm of my hand and all I can do is close my fist around the object.

Tey rubs his hands together in excitement and swaggers towards Miguel as he draws his knife from his boot. A tattooed, muscular arm wraps around my middle, drawing me closer to a warm body in such a cold environment. Dalton slides his fingers into my hand that's clenching the object placed there. Glancing down, I watch as he pries my fingers open to reveal a stuffed unicorn. I quickly glance over my shoulder to see both Dalton and Nicky staring down at the unicorn in disbelief.

"He never lets anyone touch it," Dalton whispers, and

sharply looks at Nicky who just clenches his jaw and glances straight ahead.

Shit. He's mad. I thought we were at least on a level of having a decent relationship of being civil towards each other. But Nicky likes Tey. Anyone with eyes can see that, and I might have just crossed a line by accepting to look after the tiny stuffed animal. I was right, my doom is coming.

I awkwardly let out a quiet laugh and stuff the unicorn in my bra, acting like it's no big deal. Deciding to ignore the anger radiating off of Nicky, I glance back to Tey to see what he's doing.

"Do you know her?" Logan questions, standing up to move out of the way for Tey, as he moves around behind Miguel's chair without a word and starts circling him like a shark in the water.

Judging from the wide smile spreading across Tey's mouth, this is about to get messy. Miguel doesn't say anything, refusing to speak as his lips form in a tight line and he glances around. Bad move on his part.

"Here we go," Dalton says and leans down until his chin is on the top of my head as he watches with rapt attention.

"Should I get you some popcorn?" I say sarcastically, but gasp softly as Logan lifts his gun and shoots Miguel's foot without warning.

"This is my favorite part," Dalton's voice comes out gravelly and he starts swaying us side to side as Miguel's screams echo around the freezer.

"I'll ask one more time and if you give the correct answer, I'll make your death fast. If you don't, then my brother here is going to take his time. He's an artist after all." Logan nods his head over to Tey, who just stands there biting his tongue as he places his fingers together like a frame as he stares at a whimpering Miguel.

"Tey." Nicky grabs his attention by calling his name and points to the other side of Miguel's chair. "This angle is better over here, the blood splatter will reach higher." He waves over to the tarp and watches as Tey does that thing with his hands again, as if he's really looking through a lens frame to find the perfect spot.

"Nicholas, you know me so well. I'll use this side instead." Tey blows Nicky a kiss and I catch the pink rise in Nicky's cheeks, but look away as he glares at me when he notices me staring.

Miguel wiggling in his chair draws my attention back to him, as he tries to free himself from the rope tying his hands together, but that's a useless waste of energy.

Rope is not easy to escape from, it just leaves a bad burn and scars behind. Now zip ties, that's a different story. All you gotta do is pop your thumbs out of place and it's home free.

"Are you ready to talk?" Logan draws out, checking the gun chamber before snapping it back into place and tapping the gun against his thigh in an impatient move.

"Fuck you! I don't know her, but I know of her," Miguel growls out and groans as Logan steps on his injured foot. "People talk, man, and everyone knows of the Demon Jokers. Her daddy is looking for her. I'm not the only one who knows she's here."

I can see Miguel's lips moving but can't hear anything else as it becomes difficult to breathe, every little aspect of my being focusing on that one sentence.

Her daddy is looking for her.

"No. No. No," I chant under my breath as I start

shaking like a leaf, and glance around fast for an escape route.

I need to run. Start running now. He knows I'm here.

"Calm down, right the fuck now." Nicky suddenly appears in my line of vision, blocking Miguel and pushing me further against Dalton as he steps forward.

I start struggling against Dalton's hold, needing to leave, but he lifts my feet off the ground as he holds me higher against his chest. Nicky's face is a blur. My world comes crashing down around me and hope drifts away, as I keep repeating in my head that Payne is coming for me. The sudden slap on my cheek brings the noise back all at once, letting me draw in a proper breath, and I see Nicky frowning inches away from my face.

"Do you want to help Tey?" Nicky questions and I don't understand what he means until he steps aside and grabs my chin to direct my attention to Tey as he holds up two knives, waving them like a psycho. "Miguel's a bad man who only wants to cause you harm, and hurt my family by stealing from them. Should we silence him?" Nicky makes me look at the gang member, squeezing my chin tighter.

"He'll only run back and confirm it with his gang leader. A dead man can't talk, little bitch." Dalton slides me down his body until my boots touch the concrete floor again. He unwraps his arm from around me just as Nicky let's me go.

They are letting me decide and it really all comes down to this moment. I told myself I'd stop hiding, running while looking over my shoulder for the rest of my life. This man is stopping me from living. I was trained to seduce a man with my body, but I was also taught how to kill one by the gang members who hurt me. I'm not good myself, so why try pretending? Since birth, I was a mistake, raised by a monster, and destroyed by those who I thought were family. I have nothing to lose.

I reach into my bra and place the warm unicorn in Nicky's hand as I start to walk past him.

"Guard this with your life," I repeat the same words Tey used and catch the small twitch of Nicky's lips as if he wants to smile but wouldn't dare at a time like this.

"There she is. I knew it," Dalton mutters to himself, leaving me clueless as to what he's talking about.

I walk up next to Tey, ignoring Miguel as he curses at me, and I look down as Tey offers the knife in the palm of his hand to me. I wrap my hand around the handle and take it, testing the weight as I spin it between my fingers.

"That's hot. I've changed my mind. I want to be your baby daddy right the fuck now. Pop my cherry first and then let me spread my seed in your love tunnel." Tey plays with his lip ring by flicking it with his tongue as he stares down at me with wide, blue eyes filled with intensity.

I think he's serious and I can't help but snort.

"If you're a virgin then I'm the freaking Queen of England," I tease, feeling lighter now, and flip the knife until I catch the sharp end between my thumb and index finger.

He grabs his chest, right over his heart, and staggers on his feet as if he's having a heart attack. I crack a smile at that and can't believe we are joking around. I'm going to murder a man and yet I can smile. Maybe I'm not so far off the same kind of crazy as Tey is.

The sound of the gun going off again makes me jump slightly and glance over to see Logan glaring at us before focusing back on Miguel. If you've ever seen a man cry after getting his fingers blown off, let me tell you... it's not

pretty. I'm talking about a babbling mess, some screaming, snot, the whole works.

"What gang are you from? Tell me or they will start
playing." Logan grabs a handkerchief out of his pocket
and starts wiping his hands, then his gun before slipping
the gun back into the waistband of his pants.

"Listen. Listen! I was only following orders. Steal from
the Russo family, drugs mean nothing to you guys
anyways, and confirm that she's really here. Dom-"
Miguel clamps his mouth shut, but I swear it twitches as if
he's trying not to smile even though he's bleeding
everywhere.

Something doesn't feel right to me. Who's Dom?

"Dom? Are you sure about that?" Logan questions
Miguel again and nods to Nicky, who takes his phone out
and walks out of the freezer to make a call

"Yes. He's after the cocaine. He says that you don't
deserve to run his streets, taking his clients. He's taking
back what's his." Miguel hisses out, looking paler by the
second as sweat coats his body.

"I don't like liars, Miguel. You want to know something
funny?" Logan straightens his jacket, picking at lint that
isn't there. It's all for dramatic effect, to scare Miguel.

Logan slowly shakes his head and grabs Miguel's hair
so he has no choice but to look into Logan's hard, caramel
eyes. He's really breathtaking when he's like this, a man
who has control and shows his power by just a few
actions. As long as I'm not on that receiving end at least.
That reminds me, I'm still going to make the fucker pay
for making me get on my knees.

"Word on the street is Dom doesn't deal in drugs since
he took over for his dead father. But don't worry, Miguel,
I'm setting up a meeting as we speak. I'll find out the

truth. Now, tell me... who's her daddy?" Logan asks and points at me.

"I'm her daddy," Dalton answers from across the freezer while leaning against the tarp under a meat hook. He winks at me with a smirk as he crosses his big arms over his chest in arrogance.

"Oh, please." I roll my eyes and pretend he's not there, to get on his nerves.

He likes the attention.

"Don't give me that sass. Get over here so daddy can give you a spanking." Dalton's violet, darkening eyes stay locked on mine when I look over at him again and I actually think he likes that idea.

"Sorry, biker, but Nicky already took care of that. He spanked me real good," I taunt, watching as Dalton's lips part and heat fills his eyes.

Oh yeah, he likes that a lot. Perv.

"What?" Tey's voice sounds heartbroken and when I turn to glance at him, he's actually pouting. "I can't believe he didn't wait for me. We're a team, we are supposed to make a Tillie sandwich together! I'm kind of feeling betrayed over here."

"Enough! I'll get my answer somewhere else." Logan stares me down and all I can do is look away, not liking how he plans on getting that answer. "Tey, Tillie... It's your turn to shine. Looks like you live another day, baby girl."

Logan walks over to a corner of the freezer, ignoring Miguel pleading for his life, and presses a button on the wall before walking out the door with Dalton and Nicky following behind him without another word. Music starts playing from speakers somewhere, and I can't help my surprised laugh at the choice of music.

Let the bodies hit the floor.

"You like?" Tey bangs his head to the music and casually brings his knife down into Miguel's thigh as he listens to the song.

He quickly pulls the knife out with sickening suction noise and we both watch as blood pools through Miguel's jeans and onto the floor.

"The idea is to make it last longer-" Tey starts to say, but stops as I walk behind Miguel's chair and start cutting off his fingers, only to toss them at the tarp Tey plans on decorating with blood.

"Avoid the arteries for as long as possible. Got it," I reply back calmly, almost like I'm in a trance as Miguel keeps screaming for mercy.

A monster fucks a human woman with a soul, she gives birth to a girl who's half-human and the other half is a monster without a soul. I get to keep my humanity, but sometimes I need to turn it off to survive... This is one of those moments.

I toss another finger, watching it leave a streak of blood on the tarp, and glance back at Tey to see him adjusting his pants as he stares at me in awe.

"I knew it the moment I stared into your eyes, you're just like me. Damaged, broken, but only the best are," Tey says passionately and plunges his knife into Miguel's shoulder as he walks over to my side. "Tillie, I'm going to fuck you bloody one day. I'll fuck you on your period. I'll fuck you as you bleed for me. I'll bleed for you and continue until there's nothing left." Tey gently grasps my face in his large palms and bends down until his lips are inches away from mine.

"What are you doing?" I whisper, only focusing on him and nothing else.

"Breathing, sharing the same air as you. Maybe, if I

give you my breath, you'll want me enough to stop breathing. If you give me yours, maybe it'll make me breathe long enough to stay sane." His lips graze mine, his hot breath warming my mouth and drawing in what little oxygen I have because I'm suddenly breathless.

My first real kiss and I can't even call it a kiss because it's something more. It's a give and take as we stand there, our chests falling and rising, as we breathe together in sync.

"Will you create a masterpiece with me?" he mutters against my mouth and steps back to stare down at me with the most serious facial expression I've ever seen on him.

It's like a bubble popped and I'm back in reality as Miguel sobs behind Tey, begging for his life. I almost forgot he was there. I stare into Tey's eyes, the blue brighter than usual and decide to give him an honest answer as I take a deep breath.

"I thought you'd never ask."

CHAPTER 9

Cruz

"Dance." I lean back in the motel chair and order the second prostitute I've had this week to dance a dance only one woman seems to know.

I take in the hooker I found hanging around the corner of the motel. Skimpy clothes that hang off her skinny body, and the sunken way her cheekbones make her brown eyes look too large for her face. She could resemble Tillie, but she's not her. Fear shows on her face, instead of burning hatred, and she does whatever I say without even pausing to think about it. I like my girls to fight back, rebel against me.

"Ho-how do you want me to dance?" she stutters, not looking me in the eye and scratching at the track marks on the inside of her elbow.

"Take your clothes off and move seductively. Seduce

me with your body," I order, snapping my fingers as I grow impatient and she just stands there.

At least the last hooker knew how to take an order before I strangled her. Staring at the one before me, her face transforms for a split second into high cheekbones, plump pink lips, and scared brown eyes that widen every time I'm around. The image blurs and I rub my eyes as the hooker starts taking her clothes off, slowly moving her hips from side to side. It's all wrong, everything about her keeps reminding me that no woman will ever measure up to my Tillie. I see the greed in her eyes, looking for her next hit, and she will do anything for it.

"Stop. Get on the bed." My voice comes out harsh as she quickly climbs onto the bed naked. She lays down facing me while I stand at the end of the bed.

I'll never find someone to replace that void Tillie left behind, she's the only one that satisfies my thirst. I want to mark the rest of her body, carve her up with my name so that anyone who looks at her knows who she belongs to. I crawl over her body, not bothering to get undressed as I unbuckle my belt and lower my zipper. This hooker has needle marks on her pale skin, but that's about it. She should be covered in scars to resemble my Tillie.

"Tell me you love me," I order, fisting my cock as I stroke it to get hard.

"I, uh, love you," she quickly answers, and I close my eyes on a deep inhale, trying to picture Tillie saying that to me and I feel my cock twitch at the sound of her voice echoing in my head.

The hooker tries to wrap her arms around my neck but I shove them above her head with one hand, squeezing tightly. I don't bother with knowing her name, where she's come from, who's loved her in the past. She's here for one thing only, and she'll learn that very soon.

I shove her thighs roughly open with my knee and plunge into her without any foreplay, her dry pussy making her scream at the invasion. I enjoy the pain filled cry she lets loose. She struggles against my grip on her body, which helps get my dick fully hard. I fuck her hard into the mattress while she's bone dry, as I picture another face, and look above her head as she starts to cry, begging me to stop.

"P-please," she sobs, tears running down her cheeks when I glance down at her makeup smeared face.

"This won't do. She never begged me to stop, she accepted her fate," I continue slamming roughly into her and bring my other hand up to her neck as she starts trying to get out from under me.

Squeezing around her throat, I watch her eyes widen, her face turning red as she opens her mouth to draw in a breath. I cut off her oxygen, watching as she tries to put up a fight, but her struggles cease when she takes the last breath she'll ever have.

"Tillie," I whisper as I speed up my thrusts, splashing ropes of cum inside the still warm pussy, as I pretend it's my dancer instead.

Breathing hard, I pull out and sit back on my heels to study the dead body in front of me. I think she would be prettier with my signature on her pale skin. I pull out my knife and get to work. I flip her limp body over, laying her on her stomach, so I can make a start on her spine.

Time passes by and the sound of my phone ringing distracts me from my masterpiece. Moving away from the bed with my hands covered in blood, I answer and put it on speaker without bothering to look who's calling.

"What?" I walk to the bathroom and turn on the faucet, watching the thick color of red swirl down the drain.

"The trucker is here," Nix says impatiently and hangs up without another word.

Grinning, I walk back to the bed and flip her back over onto her back, so when the cops investigate her body, they will be in for a surprise once they turn her over.

"Now you're pretty. Gotta go. Sweet dreams." I chuckle down at her unblinking eyes and move the stray strands of hair out of her eyes, while roaming my gaze over her naked body that's now covered with the letter C from head to toe.

Stepping outside the door, I close it behind me. I know she'll be found in the morning by a cleaning maid, but I'll be long gone from here. Even if she was just a nobody, the police won't bother putting much time and effort into the death of a hooker in a run down motel when there are other more important crimes to solve. The neon sign blinks on and off over my head as I whistle a tune, moving across the parking lot to the semi-truck.

Yesterday, Tillie's bike was called in. I went out to the desert to figure out where her head would be. I searched in the baking sun for hours, knowing she wouldn't have walked into the desert just after escaping the compound. She's a fighter, I'll give her that. It didn't hit me until I watched a lone semi-truck drive past. She must have hitched a ride. It was easy enough to track down any semi heading this way by calling a couple of trucker companies. It led me to this moment, three days of waiting for him to show up at the motel room he rents out every time he passes through town. I'm getting closer to finding her, that thought alone makes my eyes roll in the back of my head.

I approach behind the trucker as he climbs out of his cab, watching as he swipes a plaid jacket off his seat, and slides his fingers through his dark hair before turning around. He jumps in surprise and eyes me warily.

"You Adam?" I question, feeling my heart racing because this trucker is going to help me find my missing property.

"Yeah, who's asking?" He looks me up and down, pausing to glance at my cut with the Demon Jokers symbol embroidered on the front.

"Perfect. I lost something of mine and I'm going to need your help getting it back." I step closer, drawing my knife out from behind the back of my jeans as I keep repeating the same thing over and over again in my head.

She's mine. She's mine. She's mine.

CHAPTER 10

Logan

I stand at the end of Tillie's bed with a cup of coffee, watching her sleep peacefully...with Tey wrapped around her like a koala bear. He's always been the big spoon, I've caught him plenty of times in my bed, snuggling up against me while I was sleeping. I used to give him shit when we were younger, telling him to stop sneaking into my bedroom, but he said he needed to feel the warmth of something next to him. So I didn't bring it up again and pretend it's normal for my best friend to hug me while I sleep.

He's been like this for two days, since the night at the warehouse, and it worries me. I've caught him each night in here with a large grin on his face while it's buried against the back of her neck. He's becoming attached. It's what I feared from the beginning.

I walk to his side of the bed and flick his ear, stepping

back with perfect timing. His knife whips out, missing my face by mere inches as he grumbles in his sleep.

"Tey. Wake the fuck up and go home. Check on the foster kids. You know you'll regret it if you don't," I whisper and wonder why I'm trying to be so quiet.

I glance at Tillie, seeing her face completely relaxed in sleep, which is the opposite of how it usually is when I come in here to watch her as she dreams. She always looks worried, her shoulders tight as if she feels like someone is at her back, staring her down, getting ready to attack her. I like the way her parted lips look plumper, fuller than usual while she sleeps. A perfect way to wake her up would be me shoving my cock in her mouth, but I don't want my third arm bitten off. She's feisty like that. I grab Tey's knife, watching him sigh in content as he snuggles into her some more. I lean over both of them, just to fuck with her while she's fast asleep and to see what she'll do.

The moment I graze my thumb over her nipple, it hardens, peeking through her shirt. The soft moan she lets out has Tey snapping his eyes open. He's no longer pretending to sleep, making eye contact with me over her shoulder and wiggling his eyebrows.

"No. Go home. We'll meet you at school, take my car. I'll keep an eye on her." I straighten up and hand him my coffee cup as he mumbles under his breath sleepily, pouting like a baby when he leaves her bedroom.

It gives me a second to look her over without her knowing, growing more curious about her as the little wrinkle forms between her brows and she stretches her arm out like she's looking for Tey and the warmth he left behind. Every time I stare at her, she seems to know. Always looking my way, meeting my eyes before curling her lip and glancing away, as if disgusted. It could be that Paris has been hanging off my arm the last few days, following me around like a stray dog. Maybe it's the way half the school's population calls Tillie crude names as she walks by, or stuffs her locker with trash. The other day was used condoms, which set me off. No cum touches her but mine, or the guys if I allow it. I put the mark on her back and said that she's an open target for the students to go after her, but it's my way of seeing how much she can take. She hasn't backed down, not once. She takes it and gives it right back. I admire that.

My gaze slides down her body as she lays on her side, the t-shirt rising up to the curve of her bubbly ass and the blanket tangled around her feet. I could look at her toned, tan, smooth legs all day, imagining them wrapped around my waist.

"Are you going to stand there perving all day or get the hell out so I can get ready?" She mumbles out in a groggy voice, her eyes still closed before she squints them open to look at me with a raised brow.

"So what if I was staring? Just appreciating my slut. It's a nice view, I'll admit. You never did tell me how much you charge by the way. I feel like getting my cock wet again." I duck as she chucks her pillow towards my head and actually growls at me as she sits up.

"Get out before I cut off your balls in your sleep and feed them to you." She smirks as my body shudders at the idea.

"Ouch, baby girl. That would be a shame, my little swimmers wouldn't be there for the baby making." I click my tongue and head towards the bathroom door to shower.

"I'd do the world a favor, devil's spawn," she whispers

to herself and suddenly starts struggling in her sheets to get out of bed. "Hey! Let me use the bathroom first. You take forever to style your hair, you're worse than a girl," She demands as I slam the door, twisting the lock just as she makes it, her fist thumping on the wood.

"Go get breakfast then. It might be a while. The shower holds a special memory for me, so I might jerk one off." I hold in my laugh as what sounds like her head thumping against the door on the other side.

"Ass!" she shouts and goes quiet as I start the shower.

Going through my routine, I sing under my breath as I soap my body up and wrap my fist around my cock, stroking as I picture her on the other side of the door, listening to me beating one off with her on my mind. Once I come with a low groan while splashing cum on the shower wall, I stand there under the water as I take deep breaths with her still occupying my thoughts. Grabbing the shower hose, I wash the wall and decide to take forever on my hair just to fuck with her. I get out of the shower with a grin and dress simple today in ripped jeans and a grey sweater, slipping on my Rolex last as I head downstairs towards the kitchen. We have an hour before we need to leave for school.

"Oh, dear! I'd love to have lunch to chat, but that's the ladies' luncheon that day and I can't miss it. Another time? Maybe we can go shopping." Diana's voice sounds strained and that has me pausing outside the kitchen doorway, looking around the corner.

Tillie is at the end of the island, sitting on a bar stool as she eats a bagel, her smile forced as she stares at Diana like she's feeling awkward. The gold digger won't even look her own daughter in the eye, and I wonder what happened to the loving mother who fainted when she met her long lost daughter. The crocodile tears aren't in sight any more. Diana's smile is tight around the edges as she walks around the other side of the kitchen to Franco to say goodbye. She kisses him on the lips deeply, moaning loudly for us to hear, the sound too high pitched and fake to my own ears. Franco doesn't bother to touch his wife back as he leans against the kitchen counter. He doesn't do anything but watch Tillie as his wife tries to act like a porn star in front of her daughter. I clench my hand, wanting to pound my fist into his face for how he's looking at her. Like she's the juiciest steak in the universe and he's starving. What the fuck?

"That's, um, fine. We can talk about Uncle Rig and go shopping, maybe next week? No rush." Tillie coughs, takes a drink of coffee, and looks away from them as they break apart as if she can't stand the way Diana is staring at her accusingly.

"Not much to tell, but I'll share anything I know. They are painful memories, I'm sure you understand that," Diana says, turning to stare at her daughter with another fake smile, as she wipes at her smeared lipstick with a napkin.

"Yeah. Completely understand," Tillie says quietly, looking defeated as she stares into her coffee cup.

"I knew you would. Bye, dear." She smoothes a hand down Franco's chest and turns on her high heels to leave.

Diana pats her hair down and grabs her purse off the counter as she walks towards the garage door, leaving just Tillie and Franco alone. I stay hidden, waiting to see where this is going to go because I don't like the way Franco hasn't taken his eyes off Tillie this whole time. She won't even glance his way, her body strung tight, and she keeps glancing at the clock on the stove.

"You remind me of her," Franco suddenly says, breaking up the awkward silence.

Tillie looks up from her food, her bagel halfway to her mouth. She swallows before questioning Franco about what he could possibly mean.

"Who?" She tilts her head to the side, just as confused as I am.

"My first wife," he replies and walks around the island to sit down next to her, so close that his shoulder rubs against hers as she shifts on the barstool.

My body goes rigid. I must have heard him wrong.

"What?" Tillie chokes out, dropping her bagel on her plate as she pounds on her chest.

"She was innocent, too. Was never meant to experience the evil of this world, but before I could protect her, I was too late. I know who you are Tillie and I can protect you," Franco says, leaning forward and whipping a smear of cream cheese off the corner of her mouth with his thumb.

He watches her as he brings his other hand to the back of her neck and places his thumb firmly on her bottom lip. I can't move, I need to see what she's going to do. My father may run the family business, but I have to know who's side she's going to be on. Franco holds the key right now, he fucking knows who she is and hasn't shared that piece of information.

"I'm no-not innocent." She tries to lean back but he stops her with his hand gripping the back of her neck.

"If that cherry of yours wasn't already popped, I would have given you to Jin once I found out just who you are. Virgins sell for high prices. There's lots of greedy men out there who would love to get their hands on you," he threatens and watches Tillie start to tremble, pressing his thumb past her lips, into her mouth. "Suck," he commands.

Tears water in her eyes as she closes her lips around his finger and refuses to meet his gaze, looking over his shoulder at the clock again as she sucks the cream cheese off his thumb.

"The only innocence you had was taken away from you, and you didn't have a choice where you grew up. I can keep you safe, a place to come and go as you please, as long as you follow my rules under my household." Franco removes his thumb, his gaze dropping down her body, his meaning clear. But he drives the point home as he places his palm on her upper thigh, right on the edge of her shorts.

Her eyes finally stop looking at the clock, as if she was wishing time would speed up, and they start to slowly close. Knowing she's hiding her tears, so accepting of what's happening to her, that is my breaking point. I don't want to hear anything come out of her mouth because she's not one to beg, and I refuse to allow her to get on her knees for him.

She's my baby girl.

I make sure my face is completely blank of any emotion, not wanting Franco to see the anger coursing through my veins. Rounding the corner, I walk a little louder than normal to make some noise as I clear my throat. He leans away from Tillie, who sits frozen in her seat with her fists clenched in her lap. I see him squeeze her thigh one more time, even though he knows I can see him, before he stands up and grabs his blue jacket off the counter with his matching hat.

"Logan, any progress on the missing shipment or the other thing I asked Nicky to look into?" he questions, acting like he doesn't already know, and I wonder what else he's keeping from me?

I've never wanted to kill him, but right now, that's all I want. To see him on the ground, looking up at me in fear, as he finally sees who's in charge. I'll find out all of his secrets. He stopped being my father the day my mother died. He made sure of that as he beat me with his belt, or his fists, all while telling me how to be a man. He placed a gun in my hand and made me kill my first time in the warehouse at the age of twelve.

"Nothing yet, but it's only a matter of time before it comes to light." My voice is stoic and he pauses as he grabs his car keys to glance up at me.

My face stays void of any emotion as I stand there, staring at him as he tilts his head at me before glancing quickly at Tillie and back towards me again.

"I'm sure it will, Son. Oh, before I forget. Don't get caught doing anything that shouldn't be seen. Reports say federal agents have been sniffing around." He gives me one last look and walks out the door, the sound echoing around the kitchen as we listen for his car to start.

The moment we hear him drive away, Tillie lets out a deep exhale. Turning towards her, she places her head in her hands with her shoulders shaking. The first sniffle chips away a small piece of ice in my heart. I walk calmly to her side, hesitantly placing my hand atop her hair and slide my fingers through the dark strands. She stops crying and lifts her head, her watery eyes connecting with mine as I stroke her long brown and purple hair.

"Are you petting me?" she asks in shock.

"What? No. You have something in your hair," I lie through my teeth, but continue sliding my fingers through her hair while staring down at her upturned face.

"Why are you comforting me?" she questions, not looking away as my hand pauses its movements.

The question surprises me because I don't have an answer. It's not from pity. I've seen people who deserve to be pitied, but I never felt anything for them. Maybe it's the way she fights back on her own that I admire, and I don't want to see her break down, accepting the hardships that life throws at her.

Hopeless isn't for someone like her. She's different.

"I don't know, but I do know something that will make you feel better. Come with me." I grab her wrist, pull her out of her chair and down the hallway to Franco's office.

"What are we doing here?" she hisses, glancing around like we're going to get caught any moment.

"This is my way of saying fuck you to Franco. Hop up on the desk," I demand in a deep voice, sending papers flying as I swipe them clear off the desk and sit down in my father's office chair.

She eyes me for a second, before glancing at the spot I pat on the desk in front of me. Then she looks back into my eyes, with her lips twitching at the corners.

"You're bad." She bites her lip and walks over towards me with a sway of her hips, as I spread my legs for her to stand between them.

"Only the baddest, baby girl." My fingers hover over the button of her shorts before unsnapping it and slipping them over her ass and down her long, toned legs.

Standing before me in only a tank top and a black thong, I grab her hips and lift her onto the surface of the polished, cherry wood desk. By the time I'm done with her, the shape of her asscheeks and her juices will be left on the desk, as a reminder of just exactly who she belongs to.

"Spread your legs," I order, sitting back in my father's chair as I glance down at the wet material on the front of her thong.

She meets my eyes, her chocolate ones seeking mine before she slowly opens her legs.

"Now what?" Her voice comes out raspy, sexy.

"Now I'm going to eat out your delicious as fuck pussy and make you scream my name." I roughly grip her thighs, pushing them as wide as she can go, but she smacks my hands away.

She leans back on her elbows and lifts her heels off the ground to form the perfect V, with her legs straight in the air, as she grips the edge of the desk by her ass.

"Is this okay?" She smirks as I growl and lean forward, running my nose down the front of her panties.

"Fuck, you smell incredible," I groan at the intoxicating scent of her cunt, moving lower to lick right over the wet spot on her thong where her pussy lips are.

She lets out a soft moan, spreading her legs wider as I grab the back of her thighs and hold her still. I slide my hands up the back of her toned legs and back down, loving the silky smoothness of her golden skin. I look up to see her already staring down at me, as I shove her thong to the side to expose her pretty, pink, hot pussy. All of it is just for me.

"Logan," she pleads the longer I stare, devouring her slippery, wet cunt under my gaze.

"I'll give you what you want, but you have to say it first." I hover my mouth over her pussy lips, taking a deep inhale to draw her sweet scent of oranges in, and exhaling to make sure she feels my hot breath.

"I don't know what you're talking about." Her voice comes out as a purr, playing coy with me as she peeks under her lashes with a smirk, spreading her legs wider, showing me just how flexible she is.

I'm in charge here.

I sit back a little and without giving her a warning because she's not being a good girl, I bring my hand down on top of her pussy. My palm smacks hard enough to leave a sting, turning her skin a blush color. I soak up her loud moan, her eyes widening with her hunger and lust.

"Say it. Tell your stepbrother what you want," I demand, with another slap to her pussy, just to hear her cry of pleasure. I practically feel my eyes roll in the back of my head when I take my hand away, she gives chase with a buck of her hips.

She likes it. She likes the pain, a lot.

"Touch my pussy, Logan. I'm your slut, damn you." She glares at me and grasps my hand to place it back on her. "Again. Touch me. Make me come. Again!" Her tone is a forceful demand that isn't holding anything back, and the sound of her raspy voice has my cock straining against my slacks, wanting to dive right into her pussy.

She's a bossy little thing. I like that, it gives me a chance to show her how I like to deliver my punishments.

"Good girl," I say and smack her pussy suddenly, the strength a mix between hard and gentle. The sound of her slick lips gets louder and louder after each slap.

I can't hold back any longer, after seeing her juices sliding down between her asscheeks and having her breathy moans fill my ears. Diving between her legs, I lick around her ass, chuckling at her quick gasp the moment I touch her with the tip of my tongue. Her body freezes, and I look up to see her staring at me as I give her another long lick all the way to her clit, circling slowly around that spot that makes her legs shake under my hands. I pause and raise a brow at her to see if she wants me to continue. Biting her lip, she grabs the back of my neck and shoves my face back down in a command to keep going.

"More. Please. I never knew that spot could feel good instead of being painful," she whispers, sliding her fingers through my hair and holding tight.

I want to show her how good it can feel, something that she'll never forget.

I'm going to devour this girl, make her scream my name until her throat is sore and I have her begging for more.

Not wasting any time, I bury my face between her legs. Slowly licking between her folds, like I'm licking my favorite ice cream. Then I plunge my tongue in and out rapidly to hear her moan.

"Why is your tongue so long? H-how are you doing that?!" she shrieks out as I drag my tongue up to her clit and start flicking swiftly, grinning as she tries to draw away from me when the pleasure becomes too intense.

She tightens her grip in my hair so much that it's almost painful. Just seconds later she is rolling her hips to drive me closer, and pulling out a groan from me. She can't help herself, needing to feel the ecstasy that drugs us all.

"I'm-I'm going to come." She throws her head back as I glance up at her from between her thighs, and grab her waist to hold her still, feeling the tiny scars under my fingertips.

"Break for me, baby girl," I command in a deep husky voice before flicking my tongue in waves, quickly moving side to side, and sucking her clit hard so that it has her clenching her thighs together around my head.

Her body tenses up and I can't stop staring up at her,

not wanting to miss the look on her face. Her pink, plump lips part, forming a perfect O, while her eyes meet mine before rolling back into her head.

My mouth floods with her juices as she comes, making me groan and she screams loudly with her pleasure. Her whole body shakes as she rides my face in jerky movements with her hips, before she slumps back on the desk, breathing heavily.

I lick her again, loving the way her body shudders and she moans while pushing my head away like she's too sensitive for more. She slowly blinks up at the ceiling in a daze as I nuzzle her inner thigh and bite the tender flesh between my teeth. She sucks in a breath, swatting at me to stop as she mumbles something. I can't stop grinning. Did I break her?

"Baby girl?" I recline in my father's chair, licking my lips, the taste of her lingering on my tongue and I'm content enough to just sit here watching her spread out in front of me.

"Lo." She uses my nickname in this breathless voice, and I know without a doubt I broke her.

"Move your ass to the right for a second," I say and enjoy her groan as she shifts her body to the right, not bothering to cover herself.

I stroke a hand up and down her hip absentminded as I pull open a few drawers of the desk until I find what I'm looking for. Holding the flash drive up, I plug it into the computer and wait until all the files are downloaded. I'm going to find out what Franco is hiding, it's come to this point. He used to say family is everything, but I think he cares more about himself than anything else these days. Pocketing the flash drive, I turn back to Tillie to see her looking at me in question. She starts to close her legs when I don't answer but the palm of my hand stops her from moving.

"I'm not done. We have about ten minutes before we have to leave, and I'm a man who does everything to the fullest." I stand up, leaning over her body as she sits up, looking confused. "You didn't squirt for me and that won't do. You're going to squirt all over the place and clean it up with that naughty mouth of yours. Do as I say, baby girl, and you'll be rewarded." I glide my thumb over her bottom lip as her mouth pops open in shock and her body flushes hotly under mine.

Like I said, I always rise to the top by being the best. Can't back out on my reputation now.

CHAPTER 11

Franco

"Chief, that journalist is here to see you... again." Rose, my secretary, peeks her head through my door with a mocking smirk.

She knows how much I hate reporters and gains pleasure in my misery. Rose doesn't know who exactly I am, but I'm almost positive she suspects I'm corrupt, like most of the detectives in the precinct. My crimes don't stop with just me, I've blackmailed some powerful people to do my bidding but evil spreads far and wide. I didn't even have to put in any effort to get people to see my point of view. The way I use my status for handling the drugs coming in and out of my city, it's become too easy. I'm the man, set out to be the villain in my city behind closed doors, but yet here I sit, in this chair meant for someone who cares about his citizens. I should be the man behind the bars, instead, but here I am. I'll always protect my family, but I'll place myself first before anyone else. I'm too invested in this life-style to go down.

"Tell her I'm busy." I wave my hand as my phone rings, dismissing her.

She rolls her eyes and disappears, giving me the privacy to take this call without being overheard. Turning in my office chair, I look out the window with my feet propped up on the windowsill.

"Jin. You know better than to call me while I'm at work," I remind him, rubbing the bridge of my nose because I know what's coming.

"No one would dare think to cross you, Franco. I'm calling to let you know I've met the girl. She would work perfectly for the next shipment, selling for a pretty penny. I could do it, you know, take her away and she won't be a problem anymore. I'm moving the girls out tonight," Jin says in a mellow tone of voice, knowing he's serious.

He's been trying to get me into human trafficking for years now, and I think I'll finally agree. With the missing shipments of cocaine and my counterfeit money being stolen, it wouldn't hurt to dip my hands into selling whores.

"Why sell the girl when you can just hand her back over to the Demon Jokers? I heard they are looking for her, she's a special prize to the motorcycle club and I wouldn't mind negotiating terms for a trade. Her for money," I suggest, liking the idea because I need her out of my house, away from me before I give in to her.

The temptation is too strong, wanting to touch her smooth, tan, young skin. To have her big innocent-looking eyes locked on mine with adoration, just like Helen used to. Tillie needs someone like me, to guide her in this world, where evil lurks at every corner. I could teach her the ways of the world while having her youthful body by my side every night, under me. Begging for more as her perky breasts bounce when I thrust into her, showing her how a real man fucks. Diana won't utter a word, she knows better. Tillie may be her daughter, but she hasn't been in her life since she was born. There isn't love there. I will keep giving Diana my credit card, be the husband she wants in public, but if I use her daughter, she'll turn a blind eye. My wife is a good actress, the crocodile tears almost fooled me, but she loves money more. She needs this lifestyle that she feels safe in.

"It seems the boys have become interested in her. I thought my son would know by now to never let a cunt lead him around but he never learns. Get rid of her while you can, she's a weakness," Jin says in a sinister voice, thinking all women are beneath him.

I picture her in a cage, one big enough to fit a dog, her innocent eyes dulling as hope washes away. Her gaze fading while she lays in her own blood and vomit, slowly dying from being passed around, man to man, using her body for their pleasure. Jin doesn't know that Tillie is the Demon Jokers president's daughter, and I'm keeping that little bit of information to myself for now. Jin helped me in a time of need but that doesn't mean I trust him. I trust no one.

"I'll think about it. Tillie may have run from the Demon Jokers, but the girl can be under my care for now. I think I'll use her then discard her when the time is right." My brows furrow as I hear something drop behind me and I spin in my chair to see Elle, the annoying journalist from Los Angeles Times, bending down by the doorway to pick up the pen she dropped.

"I'll call you later. I might have a package for you,

sooner than later." I eye up Elle, as I hang up on Jin without waiting for a reply, wondering how much she overheard.

"Mr. Russo, I'm glad we can finally have an interview." Elle forces a smile and steps forward, extending her hand across my desk.

"I'm quite busy as I had my secretary inform you." Standing up, I button my jacket and stride towards her.

She backs up a step as I lean close to her, almost tripping on her high heels, but scowls as I reach around her to open the door with a hand gesture for her to go first.

"Mr. Russo, I would just like to ask a few questions about the rumors of corruption going on in your department." She starts to grab a recorder out of her purse but I stop her by grabbing her wrist.

"Set up an interview first with my secretary." I grip her wrist tighter then let her go as I walk away, before turning to look over my shoulder. "No recorder though."

She throws her hands in the air in frustration and stomps over to Rose, to no doubt set up an interview that I'll never allow. Maybe it's time to take care of the fucking journalist, she's been pestering Logan for years.

I'll have her swimming with the fish in no time, or maybe I'll just sell her to Jin.

Decisions, decisions.

CHAPTER 12

Tillie

I walked through school in a daze on and off all day, not hearing a word, and faces were a blur. It's all because of that arrogant jerk! The guys are slowly trying to kill me, torturing my body until I hardly recognize myself. When Logan uses that mouth of his, I either want to slap it shut at whatever spills out of it, or I could just sit on his face while he gives me the sweetest torture. Just that thought alone makes me whimper, my eyes filling with tears. I want more. I want more of Dalton's gruffness, the way he promises revenge for me as he brings me to ecstasy. The silent way Nicky stares at me, like he's stripping me bare with his gaze alone, planning more ways to give me pleasure and pain. I've thought of ways for him to place me over his knee again, he'll be seeing more sass from me in the near future. Don't even get me started on Tey, he unleashed something inside of me that's been boiling for years. I can see him by my side for a long time, just being his crazy self as he encourages me to let all my crazy out.

Sigh.

What is wrong with me? I hate them, but for some reason I can't help wanting to be closer to them. How I picture it is, when you have a stare down with a poisonous snake, they tell you to not run. To hold still and it won't attack, but your brain says fuck it. We are running, fuck the consequences. That's how I feel, staring down at a rattlesnake, waiting for it to bite me.

"Till! Tillie! Fuck off!" Nicola screams next to my ear, appearing out of the blue and almost making me piss myself.

Turning to her as we head out to the parking lot, she grabs my hair and pulls while making dinosaur noises to a group of people walking by. Her hair pulling has me screaming as I duck my head and crouch while I curse under my breath, trying to untangle her finger from my hair.

"Sorry! Sorry! Letting go." Nicola grimaces, blinking rapidly as she finally lets go and looks down at the ground like she's ashamed.

"Did you really just make dinosaur noises at a group of guys? Was that an attempt at a pterodactyl?" I snicker and place my arm through hers, dragging her with me as I walk towards Logan's corvette.

"Hey! It takes real skills to make the sounds that come out of my mouth," she brags with a shrug, but she's still not meeting my eyes.

I have the perfect way to fix that. Seeing the group of fake blonde bimbo's surrounding Logan and Nicky's car, I take this as my opportunity to show Nicola it's okay to be different as we reach the guys parking spots.

Letting go of Nicola, I mess up my hair on purpose so it's sticking up in all directions and jump around in front of the girls like a crazy person while making the loudest screech of a pterodactyl humanly possible. I chase them off, watching them scream and run in their high heels. Once they are gone, I place my hands on my knees and laugh until tears are rolling down my cheeks. Turning around to high five Nicola, I'm confronted with horrified faces and Nicola gasping for breath on her knees on the pavement.

"Honey bear, if you need a straight jacket, I have one at home you can borrow," Tey says dead serious with a nod, like he's actually thinking of going to grab it for me.

"My ears are still ringing. Make sure to use those lungs in the bedroom next time, little bitch. I'm taking this as a challenge now." Dalton rubs his five o' clock shadow, staring me up and down like he's making plans.

I'm scared and dare I say... a little turned on.

"I don't know what scares me more. Knowing that I had whores leaning against my car or that Tillie is just as crazy as Tey. Always thought I'd only have to look after one loose cannon, but now it's two." Logan shakes his head, looking up at the sky in exasperation, but his lips twitch like he's holding back a grin.

I smooth my hair down, clearing my throat as I glare at them like it's their fault I had to resort to this part of myself. It feels good to let go. I watch as Nicky stares down at his laughing sister and glances up at me in silence for a beat then helps her off the ground by a hand on the elbow. What was that look for?

"Oh God. I wish I was filming that. Thank you." Nicola hugs me fully, causing me to tense for a second before I hug her back, melting into her as my shoulders relax.

I could get used to being hugged. It's been a long time since anyone has wrapped their arms around me without a hidden agenda, like Uncle Rig used to. Hopefully one day I can do it without thinking of my past.

"Anytime. Now, are you going to tell me why you almost bulldozed me over in excitement before we decided to play dinosaurs?" I question, completely ignoring the guys as they talk among themselves, but I can see out of the corner of my eye that Nicky is leaning closer to us to eavesdrop on our conversation.

"There's a party tonight," she whispers, glancing left and right while shaking my shoulders in eagerness.

"And?" I raise an eyebrow, wondering why her eyes are alight with an intensity and a feverish look that makes my back straighten.

"The jocks are throwing the party... At Gary's house." Her left eye twitches and she glances at her brother, and quickly looks away when she notices him listening as his brow wrinkles in confusion.

I don't think Logan and Dalton have let him or Tey in on what happened in the locker room. Will they go on a murdering spree or not give two shits? I know Franco told them to stay out of trouble, to lay low... but will they actually listen?

"You know, I'm suddenly thinking a party is the perfect way to let loose tonight," I say with a grin that Nicola matches, slowly spreading across her face.

I turn to the guys, pretending I don't see Nicky straighten and glance away.

"Lo," I gain his attention, watching him pause his conversation to look at me as Dalton's mouth drops open in shock at the nickname I just dropped. "Nicola and I want to go to a party tonight. It's at Gary's house."

Logan rubs his chin, staring me down, before he glances at Tey and Nicky. Tey's hardly paying attention, talking to his unicorn as he lifts its tail and pulls stuffing out of the stuffed animal's ripped butt-hole. I watch with my mouth hanging open as he mutters under his breath, pulling out matches, the world's tiniest bottle of lube, and finally a stick of gum that he pops in his mouth grinning. Shaking my head, I glance back at Logan and have an intense, silent communication with him until he sighs in defeat.

"Fine, but you two don't wander off. You stay in my sight, even if one of us is getting our dick wet." He unlocks his car with a pleased grin and gets in before I can go batshit crazy on him.

That fucker.

I'll cut a bitch... wait. Why the fuck would I care? It's not like I want him to... seriously like me. Any of them. I don't need anyone. I need to stick to my plan of turning all four of them against each other and have them begging on their knees in front of me. Suddenly in a bad mood, I'm about to climb into the backseat when Nicky stops me by the elbow.

"Why are you asking permission? Why would you want to go to the party?" Nicky asks with suspicion. I swear nothing gets by him.

Plastering on a smile, I stand on my toes and whisper in his ear. His hand tightens on my elbow as his jaw moves back and forth when my body brushes up against his. Sucker.

"I'm looking to get spanked again, so what better way than to be bad at a party full of raging hormones? Besides, I want to let loose since I'm likely to die soon. I want a drink," I lie through my teeth, grinning up at him innocently.

He takes a deep breath and lets go of me, walking towards his car only to turn back then change his mind with a head shake. Guess he wasn't expecting that. Half of what I said is true, I wouldn't mind a spanking from Nicky again.

But tonight is about putting someone in their place. Gary's been walking around with a bruised eye for a week with a cocky grin, thinking no one can touch him. He doesn't get to have that freedom. I won't let another girl fall into the palm of his hand just to get hurt.

I'm the one who's finally going to be doing the hurting. Instead of receiving it, I'll be delivering it.

Time to party.

I've never been to a high school party before but it's exactly how I pictured it as we stand in the doorway. Cheap beer, barely clothed girls, and a makeshift dance floor with guys grinding on girls, attempting to lure them into sex with all the wrong hip moves. The thought makes me shudder in horror at the effort these girls go to just to flirt, half of them are younger than me. At that age, I was sliding down poles while taking my clothes off. Everyone's mostly innocent here, never experienced true pain that makes you wish you were dead.

"If you're trying to kill me, you're succeeding," Nicky says behind me in disgust, pushing away a drunk kid stumbling out the door just in time as he vomits on the porch.

"I wanted, uh, to party," I grimace and can't look at

him, knowing he's going to see right through me. "Let's get a drink."

I quickly step through the door, heading to the kitchen as my breathing picks up. I need at least one shot to get me through this night, before I bring out the other Tillie who knows how to seduce a man with just a smile. So many bodies stuffed together in one place, the air heavy with sweat and liquor. Squeezing between people, I finally make it to the kitchen where all the drinks are set up on the counter with spilled liquor and red solo cups. Feeling the guys behind me, watching my every move... I grab the nearest alcoholic drink and twist the cap off. My hands shake slightly as I start chugging the cheap beer, hating the taste that goes down, but it instantly mellows me out.

"Is someone going to tell me why we are here, mingling with the riffraff?" Nicky snarls at the partygoers, the music getting louder and causing them to form a circle around me as the kitchen fills up.

"You'll find out soon enough but when you do, you can't interfere. That goes for both of you." I point my now empty beer bottle at Nicky and Tey, glaring to get my point across.

Don't mess with my shit, it's mine to take back.

Tey swaggers over to me, throwing his arm over my shoulder and grabbing the nearest bottle of whiskey within reach. He has his poker face on, not giving me a hint of what he's thinking about, but I can't stop watching as he tilts his head back and brings the whiskey up to his wide lips. His Adam's apple bobs with the first swallow, but he grabs the back of my neck with his other hand and forces my head back as he leans over me. With his face inches away, he puts pressure on my neck until I open my mouth to ask him what the hell he's doing.

"What-" I start to say but I'm cut off as Tey rest his plump, soft lips against mine and opens his mouth as I gasp.

Warm, smooth whiskey flows into my mouth, the taste tickling down my throat as I swallow. I don't know when I closed my eyes, but when I slowly blink them open, it's to see Tey leaning slightly back with a small wicked smirk.

"I have a feeling tonight's going to be fun. If you need me to get rid of a body, I'm game." He wipes a drop of whiskey off the corner of my mouth with his thumb and turns his head to glance at a scowling Nicky. "Nicholas, come here."

Nicky glances between us, his scowl deepening but he pushes off the opposite counter to make his way over to stand behind me, placing my body right between theirs. Tey takes another drink and winks at me just as he pushes up against my shoulder, squeezing me up against Nicky's chest. I watch as Tey does the same thing to Nicky, grabbing the back of his neck and pulling him closer until they are both leaning over me. My breathing picks up as my panties grow damp, seeing how Nicky's eyes drop down to Tey's mouth and stays there. I let out a breathless moan as Tey tilts Nicky's head and places his mouth against his, the same way he did to me. A hand skims my hip while another slides across my ribs, grazing the curve of my breast, but I can't pull my gaze away to even look. It could be Tey holding me in place or Nicky pulling me closer, but the thought of both of them touching me at the same time sends my heart into overdrive because I want that real fucking bad. All I can see is two hard, muscular as hell bodies moving closer together and making me a tight sandwich as I grip fists full of their shirts to stop myself from joining. Strong jawlines move as they fight for dominance, neck muscles tight and lips locked as Nicky swallows the whiskey down from Tey's mouth as he lets it flow out.

"Get the fuck out," I hear Dalton growl from somewhere and hear a girl squeak in fear before the kitchen goes quiet.

That seems to make everything come back in full force. The music, the party happening around us, and the way Nicky shoves away while looking around frantically in panic.

"Do you have a death wish?!" Nicky yells, licking his lips as he glares at Tey. "If that gets back to Jin..." Nicky runs a hand through his hair, turning his back to us as he tries to gain control of himself.

"You need to relax. It won't get back to him."

I peek around the kitchen, surprised to find it empty. Dalton stands in the doorway, practically growling at anyone trying to come in. That explains that. Logan appears out of nowhere, I wonder when he left to begin with? Maybe he went to see if Nicola and Evan finally made an appearance. I hope as fuck they are already here, someone has to keep an eye on the rest of the party incase shit goes south. Logan curls his index finger at me and nods his head to the side to follow him. Looking between Nicky and Tey and seeing them talking to each other in a low voice, I quickly duck around Dalton to Logan's side.

"I'll distract them as long as I can, but don't hold your breath," Dalton grumbles and crosses his arms with a mean curl of his lips as another group of boys try to enter but they quickly retreat like dogs with tails between their legs.

I pat his bicep and quickly catch up to Logan who goes into the living room, leaning against a wall with his ankles crossed. I slide up to his side and follow his gaze to see what he's looking at. Brown eyes connect with mine, a cruel smirk on his mocking lips.

Gary.

Surrounded by his jock buddies on the couch, he tips a beer back as he stares daggers at me, like I was the one to somehow wrong him, when in reality he's the problem. It's not my fault he's a rapist. I hate men like him. Thinking women owe him something, that it's all our fault for wearing clothes that show too much skin to tempt him.

"Go upstairs, last door on the left. It's his room, he'll follow because he can't help himself. Stumble up the stairs on your way, act drunk. I'll give you five minutes, Tillie, before we come in. I'll have Dalton round up his two little friends," Logan says with a stony facial expression and pushes off the wall to walk out the back patio.

Never taking my eyes off my prey, I roam my gaze along the bruise over his right eye, noticing it fading along with his busted lip. It's really not fair that his bruises can fade and mine seem to always linger, even years later. I'm trying to decide how I want to play this. Do I hurt him like he did me by taking his dignity away, or worse? Out of the corner of my eye, I see Larry playing with some girls' hair, distracting her as Stan slips a white powder into her solo cup.

This is going to be the night I turn it all off, to play my part in this world. Eighteen years ago, a monster was born from the Devil himself. It's time I spread my wings, accept this is who I am. No more running, I'm sprinting full force at those who have done me wrong.

I came here with a plan, to lure him away with seduction, get him into a quiet place away from all the prying eyes, so I can do what needs to be done. He just has to take the bait and I know just how to convince him. Grabbing a beer from a cooler at my feet, I chug half of that in one go and grin with my eyes closing. Justin Bieber's song "Peaches" comes on over the speaker, making some of the girls surrounding me scream in excitement and start dancing. Deciding this is my chance, I make my way into the middle of the dance floor and can feel Gary's eyes on my back. My hand travels up my body, sliding into my hair as the music takes over and I move my hips to the beat that just comes naturally.

When was the last time I danced this freely without having to take off my clothes? It's been awhile. Tossing my hair to the side, I peek over my shoulder with a seductive smile as I glance directly at Gary. He roams his gaze up and down my body, his lips still curled in a sneer, but he can't help following my body's movements. Giving him one last look, I drain the rest of the beer and pretend to wobble in my heels. I stumble into a couple and laugh loudly like I'm drunk. With my back turned away from him, my smile drops instantly and I make my way towards the stairs. Pausing at the base of the stairs, I take a deep breath and grip the railing. I know he's following, I can practically feel him giving chase. The thought makes me shiver with disgust.

Finding his room easily just like Logan said, I stumble into through his doorway and instantly, the smell of overpowering cologne hits my nose but confirms I'm in the right bedroom. Why do guys think that you need to soak in body spray like it's going out of style? It's like he dumped peppermints with spearmints inside someone's granny trunk in an attic filled with mothballs. I leave the door cracked behind me and quickly shove the window wide open to air the place out before sitting on the checkered pattern bedspread with my legs crossed as I wait.

Hook, line, and sinker.

I lean back on my hands as the door silently closes, my gaze directed at my sequined heels that match my stockings. Logan picked out this outfit, a sequin halter top that pairs nicely with the short satin skirt that ends mid-thigh. Apparently, Gary likes it, too.

"I knew you wanted it. Sluts like you pretend you don't, but here you are. On my bed. All alone," Gary states cockily, crossing his room to sit beside me and tucks my hair over my shoulder. Sliding his fingers down my arm, he stares at my thighs while licking his lips.

"You have it all figured out." I giggle, pretending to be buzzed, and he smirks this evil smile that makes me want to slap it off his face, but I restrain myself, by some miracle.

"Now, do what you do best and spread your legs for me," he says and turns to place his wallet and cellphone on his nightstand. He thinks I don't notice how he turns his camera on and positions it towards the rest of his room.

He's recording this. Good, something to look back on years from now, and maybe he'll learn his lesson by watching it over and over again because he won't be able to help himself. That one time his world crashed around him, and he needed proof it really happened.

This guy is no foreplay, he turns back to me and starts slobbering all over me. He starts kissing down my neck, his mouth sloppy and rushed. He grabs the clasp around my neck as I hold still, not making a sound as my top pools around my waist. My breasts are exposed, the cool AC making my nipples pebble, and he takes that as a sign to grope me with one of his hands. His touch and groan makes my muscles lock up tight, I keep telling myself it's no different compared to the strip club.

"I've been told I give the best head by multiple men. Why don't you lie back and I'll show you." Before I'm done even talking, he's unsnapping his khakis and laying down on the bed with his hands behind his head.

"Well, get to it, cunt," he draws out, nodding towards his flaccid dick that has me swallowing down the vomit threatening to climb up my throat.

Standing from the bed, I unzip the back of my skirt to let it fall to the ground around my heels. I stand in front of him in high heels, diamond stockings attached to a garter strap around my thighs, and lacey, hot pink panties that look good against my skin. He glances over my body with a scowl and looks back down at his dick that still isn't hard. Seems to me if he's not pinning a girl down, it doesn't work for him.

"How about I put on a little show for you? I'll be so wet for you." The tone of my voice is raspy and breathless, letting him think I actually want this.

"Hurry the fuck up and then suck my dick." His voice grates on my nerves, but I climb back onto the bed until I'm sitting on his calves.

Far enough back that he can't touch me, and so if he tries to go anywhere, he can't. I'm going to distract him long enough that he won't see the dagger tucked nice and comfy into the back of my garter until it's too late. He won't see me coming for him.

I slide my hands slowly up the curve of my hips and cup my breasts in both hands under his watchful gaze for a second, before running my fingers through my hair as I tip my head back like I'm experiencing ecstasy. He doesn't once glance at my face, his focus is completely on my body. I lean back, bracing one hand on his calf as my other slides down my taut stomach towards the edge of my panties. Slipping my fingers inside, I try to think of something else to distract me.

Dalton comes to mind, the last time he made me gush all over his skilled fingers. With him taking front and center in my head, it's easier to glide my hand into my panties and start rubbing my clit in tiny, fast circles. Taking my gaze away from the ceiling, I glance down to see Gary gazing at my moving fingers with lust, his panting breath loud as he grabs his balls, trying to get hard. It gives me a chance to slip the dagger out. He doesn't know what the feeling is at first, when I move my hand out from behind my back to place it on his upper thigh... right next to his dick, that was just starting to rise to the occasion. I'm still not impressed by the little guy, he's definitely not a grower.

"What is-" he starts to say absentmindedly but his whole body freezes when he glances down. "You fucking bitch!" he hisses, attempting to look menacing, but for once, I hold the power with a man under me.

"You're not allowed to call me bitch. That's reserved for someone else. I'd watch what you say to me. After all, I could cut off your dick with just a flick of my wrist." I bite my lower lip, inching my dagger closer to said dick and start to slip my fingers out of my underwear. Dalton gave me the dagger before we left for the party, so I was prepared.

"Well, don't stop on our account. It was just getting good, little bitch," Dalton drawls out from the doorway, making me jump slightly and causing Gary to hiss out in pain between his teeth as I accidentally cut him on the thigh.

Turning my head to look behind me, I watch as Dalton leans against the open doorway with Stan and Larry on either side of him. I can see from here that both of them are shaking with fear. Logan enters next, with Tey and Nicky coming to stand on either side of him, as he shuts the door. I didn't even hear them come in, sneaky bastards.

"What the fuck is going on?!" Nicky exclaims with a growl, taking a step towards the bed as if to grab me and throw me over his shoulder caveman style, but Logan stops him with a hand on his shoulder. Tey gives me this look like he's deeply wounded that I'm having fun without him. There's betrayal in his ocean blue eyes as he gazes to the knife and back at me sitting practically naked on top of another guy.

"Get this crazy cunt off me! She was asking for it just like last time, but I swear she came onto me. I found her in my room!" Gary shouts in panic, seeing he just might not make it out of here alive.

"Last time?" Tey says in a deadly, quiet voice, his face wiping away any facial expression.

"You should have kept your mouth shut," I tell Gary, shaking my head with a sigh.

Before I can blink, Nicky grabs Larry and twists his arm behind his back, so that his body is arched at a weird angle as he stands on his toes. I hear a snap, a cracking of a bone, and Larry's short cry of pain.

"Start talking," Nicky threatens, his voice harsh as he puts more pressure on Larry's arm.

Stan stands there frozen, sweating bullets as he glances around like he's looking for a way out. Dalton slaps a hand on his shoulder, making the guy almost piss his pants.

"Don't say a word, Larry!" Gary shouts in a strained voice, his face turning an ugly red as he glares up at me while his hands fist the comforter under his tense body.

I'm betting he would love nothing more than to hit me, to put me in my place. I just grin like a little shit and dig the dagger in a tiny bit, enough to draw a line of blood from his inner thigh. He cries out and I can't help rolling my eyes, I've had way worse. That shouldn't even hurt him. Big baby. I don't need to look to know that Tey is suddenly standing at the foot of the bed, glancing over my shoulder.

"I'm mad at you, buttercup, but keep doing that and you might be forgiven," Tey whispers softly into my ear before biting down hard on the tender flesh. Ignoring my sharp inhale, he places his chin on my shoulder with a pleased sigh as he watches from behind.

"Hey! Don't stare at her, look at me," Nicky's voice goes deep, his anger coming through as he slaps the back of Larry's head.

"It wasn't my idea! I was just told what to do and did it. I only held her down while Gary touched her," Larry says in a scared, shaky voice as he stares at the bedroom wall so he doesn't have to look at Nicky.

The expression that comes over Nicky's face is scary yet beautiful. His face is smooth, void of any expression. You would think he's numb to everything, but his eyes give him away. Bright emerald green eyes start to turn a darker shade, almost appearing black as his pupils pulse before narrowing on his prey. That prey would be the guy who's deadly still under me.

"Listen! We thought she was fair game, you guys said it

yourself to the whole school. It was a joke. We didn't even touch your sister before she stepped in. It's all a misunderstanding," Stan tries to argue, looking for any way to get out of this.

"Oh man, you really shouldn't have brought up Nicola. Logan, I'll see if I can get a few club brothers over here to help dispose of the bodies," Dalton grunts, reaching for his phone in his pocket.

"No need. I have some empty tanks at the warehouse, they can decay in those for a couple of days. Limes should help the skin tissues dissolve faster," Logan suggests, his brow wrinkled as if he's thinking of another way to get rid of the three idiot jocks' bodies.

If I was any ordinary girl, this type of talk would have me screaming for the hills, but I secretly like it.

It's empowering.

Exhilarating.

Well, at least I think so, not everyone agrees with me.

"What the... yo-you can't do that!" Gary stutters in disbelief. He starts to swing his arm back to hit me, but freezes when I get too close to his dick with the blade and chop off some of his pubes with a quick flick of my wrist.

"We can do whatever the hell we want to. Nicky, let him go. This is Tillie's show and I have to say, I'm here for the view." Dalton rubs his hands together and eyes my bare breasts with a pleased smirk stretching across his plump lips.

Men.

Stan and Larry are shoved to their knees, facing the bed so they have the perfect view of me as my guys line up behind them, menacing like fallen angels about to wreak havoc with just one word from me.

"What are you going to do first?" Tey asks, like the

devil on my shoulder, all too happy to watch my handi-work and make me listen to his suggestions.

Gary's wide brown eyes shift down to the dagger drag-ging closer to the family jewels and his eyes start to water at the corner. I want him to beg for mercy.

"Should I cut off this pathetic thing between your legs?" I skim the sharp blade lightly across his balls, feeling a shiver travel down my spine in delight as he whimpers in fear of having the baby makers snipped off.

"Ple-please. I won't ever d-do it again." His plea makes my ears ring, echoing over and over again, words I once used that never helped me in the end.

Begging gets you nowhere.

"Do you think because I have a pussy it makes me weak? Look at you. You hopped in your bed so fast and couldn't even tell the danger you were in, just because I have breasts." To prove my point, his eyes flicker down, of their own accord, to my chest and stays there even with the knife inches from his most important body part.

Tey reaches around me to lightly slide his fingers across my collarbone before trailing down, circling my nipple as if he has all the time in the world until he pinches hard with a twist. A loud moan slips past my parted lips, giving away how much I like the tingling feeling mixed with a sharp pain, spreading through my body and causing a damp spot in my panties. Gary's body twitches under me and I ignore the wet, babble noise coming out of his mouth as my dagger keeps slicing into his skin.

"Keep watching. See what's going to happen to you," Logan orders in an authoritative voice, making Stan and Larry watch as he grabs the back of their necks and squeezes so they have no choice but to look where he wants them to.

"Answer her," Tey demands in a sharp tone as he climbs onto the bed behind me and sits on Gary's legs before reaching around my shoulder to smack Gary hard on the cheek.

With Tey sitting on Gary, he won't be able to move at all, even when he starts struggling with the pain I'm about to put him in.

"All women are the same," Gary suddenly growls out harshly, his lips curled as he sneers up at me. "Sluts."

"I know what you are. I've been around men just like you all my life, and I'm going to leave a reminder each time you look in the mirror. You're going to feel my pain and carry it with you the rest of your miserable life, just like I have to." My voice comes out robotic, trying to shake off the memories, and control my shaking hand as I raise it to his chest.

I pause, the tip of the blade inches from his skin, but for some reason I can't bring the blade down to do what needs to be done. I stare down at my hand wrapped around the dagger, willing myself to just do it. A warm chest presses against my back, bringing warmth to my chilled body. Tey rests his chin back on my shoulder as he reaches around my waist with his other hand to close around my hand holding the dagger.

"I'm going to step into your world, just this once. Take some of my strength," Tey says quietly in my ear, and I soak his words in as I take a deep breath.

Feeling calmer than I've ever felt, I bring the blade down the rest of the way as Gary starts screaming in panic and pain. Music thumps from downstairs, drowning out any noise coming from this room. My hand glides around

Gary's skin with ease, Tey never letting go. Blood soaks the sheets, traveling down the sides of Gary's chest as he gasps for breath through his tears.

Straightening, I take in the ridged cut of his skin, where my blade slipped a couple of times from the blood, but it's clear enough to read.

Rapist.

"Tillie, let him up," Logan suddenly says, his voice angry and gruff.

Almost like I'm in someone else's body, I move to get off the bed with Tey helping me with a hand on my elbow. I don't understand why they are helping me deliver my payback, letting me take the ropes, but for once in my life... I have someone to lean on, just for a little bit, until I can find my strength.

Don't get me wrong, revenge is still in the back of my mind, but it's on pause for right now. This is about living before I die. That death can be any day now and I can feel it trying to creep up on me.

The moment we're away from the bed, Gary struggles to get off his mattress and ends up tangling his legs in his sheets as he rolls off onto the floor.

"Please, we won't ever do it again. Just let us go, man," Stan pleads, clenching onto Nicky's pants leg, and doesn't let go as Nicky tries to shake him off with a curl of his upper lip.

"I've changed my mind. You'll live for today, but just remember those tanks have your names on them," Logan says, ignoring the hard look Nicky gives me and the way Dalton pushes off the wall like he's going to argue.

"Thank you! Thank you!" Larry cries and he misses the way Tey starts chuckling darkly, right by my ear.

"Dalton, line up Gary right next to his buddies. Oh,

and hand Tillie that baseball bat from next to the night-stand." Logan grins as he checks his Rolex and starts rolling up his sleeves to his elbows, which is very distracting.

Didn't know I'd be getting an arm porn show today, but I'm not complaining, especially as Nicky starts to do the same thing.

Dalton does as he's asked without complaining, dragging a groaning Gary next to his two buddies and making all of them get to their knees. Next, he walks over to the nightstand with a cheerful whistle and grabs a baseball bat tucked behind there, handing it over to me with a wink.

"Swing hard, little bitch... makes your breasts jiggle more. You may not know this, but I'm a breast man, and you've got some fantastic ones on you." He tweaks my nipple as he walks by, making me gasp.

He goes to stand behind the three jocks that are about to be in a lot of pain and gives me a nod to get started. Testing the weight in my hands, I look up and stare into a pair of honey eyes that narrow on me as I just stand there.

Right. Okay, I can do this.

Gripping the handle of the baseball bat, I stare down at Larry and picture all the women these three men have hurt. Raped. Abused. No more.

The bat makes a low whistling noise as it swings through the air, but the sound of bone crunching under the solid wood brings back memories of Payne using his fists on me. The time I had two cracked ribs. A broken nose. My stomach black and blue from being beaten, the shape of a boot print outlined on my skin. I didn't even realize I closed my eyes at some point until I blink them open, as I lean over Larry and keep bringing the bat down.

His cries cut off and I know he's either passed out from the pain or I may have hit him over the head. I can't remember.

Breathing hard, I straighten from my crouched position over Larry's body and blow the hair out of my face with a grin as blood trickles down my cheek. Pure bliss shoots through my body at seeing the strange way Larry's leg is bent, the odd angle of his arm, and his face bleeding... I took my rage out on them.

It felt fucking fantastic.

I glance up and see the two horrified gazes of Gary and Stan hugging each other as they stare in shock at the blood surrounding me. I probably look crazy but could care less. Tey doesn't seem to know where to look, his gaze going to the blood I'm covered in and flickering down to Gary and Stan whimpering at my feet. Nicky keeps eyeing my bat, his fists clenched at his sides, but his gaze stops at the scrap of lace between my legs like he's going to rip it off of me with his teeth. I notice Logan next to him, his chest heaving up and down as he tries to hold himself back, but the passion in his darkening gaze makes my thighs squeeze together to release the pressure building there.

"Nicky," I absently say, making eye contact with Dalton, his whole body vibrating like he's seconds away from grabbing me.

"Tillie," Nicky growls, his voice deep and oh so dangerous.

"It's your turn." I glance at him and hold out the bat, waiting for him to take it.

He needs an outlet too. It could have been his sister in my place in the locker room and I know how much he cares for her. He doesn't say anything as he grabs the baseball bat and swipes my hair off my shoulder to caress that tender spot between my neck and shoulder as he walks by. Stan whimpers as he tries to crawl away, but Nicky grasps the back of his collar and slams him to the ground just before he lifts the bat. Screaming pierces my ear and the sound of more bone crunching fills the space as Nicky beats the shit out of Stan, but I can't seem to focus on anything. I feel anxious, jumpy, like I need to run and keep going until I can't breathe.

"Get down to your knees, little bitch," Dalton says in a gruff voice, his violent eyes heating as they trail over my body.

I tilt my head, not understanding why he's suddenly bossing me around and wondering what exactly he's up to, especially when he grins that stupid smile. Stupid dimples.

"On your knees and crawl." He points to his boots, his hard tone telling me to not bother arguing with him and I better listen.

I hesitate for a split second and slowly sink to my knees, my breathing coming out easier once I'm kneeling on the carpet. My whole life I've been told what to do. I craved freedom, but having that moment of control actually scared me. I don't know how to handle these feelings. Fear of the unknown sneaks up on me and I need something to ground me back to reality. Eyeing Dalton's boots, I get on my hands and knees and do something that really lets me know I've gone off the deep end. I crawl over to him, my hips swaying, and I know the guys are getting an eyeful of my ass and the wet line right over my pussy lips.

Stopping at his feet, I stare down at his biker boots and slowly drag my gaze up his tall, built body, until I'm looking into violet eyes that are enjoying every moment of this.

"I think we've allowed you enough freedom, don't you think?" Dalton mutters, resting his hand on the top of my head... Is he petting me?

He is! It's strange, but I'm kind of loving it. His fingers keep sliding through my hair, pulling slightly at the locks making my scalp tingle, and my eyes try to slip closed at the feeling. I'm trying not to lean into his touch as his expression turns arrogant, like he knows what's going through my mind and it's hard to keep my cheeks from flushing with lust.

"Kiss my boots." His voice gets gravelly, as if he likes the idea a little too much.

I can only glare up at him and turn my head away with a scowl. I notice Nicky has stopped beating Stan with a bat, his white shirt covered in blood but he's actually smiling like he's enjoying himself. He puts his messy hair into a bun and helps Tey drag a passed out Gary over to my feet face down.

"Don't look at them, look at me," Dalton orders, placing a finger under my chin to direct my gaze so I'm staring up at him. "I did promise you something, didn't I?" He shifts his eyes over to Gary and then looks at me again... it suddenly clicks what he is referring to.

I did, after all, admit my fantasy to Dalton in the dark closet that day, and now he's making it come true. He's also messing with me, just like the garage all over again, and he expects me to actually kiss his biker boots. Logan's leaning against the wall right beside us, silently watching me with that intense, cool, honey gaze, to see what I'll do.

I decide to play along, but on my terms. I'm taking control of my body, and right now, I want to use Dalton for my own personal gain. I start to lean down towards his boots, making sure my back is arched enough for Tey and Nicky behind me to see how wet I am, my thighs parted enough for them to make out the line of my pussy lips through my panties. Just when my breath is fogging the tip of his boots, I quickly straighten and have Dalton's belt unbuckled in seconds before he can try to shove me back down. He groans low in his throat with desire, wanting me, craves this, as I unzip his jeans and reach in to grasp his big, hard cock.

My fingers don't wrap fully around his girth, the texture smooth and velvety soft. When I finally take him out, his chest heaves up and down as his fists clench by his side, trying to stop himself from shoving me down on his big cock. His dick really is so large that I'm pretty sure a lot of women can't handle him, but he's lucky because I'm not like most women. I can't help leaning forward to feel the warmth of him on my tongue. I lick him leisurely from base to tip, my tongue dragging along him and making him groan again as he tilts his head back in pleasure.

"This is what you wanted, right?" I purr, wanting him to beg for it.

I pause around the tip of him as a drop of pre cum leaks out, my mouth wide open but I don't take him in. My hot breath fans the underside of him, and his breathing deepens as he stares down at me, running his tongue along his upper lip.

"I love it when she gets sassy, but I love it more when she's covered in blood," Tey mumbles absentmindedly behind me, running a finger down my spine.

"I think she's using you, Dalton." Nicky says in a deep, throaty voice, and he gives a swift kick to Gary's ribs just because he can.

"Why don't you tell him what you really want, baby girl," Logan muses, crooking an eyebrow at me as he draws my head back by fisting my hair.

This view allows me to see all four of them towering over me, making me feel small and surrounded. I'm back on my knees, but I can see the difference this time. I'm fucking wanted... desired, but I can stop this at any time and walk away.

"Say it," Dalton demands in a growly voice, as my neck strains at the position.

"I want you to fuck me. Make me feel good, numb my mind," I admit in a raspy voice.

I'm yanked to my feet and spun around before I can blink. With my back flush against Dalton's front and his cock grazing my lower back, he slides his calloused hands up and down my sides, giving me goosebumps. Logan tightens his grip in my hair and controls my movements, making me bend over until my eyes are level with the front of Tey's pants zipper. Glancing up, Tey gives me a sinister smile. He wipes something off my cheek with his thumb, and brings it into my line of sight so I can see the blood.

"I did tell you that I'd fuck your mouth next time when you're covered in blood." Tey nibbles on his lip ring, as he unzips his pants and pulls out his cock.

I can only stare and stare some more. I'm pretty sure my mouth is wide open in shock.

He lifts his shirt off over his head, giving me a view of his six pack of hard ridges that shift as he moves. He starts stroking his hard as steel cock in front of my face, his long length growing bigger the more I stare. My eyes widen as his fist moves away from the tip of his cock, the shiny metal making my mouth water. I want to see what it feels like sliding against my tongue, see if it's cool and smooth as it looks. His cock is pierced with a barbell. I understand the term big dick energy but these guys really don't mess around. Long and thick, big enough to make me choke, especially with his penis pierced. I wonder how it would feel while it's moving inside me, in and out, hard and fast. The thought makes my pussy flutter and I kind of hope to find out soon.

"Damn, Tey," Dalton whistles as he, too, stares at Tey's cock. "Did you and Nicky go together or something? You get a piercing while he gets his cock tattooed?" Nicky reaches over and slaps the back of Dalton's head with narrowed eyes.

"Shut the hell up. Make her moan and I'll stab Gary each time she makes a sound. Oh, and she likes her ass spanked. That should get her going." Nicky grins as Dalton glares at him. Nicky goes to sit at our feet, pulling out a knife.

Guess he's serious about the stabbing part. I roll my eyes as they banter back and forth, glancing away from Tey's cock to plead up at Logan, but the fucker takes me by surprise. His hand was lightly massaging my scalp at one point with his long fingers but his grip tightens and shoves me forward. My mouth opens on a gasp and my lips are suddenly wrapped around Tey's cock. He groans loudly when he reaches the back of my throat, the metal piercing sliding smoothly along my tongue as I suck on him hard, and I can't help the pleasure hum in my throat. My eyes start to water when he pushes deeper into my mouth, pausing, and I struggle to not gag. Logan won't let me up to breathe as he holds me there, whispering in my ear to keep going while I breathe through my nose. My forehead touches Tey's abs as I calmly hold still, relaxing under the pressure even as I choke on him. Logan brings my head back and I get one large breath, filling my lungs full of air, before I'm shoved back down on Tey's cock again.

"Fuck. That feels good. I can feel your throat trying to swallow around me," Tey says in wonder. He grabs the hollow part of my cheeks with his thumbs as he holds my head to thrust roughly in between my lips, before slowing down to drag his cock back and forth, as I drool all over him.

I can't help the small moan in the back of my throat as I feel him slide in and out of my mouth, knowing the metal ball at the tip of his cock would feel amazing inside my pussy. Once the sound of me moaning slips out, as I'm let up to take a deep breath, Nicky slices a thin line down Gary's side, right under his armpit to his hip, drawing blood.Nicky is grinning like a madman as his victim lets out a moan for an entirely different reason.

"You sick bastards! All this for a fucking slut," Gary explodes and turns his head to glare death daggers up at me.

"Watch your fucking mouth," Logan snarls like a rabid beast and lets go of my hair to bend down, grabbing Gary's left hand and casually breaks two of his fingers. "She's our slut. Show some fucking respect."

I reach out and place my hands on Tey's upper thighs to steady myself, as Dalton keeps his hands full of my ass cheeks, gripping them. I stare in wonder at the men surrounding me, they won't ever know that being wanted like this means everything to me. I know I look like a whore right now. Half naked, letting the guys touch me, use me. My lips swollen and red, and my eyes watering, but damn if I don't feel pretty fucking special right now. I glance over my shoulder, needing to feel Dalton's big cock pounding into me before I lose my mind.

"Daddy," I whisper, my voice husky. His eyes roam over to me, like he has all the time in the world, as his hands grip my hips tight enough to bruise.

"What did you say?" he growls, his gaze bright and violent as his pupils dilate.

"Punish me, use me. Fuck me, please... Daddy." Never would I have ever thought that just calling him daddy would get this reaction, but I'm going to be calling him that from now on.

"Logan, let me see your gun real quick." Dalton doesn't look away from me, until he shoves my head back around so I can't see what he's doing and my gaze connects with Tey's cock like two lost lovers.

Logan chuckles under his breath and reaches into the waistband of his pants to pull out his gun, handing it over to Dalton as he reaches across my back for it. My panties are pulled tight for a second until the lacy fabric falls apart easily, dropping around my ankles.

"This is my favorite part," Tey says, running the tip of his cock back and forth over my bottom lip. I can't help circling my tongue around his tip as Nicky watches with rapt attention from beside us on the ground while he randomly cuts into Gary's skin with the knife, without even bothering to look at him.

I moan on purpose and get a sick sense of joy as Nicky breaks the rest of Gary's fingers on his left hand, making him scream until he shoves a dirty sock in Gary's mouth to shut him up.

"Naughty, Tillie." Nicky grabs my ankle, spreading my legs further apart as he glances behind me. "Ever played life or death?" he asks just as I feel a cold object run down my spine, sliding between my ass crack, and stopping at the entrance of my pussy.

I freeze, my breath stilling in my chest and I know exactly what Dalton has in his hand right now. It's not the first time I've had a gun in my face or placed against my skin. Won't be the last, either. I just was not expecting them to play a game by using one inside of me.

"Every day is a game of life and death. I have nothing to lose," I admit on a gasp, feeling the barrel of the gun slip a little into my pussy, the cold steel making me shiver.

"How wet are you, baby girl?" Logan asks, twisting his fingers in my hair again, to hold me still with my head tipped back painfully, until all I can see is the bright blue of Tey's eyes. "I'm betting you're soaking. Are you going to squirt for him?" He hums in the back of his throat, like the thought pleases him, and crouches on his heels by my leg, the opposite side of Nicky.

"Touch her, Lo, spread her wide for me." Dalton puts pressure on the bottom of my spine, making me arch my back more, so he can see the gun slipping in and out of me.

Logan grabs the inside of my thigh, caressing the sensitive spot that makes my pulse pound, before gliding his hand up further and rubbing his palm back and forth over my swollen clit. He and Nicky make me spread my legs wider, until it's a painful strain, but the pleasure over-rules everything else. At the same time, Dalton eases the gun into me halfway and pauses before sliding it back out.

"Goddamn, you fucking like this. I'm going to make you cream all over my big cock, little bitch." Dalton groans loudly, his voice tight and deep, like he's holding himself back as if he's actually worried he's going to hurt me.

I don't want any of them to hold back with me. I want

to feel, to come apart until I'm crying because this moment is mine and mine alone.

"Stop," I rasp out, all of them pausing when they hear me. The one word I've screamed before in a room full of bikers, that always falls on deaf ears, leaves my lips and I can feel all of their eyes on me, but they do as I ask. Tey cocks his head to the side in question. "Stop messing around and hurt me, fuck me. I'm not a fragile object, do your worst." The smile that comes across Tey's face will forever be seared into my head.

It's dark, dangerous, and a tad mad, but it's a smile that says your soul isn't alone anymore. It whispers *mine.*

"Are you sure about that, baby girl? You don't know what you're asking for, but I'm more than happy to give in to your demands," Logan says in a menacing tone, but I swear I hear admiration in his deep voice

"I've never been more sure about anything. I still hate you guys, though." I inhale sharply on a gasp as I feel something cold and yet familiar skimming across my neck, barely touching me.

"You move and you die. Be a good girl and do as you're told," Nicky warns, the small knife he has against my throat is pressing in a little to prove his point.

I can only stare at Tey with wide eyes, swallowing hard, and giving him a small nod, which causes the knife to dig in enough to cut a thin line on the side of my throat.

Tey groans, his gaze shifting to the drop of blood trailing down and between my breasts. Logan starts moving his fingers with no mercy or fucks given to my throbbing clit, destroying me and making me tremble as I hold back on orgasming.

My loud moan has Nicky laughing quietly to himself, and I know he broke something else on Gary as I hear a

loud crack followed right by a scream of agony around his
sock gag.

"Tey, fuck her mouth and keep her quiet. I'm going to
wreck her pussy," Dalton says in a gruff voice, slipping the
gun out to replace it with something warmer, bigger, and
the thought of his cock inside me almost scares me.

I've seen the monster. It's fucking huge, thick, and I
know it's going to be a tight fit. Tey rests either hand on
the side of my face and runs his thumb over my bottom lip
to open wide for him. He leans down slightly, his breath
hot against my lips just before he spits in my mouth.
Taking that as a sign, I put everything into giving him
head as I lap at his precum, rolling my tongue around the
fat mushroom head. My cheeks hollow, sucking him deep
and closing my lips tight around him as I go down on his
cock, feeling the slight pressure of the knife each time I
move. Dalton presses in close behind me, his big hands
gripping my buttcheeks, massaging me in a way that lets
me know he's a butt man instead of boobs. Moaning in the
back of my throat, he spreads my cheeks wide to watch his
dick start to slip inside of me inch by thick inch. He's so
big, the feel of him stretching me is painful before he's
even all the way in.

This isn't going to work.

I keep bobbing my head up and down on Tey, as I
glance out of the corner of my eye, my gaze connecting
with Logan's as his grip in my hair pulls tight. I raise one
eyebrow at him and wink, which confuses him until I
extend my leg out, bending my knee so that I'm resting my
high heel on his shoulder to spread my legs wider for
Dalton to fit. I'm flexible and this gives Logan a view of
everything from my swollen clit to my pink glistening lips

as Dalton lines up behind me. I guess Nicky has a good view too, as he makes a choked sound.

"Fuck," I hear Nicky curse silently on my other side and something that sounds like punching but the knife stays steady the whole time against my throat.

"I always live up to my promises. Nicky, flip him around so he has no choice but to watch. He'll get to see how a real man fucks a woman," Dalton orders as he bends over my back, placing a small kiss against my spine as he skims his fingers down my arms leaving goose-bumps in their wake, and grasping the inside of my elbows.

My hands that were gripping Tey's thighs are suddenly being pulled back behind me until I can't move from the grip Dalton has on each of my arms as he straightens back up. Logan releases his grip on my hair and leans forward to bite the side of my boob, making me suck in a sharp breath. Nicky does the same thing, but decides to make my body tremble in fear and arousal by running the blade down my collarbone and taking his time as he switches the knife between my breasts before circling my nipples that pebble into hard points at the coolness of the blade.

"Suck me harder," Tey demands as his head rolls back on his shoulders, a sexy groan of pleasure escaping his wide lips.

My body feels tight like a bow as Logan quickly moves his fingers in a blur over my clit just as Dalton slams the rest of the way into me with a grunt. I feel like I've been ripped in half, the wide stretch of his cock inside me has my eyes watering just before I close them.

"Eyes on me," Tey whispers, pushing his fat cock farther down my throat as Dalton slowly slides out and quickly snaps his hips forward, jerking my body towards Tey.

My eyes open wide in shock and I can only moan around Tey's cock, his piercing touching the back of my throat. I can feel my juices leaking down my thighs and have to wonder if it's normal to be this wet. Each time Dalton starts to pull out until he's right at the opening of my pussy, I clench around him as if to make him stay. He only chuckles deeply, thrusting back in hard and rough. The feeling is almost indescribable, but I do know I'd kill anyone right now if they try to take it away from me. My breasts jiggle with the thrusts of Dalton's cock, pushing me further onto Tey.

"Fuck, Tillie, I can hear how wet you are for us. I'm going to coat your throat with my cum, suck harder." Tey's hips jerk in quick thrusts, becoming faster as I suck him, running my tongue around his length each time I pull back.

"You see her, fucker? See how she wants to please both of them, willing to do anything? That's how you make a woman desperate for you," Nicky growls at Gary who whimpers in pain around the sock in his mouth, and that sound alone fuels me like gasoline on fire.

When Dalton slides almost all the way out, I slam my ass back against him. My ass smacks against the V of his hips with a loud slap, causing him to grip my elbows enough to bruise. He stops holding back, fucking me hard and fast in a way that has my legs shaking. Sliding in and out, our bodies slapping together mix in with the sounds of moans and silent cries of pain.

"You better fucking squirt," Logan commands right next to my ear, slowing his fingers on my clit, and making me whimper around a mouthful of Tey's cock.

Nicky hasn't stopped littering Gary's body with cuts from the knife or breaking his bones, the guy is going to be unrecognizable by the time I end up coming. Nicky somehow seems to know what I need to get me there because his fingers suddenly wrap around my throat, squeezing until I can't breath just as Logan pinches my clit hard. My vision blurs, it feels like I'm floating, yet my senses are all overloaded at once as I come around Dalton's cock. My core tensing, feeling a gush of liquid build and release as my whole body trembles with my eyes rolling to the back of my head.

"Christ!" Dalton growls and quickly pulls out, watching me squirt all over his cock before he shoves back in with a deep, long groan.

He starts to come, splashing my insides with jet after jet of cum, and grunts as I squeeze him with my pussy when Logan finally lets go of my clit. The pressure releases and it just makes my orgasm last longer. Nicky finally releases my throat at the same time, letting me breathe for a split second before he's shoving me down on Tey by the back of my head. I gag and close my eyes as Tey coats my throat with his cum, giving me every ounce of his pleasure. He keeps coming even as he draws back with a moan, filling my mouth up and overflowing past my parted lips.

"Don't swallow," Tey grins wickedly and bends down, grabbing Nicky's chin between his thumb and index fingers. "Kiss her."

Dalton let's go of my arms, wrapping his forearms around my waist so I don't collapse. I eye Nicky, seeing the hungry look in his green eyes even when his face is a blank mask. Resting my hands on his broad shoulders, I lean forward and he meets me halfway with his gaze on my lips.

When I say I was devoured, what I mean is Nicholas has taken control of my soul and ripped it to shreds as he grabs the back of my neck and kisses the living hell out of me. His lips move against mine passionately, sliding across my bottom lip until my lips part and he takes the opportunity to plunge his tongue in. Smoothly sliding his tongue against mine, with the taste of Tey still filling my mouth, we have a push and pull as he swallows every drop I give him.

Pulling away from him, he stares at me as he licks his perfectly sculpted lips and without looking, he stabs Gary's thigh as he tries to pathetically crawl away towards the door.

"Yes, bring the van around the corner and we'll dump them on the west coast. Make it look like rich kids in the wrong neighborhood," Logan barks out orders into his phone, breaking the connection between Nicky and me.

I straighten up with Dalton's help, a whimper slipping past my lips because of how sore my pussy is. It's throbbing with a slight twinge of pain, I just know I'll be walking unsteady for the next few days. It takes awhile but he slips out of me with a groan that sounds like he wants to push right back in. I hear his zipper and breathe a little easier because I'm not ready for a round two with that monster between his legs.

"Magic pussy." Dalton shoves his face into my neck, nuzzling me on the sensitive spot and whispering to himself. "She took my whole fucking dick."

I cough to hide my laugh, instantly regretting it as my throat pings with soreness. I'm used to hurting but this is a different kind of pain, one that I'd gladly take anytime. With Tey shoving his cock back into his pants, he roams his ocean blue eyes over my used and deliciously abused body with a smirk. He goes to grab Gary's feet as Nicky grabs his arms and they place him on his bedroom rug. Then they start rolling him up in the rug, ignoring Gary the whole time as he groans in agony, screaming around his gag. Really? A rug? It's so obvious there's a body in there, how mafia of them. That reminds me.

"Daddy," I rasp out, my throat raw in the back.

"Hmm," Dalton grumbles into my neck, not moving an inch.

Rolling my eyes, I turn around in his arms and loop my hands behind his neck. He lifts his head with a lopsided smile, looking relaxed as fuck. I bite my lip and look up at him under my lashes.

"Daddy," I say again in a husky voice, trying not to smile as he places his forehead against mine with a dazed look in his violet eyes that remind me of clouds rolling in, just before it starts to storm.

Something you can't stop looking at, mesmerized and slightly breathless as the air changes, the possibilities.

"Yes, princess?" His chest rumbles against mine like the vibration of a motorcycle.

I start to smile, probably creepy enough to throw me into an asylum but I just keep smiling until my cheeks hurt. His expression turns confused as he leans back to look me fully in the face.

"I'm going to fucking destroy you, use you, and by the time I'm done... all four of you will be kneeling." My smile vanishes just as quick as it comes, making me look more crazy, but I don't care. "Don't think just because you've been inside my pussy that I've forgotten exactly who you are and what you've done to me." I deliver that message but with a little extra spice to prove my point.

I draw my leg back and slam my knee into his balls, watching as his expression turns blank just before his whole face turns red as he drops to his knees.

"That's more like it." I pat his cheek, pretending I don't see him giving me a death glare.

"Jesus!" he chokes out, cupping his dick as he glances up at me towering over him. "Are you trying to make sure I don't have kids?"

I turn away from him to slowly bend down in front of his face to grab my clothes off the floor, giving him a view of his cum leaking out of my pussy and leaving me sticky between my thighs.

"I'd be doing the world a favor," I sass at him with a hair flip over my shoulder.

The whole time I dress, he doesn't say a word, his breathing deep behind me as he watches. Tey and Nicky are carrying Gary's rolled up body over to the window sill but they keep *accidentally* dropping him on his bedroom floor. I pause, zipping up the back of my skirt, watching Logan as he picks up a passed out Stan and chucks him out the window like he weighed nothing. Logan is such a gangster as he repeats this process with a knocked out Larry, then Gary is next and he screams the whole day down. His body makes a thumping sound outside the window as he hits the ground. With a head shake, I smooth my top down of any wrinkles and toss my hair over my shoulder as I turn towards Dalton.

"Where have you been hiding my entire life?" he asks with a wince, shaking his leg out with a relieved sigh as he climbs to his knees and pulls a hair tie out of his jeans pocket.

My eyebrows raise to my hairline... why is he carrying a hair tie around? He grips my arms and turns me back around, sliding his fingers through my long hair. The feeling makes my eyes slip closed in pure bliss, I've never had anyone play with my hair until these beautiful, vicious douchebags. It surprises me when he starts to braid my hair with skilled fingers and ties it off at the end within minutes. The bedroom door flies open with a bang and in charges Nicola with a kitchen knife in her right hand. Her hair is mussed and she's breathing hard, her lipstick smeared across the corner of her mouth. I tilt my head and almost burst out laughing as Evan appears behind her just as frazzled and bright pink lipstick on his lips.

Oh no...

My gaze shoots to Nicky, seeing the hard glare he's giving Evan, as if he's planning my buddies death. There's this dark cloud over Nicky that walks in his shadow and without a doubt he will do anything he wants just like death himself. I kind of feel bad for Nicola at the moment, but at least she'll always have a protective brother.

I glance over my shoulder with both of my eyebrows raised, Dalton is already staring at me as he waits for me to answer him while he plays with the end of my braid between his fingers.

"Trapped. I was trapped, but never again," I admit that much with a deep inhale.

I walk over to Nicola, not wanting Dalton to ask any more questions. I don't want to reveal what I've been through. These guys don't know and I don't think I can stand to see the pity in their gazes if they ever find out. Once those words come out of my mouth, I'm only seen as the victim. I promised myself I'd never be that person again.

"Seems you've been having some fun yourself." I swipe my thumb over my own lips, checking for any cum around the corners of my mouth, and grin as her eyes widen in panic as she swipes her arms across her face.

"Ladies, ladies. You can talk later about the best night of your life. Kitten, we have to get you ready for tomorrow night," Tey announces, steering me towards the door with a swagger in his step, and swipes Gary's phone off of his nightstand with a wink at me.

Cocky fucker. It was recording the whole time and he knew it.

"What's tomorrow?" I ask curiously and make sure everyone's following us so we leave the party as a group.

Less suspicion and an alibi in case anyone asks. Logan's whisper yelling out the window at someone below, I'm guessing whoever is dropping the asshat jocks to the west side. Nicky is talking into Evan's ear, who is turning paler by the minute. Nicola is trying to stand between them, while repeatedly smacking Nicky on the back of the head, and he places his hand on her forehead to hold her away as she tries to reach him. Dalton follows closely behind Tey and I on our heels, almost like he doesn't want to let me out of his sight ever again. *Strange,* I muse to myself.

"Ever been to a rave?" Tey chuckles darkly, like he has a secret.

Oh hell.

CHAPTER 13

Payne

"Have you heard from Nix?"

My question that's aimed towards Poe is met with silence, telling me that he has no news. I can feel my days coming closer, it's only a matter of time before Cruz finds her. I pick up my tequila glass and chuck it behind the bar at the mirrors lining the wall, with a hoarse scream of fury leaving my mouth. The mirrors crack like a spider web, making my reflection hazy and disoriented. Silence meets my rage, the club members knowing better than to question me, but I can hear the grumble of whispers.

"Not fit to be our president."

"He's losing it and caring less about our club."

"Cruz should be wearing that president patch, not the old man."

Each whisper, alongside the sound of cue balls ringing together on the pool table to distract themselves, so they don't have to look at me, that tells me enough. They're going to turn against me. Everyone is turning their backs on me, they're out to get me.

"You okay, boss?" Whiskey mutters, starting to pour me a new drink of tequila, but I smack his hand away and take the full bottle from him as I storm out of the main compound of the club, heading towards the stairs.

"Call Nix and don't disturb me unless you have something to report back," I tell Poe, already climbing the stairs without a reply back, he knows the drill.

I'll shoot him dead if he doesn't have any news for me, what I say goes. My word is law and I'll do whatever the fuck I want, no matter what the consequences are. It's been weeks and I'm still no closer to finding Diana, fucking slut. I'm getting desperate, my thoughts are only on finding her before Cruz. I've become obsessed, nothing else matters. Cocaine doesn't stop my mind from swirling with thoughts that keep me up at night, I can't sleep or eat. I tip the tequila bottle back, chugging and not giving a shit as it spills past my lips, soaking my beard. Some sweetbutt will be waiting in my bed, naked and willing to do anything to please me, but I don't want her. I want what's been denied from me for the past eighteen years. She's mine to take.

I walk by Rig's old room that's been closed for years, and stop in the middle of the hallway, stumbling back drunkenly to stand in front of the door. I eye the locked knob, taking another drink from the bottle, and can only wonder what else Rig was hiding from me. I know he helped Diana escape with fucking Doris right by his side. Traitors. I kick the door open with my boot, pitching forward as it easily gives way. It still looks exactly the same here. I never changed the room, his stuff is still here, as if he'll be back any second. The club doesn't really know what happened to Rig and it has to stay that way. He was my little brother, after all. Blood in, blood out, and that means something to a motorcycle club. If they only knew...

A simple room with a queen bed, small bathroom, and a dresser. I never bothered coming in here after he was gone, none of it matters to me. I sway on my feet, drinking more from the bottle until it's almost empty and then sending it flying across the room to watch it shatter above the dresser in a mess of tequila and broken tiny pieces of glass.

"Where did you send her, Rig?" I mutter to myself in anger, catching myself on the edge of his bed before I trip, sending up dust as I lower myself to the mattress as the room spins.

Taking a small baggie out from the front breast pocket of my leather cut, I dump the white powder on his night-stand and scrabble through the rest of my wallet to cut the cocaine into a thin line, but can't find my credit card. Opening the nightstand drawer, I rumble through the contents until I come across a photo.

Finally.

Feeling my hands shaking, I quickly line up the pure coke and bend down to snort it through my nose in a straight line. Taking a deep breath, I fall against the mattress and stare at the ceiling with thoughts of how I should kill Cruz. I can make it seem like an accident. No one would be able to understand why I just shot my vice president for no reason, and I can't tell them the truth. I have too much at stake. I clench my fists and feel something dig into my palm. Bringing the object up to eye level, I squint at the photo. It's Rig, taken probably a decade ago at one of our yearly cookouts that the charters throw every once and awhile. It's always been a waste, but Rig argued it's a way to keep your enemies close, to find out what they are up to behind chained fences. He should have taken his own advice. He's always been a smart man. I sent him to the other clubs to talk business and it looks like he had some other charters on his side. The other man in the photo seems familiar, tan and tall with brown and purple eyes. Where have I seen him before? Did we do business with him? The longer I stare at the photo, the more the patch on his cut becomes clear.

Hell's Devils.

That's where Doris was before she came to my club. I remember Rig talking about that territory charter once. We did some trading, guns I believe, but I never knew Rig was that close with the prez. A throat clearing in the doorway has me looking away from the photo to see Poe glancing around, inspecting the damage with a raised eyebrow. He won't say shit. He knows his place.

"Better be good," I say harshly, staring at him with murder on my mind if he doesn't start talking.

"Cruz followed a trail, they met up with a trucker who dropped off a girl at a bus station downtown. Nix believes it's Tillie but here's the thing. An employee at the station gave her two tickets, one for New York and another for Los Angeles. Cruz is leaving a trail of bodies in his wake-" Poe keeps talking but my attention is on the wrinkled photo in my hand.

He stops talking as I chuckle, grabbing my stomach until tears roll down my face and into my beard.

"Prez?" Poe asks warily, taking a step out of the room as I turn to grin at him like the cat that ate the canary.

"Get Whiskey, we're going to visit another charter." My

voice comes out eager, ominous as I stand up with a stumble, and my boots crunch over the pieces of glass on the floor.

You thought you were smarter than me, brother, but how wrong you were.

"Which charter?" Poe asks, eyeing me as he texts Whiskey on his phone.

"Hell's Devils, Los Angeles."

You can run but you can't hide from me.

CHAPTER 14

Tey

"Why are we here again?" Tillie asks, her breath hot against my ear as we walk deeper into the tunnel side by side

"Quiet, sugar butt, or you'll scare the rats away," I snicker as she yelps as something skitters across the ground and she grips my bicep, her nails digging in.

"I hate you," she hisses, but I notice her breathing picking up in short pants and she's plastered to my side like she wants to crawl into my skin.

I'd allow that, let her carve me up so she can crawl inside. I'd be able to keep her close.

"It's just a rave, nothing to worry about," I lie, there's plenty to worry about tonight.

It took days but Logan finally got a response back from Dom. This is our first meeting, the first time coming face to face with the man that looks just like Logan's mom's killer. I've heard on the streets that Dom is the spitting image of his father, and my gut is telling me that blood will be spilled tonight. I don't know why I have an obsession with blood, but it always leaves me in a trance where I can't look away. It excites me.

I think my very first memory of seeing blood was when I was just four years old. It's also the oldest memory of my birth mom. Her face is always blurry in that one memory but I know it's her by the sound of her voice that still plays in my head, the sweet scent of vanilla that always seems to make me pause to breathe in deeply. I can't remember much but I'm pretty positive I was at a carnival that day. Flashing lights, laughter, cotton candy, but what sticks out most is when my mom put a bandaid on my knee after I fell off my bike. Her voice is so clear that I sometimes stop and look around as if she's right there with me.

"There, there, little bug. It's only a tiny scratch." She blew on my scraped knee that dripped with blood, cooling the sting.

"But it hurts." Tears fall down my cheeks as I stare at the blood pooling out of my skin, looking like it will never stop.

"For now it does, but you know what? It's going to stop. It's going to heal, and one day it will be completely gone, like it was never there to begin with." She places the bandaid right over my cut, covering the blood so I can't see it any more, as if it was never really there, just like she said.

I think my obsession all started from that moment because whenever I see blood, I don't want to cover it. I want to see why it's seeping out of the skin, I want it to never stop. She was right, my mom, it does heal, but only for appearances. Years later you can still feel the pain like it was just yesterday. I want to feel pain everyday, it's the only reason I know I'm still breathing.

I'm fucked in the head, but then again, who isn't?

"Hey, you okay?" Tillie asks, her body shivering next to me as her eyes dart around the dark tunnel.

I realize I've stopped walking, the guys shadows keep moving ahead as they follow the glow sticks placed on the ground to find the tunnel with the rave. I can hear Tillie gulp loudly and she shivers again.

"Are you afraid of the dark?" I ask seriously, knowing we are all afraid of something.

"Yes, but don't tell anyone I said that." She squeezes my arm and squares her shoulders before walking in front of me, her heels clicking on the wet cement.

She sticks out like a sore thumb, even in the dark. She's the only one wearing white and black while the rest of us are dressed in black from head to toe. The mesh, black, fishnet crop top over her white bra is making my brain run in circles. Anything white would be pretty splashed in red. It's the same for her spandex, tight white shorts that ride up between her buttcheeks. It's enough that I can see her asscheeks peaking through each time she takes a step. I'm tempted to kill Logan for picking out this outfit. Did he really have to pick out white clothing that looks incredible and sexy against her smooth caramel skin? The white high heel boots that stop just below her knees are driving me crazy, I keep picturing them wrapped around my waist. I shake my head and jog to catch up to her.

"Why the dark? It's the perfect place to hide." I love the dark, knowing I can be there without being seen.

"Bad things happen in dark places. You could be stuck there and never see the light of day again," she whispers softly and almost bumps into Logan's back as he pauses at the edge of the tunnel.

Loud music thumps ahead, making the ground

beneath our feet shake... who knew the tunnels under the city could be used to party? I wonder if we can use them to transport drugs? I'll have to ask Logan later. Three people with black clothing and white masks stand in front of us. Their bodies are covered in neon paint that stands out against the dark, and I'm guessing by the buckets of paint at their feet, we're about to be covered too.

"La Demonio." Logan's voice comes out stoic yet hard, and I can see his muscles tensing.

It's going to be a long fucking night.

One of the masked guys pulls out his phone, the whites of his eyes staring at us as he mutters in Spanish to whoever is on the other line. After he hangs up, he reaches down and grabs a paint brush from the bucket with neon colors of pinks, oranges, and blues. He flicks the brushes at us until our bodies are covered from head to toe before walking away from us, not saying a word as he disappears farther down the tunnel where the music is coming from. I guess we're meant to follow after him. I'm tempted to put these assholes in their place for showing us disrespect, but Logan hasn't given me the go ahead... yet.

"Don't wander off. Stay with one of us at all times," Nicky tells Tillie in a serious tone and doesn't look away from her until she nods in agreement.

I bite my lip ring, trying not to laugh because he's pretending to not give a shit what happens to her, but he can't hide from me. I see right through him. The moment we enter the rave, it's like a sea of moving colors and loud techno music as our paint starts to glow under the lights. High domed ceilings with flashing, strobe, colored lights shine down on men and women dancing with splattered glowing paint covering their bodies.

I grab Tillie's hand as we start to push through the crowd of people jumping up and down to the music, dancing, as we move towards the other side of the room with the DJ hyping them up. Half-naked girls dance with a drink in their hands as shirtless guys grind up behind them, and a lot of them look blissed out of their minds on ecstasy. Dalton stays in front of us, causing people to move out of his way and give us a clear path. Tillie gasps behind me, making me spin around with plans of murder on my mind.

"Tey, I really want to dance." She grins so wide as the music thumps louder, making everyone scream. She actually pouts when I pull her in front of me to walk towards the guys.

"Later. You can dance your heart out, later," I whisper in her ear and heave a sigh in regret as we stop in front of a group of guards blocking us from going any farther.

"Logan Russo," Logan says, his stance casual as if he's bored.

Nicky stands right next to him, his eyes glancing around everywhere looking for a threat. Just being here is a threat to us. The biggest of the guards eyes us up and down, his gaze pausing on Dalton who just raises an eyebrow in return while crossing his arms over his chest. Basically saying fuck you. I like that.

"Let them through," a deep voice says, with a hint of a husky, smooth Spanish accent.

The guards part like the Red Sea, their jackets pulled back to show they're armed with guns, but I don't give a fuck. I'll kill them all, snap a few necks, and maybe get to use my knife with unicorn tonight. One can only hope. Once the guards move out of the way, red velvet couches are revealed with a large glass coffee table in front of it and sitting right in the middle of that couch is none other than Dom. I'd be able to spot him without ever meeting him. It's the cold, hard look in his eyes that reminds me of myself.

Very interesting.

Dark, almost black eyes roam over our group, and it's like staring into the night sky without a single star in sight. He almost doesn't have any fucking paint on him, damn it, and it makes me roll my eyes as he reaches into the front of his pants, pulling out a gun to place it on the coffee table. Dom pauses his stare on Tillie for a long, hot second, looking her up and down with a small smirk forming at the corner of his mouth, showing his interest. That makes me just pull her closer to my body, claiming my ownership. I'm not afraid to admit when a guy is hot. But I don't want him to be hot, I especially don't want Tillie looking at him. Tattoos start at his knuckles, continuing up his sleeves, and the one symbol at the base of his neck that disappears into the collar of his shirt tells me it's his gang sign. The devil.

He notices me staring at him, and he runs a hand over his dark brown hair that's shaved close to his scalp on the sides, in a way that shows it's a habit of his. Is he nervous or is he trying to give himself something to do instead of reaching for the gun in the middle of the coffee table?

I'm not sure exactly, but I would guess he's in his early twenties. I know he took over from his father at a young age. His light brown skin looks flawless with his black suit and red shirt underneath, making his sinister eyes all the more darker, as if they can see into your soul.

He won't be able to find mine.

He moves his gaze over to Logan and stops there, his eyes narrowing the tiniest bit at the sides, giving away his thoughts. He wants my best friend dead and six feet under for just being in his presence. I knew there would be tension, and trigger finger emotions, because Logan and Dom shouldn't even be in the same room. One of them will probably end up killing the other, one day. Logan won't be the one dead, not going to happen on my fucking watch.

"Russo," Dom says in a bored tone and gestures for us to have a seat as he leans forward with his elbows on his knees... it brings him closer to his gun.

That says a lot. He doesn't trust us and he rightfully shouldn't.

"Do you know her?" Logan cuts right to the chase and points at Tillie as we all sit down like we're in a fucking meeting.

"What?" Tillie asks in confusion and tilts her head as she gazes at Dom.

"We haven't met but, Mama, we should get acquaint-ed." The fucker purrs in that sexy accent of his and flashes her a smile.

I glance at Nicky, his emerald eyes practically glowing with contained rage and he reaches into his jacket, pulling out his gun from the holster to slam it on the table. It draws everyone's attention to him with the guards closing in, and my Nicholas looks seconds away from shooting everyone. I reach out and grip the back of his neck until he glances at me from the corner of his eye.

"Calm down, she's the filling of our oreo. Don't worry." I squeeze his neck one more time. He takes a deep breath and relaxes somewhat while still keeping an eye on everyone.

"Listen, Papi," Tillie says sarcastically and crosses her legs slowly to draw Dom's gaze there. "We won't be getting acquainted. I'm just a whore who will be leaving soon. Let's stick with that shall we?"

"Ah, don't say that, little bitch. You're not just any whore, you're our-" Dalton starts to say, but Logan cuts him off with a quick glare.

"I'm going to cut right to the chase. I don't fucking want to be here and would rather get this over with because I have better things to do." Logan's voice comes out hard and deep, his right trigger finger twitching on his knee. "I've had *shipments* suddenly disappear in the last month, and then more kept going missing. I caught a rat that sang your name, Dom. Are you selling drugs on my streets?"

Dom stares at Logan and rubs his thumb over his lower lip before he busts out laughing. He wipes a few tears from his eyes and slams his fists on the table a second later as his facial expression shifts into fury.

"You have some fucking nerve coming onto my turf, Ese. Are you saying I've been stealing your drugs? Fuck you. Why don't you ask Franco? He knows after he killed my father that I don't deal in that shit. He wouldn't lie to you, his own son. But then again, you can't trust him now, can you?" Dom smirks as Logan grinds his teeth, anger getting the better of him.

His switch is about to flip.

"What the hell do you know?" Logan's face smooths out and he straightens his tie, making sure it's sitting perfectly.

"You don't know?" Dom slowly shakes his head and leans back into the cushions at ease with his arms spread wide on the back of the couch. "A little birdie told me that Franco is getting his hands in too deep, Jin right by his side, as they are both making deals with the Los Muerte gang. Right in your own house, Logan and it's Nicky, right?" Dom questions as he turns his head to look at Nicky.

Shit.

"You're lying. Why would he steal from himself?" Nicky stands up, his fists clenched at his side as he stares down at Dom in anger.

"Isn't it obvious? Power. To start a war. What would it look like to the media if Franco, Chief of police, stopped a gang rival without anyone knowing he's linked to it. I imagine it would help him climb up the ladder." Dom raises a single dark eyebrow as Logan tugs Nicky by the wrist to sit back down.

"He wouldn't do that. The business would link back to him." Logan's voice sounds off, distant.

"Would it? Or would it come back to the person who's running the show as Franco stays behind closed doors? Guess you can never trust who you live with. Makes you question what's true or what's not. Maybe you should be asking how your mother really died," Dom taunts, looking for just the right thing to say for Logan to lose it.

It worked.

Logan quickly stands up, his whole body shaking in anger, and he starts to reach into the back of his waistband for his gun just as Tillie jumps to her feet. She pushes my legs out of the way until she just stops and stares as someone else beats her to Logan's side. *This night has taken a downhill for the worst,* I think to myself with a groan.

Fucking Paris.

CHAPTER 15

Tillie

I've had enough. I can only sit here and be quiet for only so long before these idiots kill each other. I'm usually one to sit back, not get involved from years of lessons to mind my own business. I was just about to get in between them, not fully understanding what's going on, except that they are in the middle of a fucking rave with plenty of witnesses. I doubt most would open their mouths, I mean, hello... we're surrounded by men who keep flashing their guns around. But I never get the chance to tell Logan to sit his ass down because a flash of pink and blonde hair launches at him and glues itself to his side.

Paris.

What the hell? Why is she here? Did he... no. He wouldn't have asked her to be here, not after what we did in Franco's office. Then again, he keeps hurting me when I least expect it, and I continue to fall for it with the guy who acts like he gives a damn about me. I need to knock some sense into myself, this is temporary, and I don't need to keep looking like a fool. Love is for fools. Hope is for fools. I should know better.

"Baby! I'm here! I knew you couldn't stay away for long," she says in a snotty voice, petting the front of Logan's chest, and he just stands there with his whole body tense. He looks down at her with a stiff facial expression, without saying a damn word.

He makes eye contact with me and quickly glances away as he sits back down with a relaxed posture. He fucking pulls Paris onto his lap, her arm wrapping around his neck in a possessive gesture as she smiles smugly at me.

"What the fuck knuckle?" Tey growls so quietly under his breath, I don't think I was supposed to hear him.

But yeah! The fuck knuckle is right. I'm embarrassed and hate the way the rest of the guys keep glancing back and forth between us like they expect me to explode into an act of violent jealousy. As if! I don't stoop that low, but I can think of ways to rip out Paris's hair one piece at a time. My fingers are fisted at my side so I'm not tempted to launch at Logan, kick him in the balls until he's singing soprano, and rip apart Paris like a rabid dog. I'm a freaking lady so I'll just sit here with a smile plastered on my face like nothing is wrong.

"I'll only say this once, Dom. One time for you to understand. Don't underestimate me. If you try to cross me, or what's mine, I'll end you." Logan makes that warning clear, never taking his gaze off Dom.

"What's yours? Your business means nothing to me, I have my own. What could I possibly take away from you? Not them, they can handle their own. I've heard stories,"

Dom wanders his gaze to Nicky, Tey, and Dalton, then finally pauses on me with a small curl of his plump lips. "Her? Does she mean something to you, Ese?"

I'm about to answer him, tell him to mind his own Goddamn business, but Paris opens her mouth.

"Her?" She points towards me and laughs while stroking the back of Logan's neck with her other hand. "She wishes. Tillie here is nothing but trash, straight from the gutter. She follows them around like a lost puppy and they only keep her around because she easily spreads her legs. They'll get over you soon and I'll be here still." Paris grins like she's won, and maybe she has.

My breath stalls in my chest, I swear the music stops, everything narrowing down until only Logan is in my sight. I stare at him, willing him to say something. Anything. But he just glances away from me with his jaw ticking and holds Dom's stare as he answers him.

"She's just a slut, like Paris said. She won't be around much longer. Sit down, Tillie, you're embarrassing me," Logan says without looking at me as Paris giggles, whispering something in his ear.

After hearing his words, I realized I never sat back down. I'm standing here like a pathetic person, wishing for a different answer, one I'm probably never going to get. When I glance around, I notice Nicky glaring down at his gun with his hands curled into fists on his knees. Dalton and Tey are on the edge of their seats but neither of them says anything either, not looking me in the eye.

"I see," Dom slowly nods, his dark eyes staring a little too closely at me... seeing everything.

That's when anger starts to boil under my skin, causing my heart to race and my only focus is to make Logan, all of them, feel my pain. Step one of revenge, make these assholes jealous and I know just how to do that. They aren't the only ones who can give me pleasure, my body is awakening and I'm testing my limits tonight.

The DJ starts playing *Pony* by Ginuwine and my center of attention rests on the sexy, dangerous man that hates Logan. I plaster a fake smile on my lips, making sure to look at Logan, who narrows his honey eyes like he knows I'm up to something and I reach behind me to untie the mesh skirt around my waist.

"Of course, Logan. I'm a *slut* so it only seems natural that I act like one." The skirt drops to the ground as I place a knee on the coffee table, leaving me only in the tight white booty shorts and fishnet top covering my matching bra.

"Don't even think about-" Logan stops himself from saying anything else and puts his hand up to stop the rest of the guys as they start to stand. "Let her be. She knows her place."

I flash him an innocent smile, my grin spreading across my face until it hurts and I turn back to look at Dom. He sits here with his legs spread, leaning back into the cushions and raises an eyebrow at me with a smirk. He knows what I'm going to do, crooking his index finger at me. My body relaxes, letting the music take over like it's always done. Placing my other knee onto the table, I start crawling across it slowly towards Dom and pause in the middle of the table. Running my hands up my body, I grab the hem of the fishnet top and drag it over my head to toss towards Tey's face.

"What the hell is she doing?!" I hear Paris screech, but I'm hardly paying attention, making sure to not break eye contact with Dom.

I uncurl my legs from underneath me, bringing myself

into the splits as I toss my hair with a flip. I hear Dalton groan from behind me as my ass bounces up and down, knowing he has a clear view of me. Good. He deserves to be tortured for not saying anything to defend me. Coming to my knees again, I spin around on the table and glare at Logan before laying down. Arching my back, my eyes catch Dom's as my head tips back, and I can see that dark, glistening look of lust in his eyes as he stares at me. Why does that turn me on, making my shorts damp. Sticking my feet straight in the air, I spread my legs wide and run my hands over my breasts.

"Tillie," Nicky growls low in that deep voice that never fails to make me shiver.

"I'm going to come in my pants," Tey says with a moan.

I ignore him, everyone around me. I can block everything out surrounding me when I'm like this, in my element. Putting on a show. It's like an instinct that never goes away. Flipping back around, I crawl the rest of the way across the table and climb to my feet, standing between Dom's legs.

As the song blares the lyrics, '*Someone who knows how to ride, without even falling off*,' I quickly drop to a crouch facing him. Grabbing his strong thighs, I spread my legs and tip my head back as I slowly move my hips side to side to give him a clear as hell view of my body.

"Beautiful," Dom mutters in a thick, harsh voice and stares down at me with hooded eyes.

I almost slip, catching myself, because I've been called a lot of things while dancing for strangers but not beautiful. Climbing to my feet, I place my knees on either side of his hips and feel his big hands slip around my waist towards my ass. He grabs a handful, bringing me closer until my asscheeks are resting right over his dick. I notice right away how hard he is through his pants, the long length thick running down his thigh. I roll my hips in sync with the song, grinding down on him as I lean back while running my hands down my stomach. Quickly popping back up, I grasp a fistful of his hair until he has no choice but to look up at me. He flashes a lopsided grin and squeezes my ass, making me shift my hips again over him. My body moves, rolling my hips in a figure eight to the song and actually loving every second of it. He's going to have a wet spot on the front of his jeans by the time I'm done. My shorts are riding up the front each time I grind down on him. The fabric causes friction and his dick hits my clit in just the right spot each time I shift over him. It's hard to hold back a moan of pleasure. I release my hold on his hair and bend backwards again as I quicken my pace, grinding hard. He chuckles darkly at whatever he sees over my shoulder and leans forwards to lick a long line, starting between my breasts and making his way up to my throat with the flat of his tongue. God, he smells good.

"That's enough!" Logan shouts behind me, the sound of his tone is hard and angry, with an underlayer of jealousy.

Good. He deserves worse.

Climbing off of Dom's lap, I turn away to face the man who gets on my very last nerves. He's standing on the other side of the table, breathing hard like he just ran a marathon, and ignoring Paris who is shouting at his feet where he seems to have dumped her.

"It was just getting good," Dalton mumbles, ever the pervert.

"You cunt! Why can't you just leave?!" Paris screeches at me and jumps to her feet, literally stomps her foot like a spoiled princess as she glares up at Logan for him to do something.

"You have something to say?" I raise a brow and cross my arms as I wait.

His finger twitches on his thigh, his eyes hard and lethal as he stares at me without ever opening his mouth.

"Fine. That's what I thought," I say with a fake smile and uncross my arms as I lower my body, planting my ass right on Dom's lap again, but facing forward this time. "Papi." My voice comes out raspy and suggestive.

Dom slides his fingers through my hair, moving it over to one side, leaving room to rest his chin on my shoulder as he slides his arm around my waist while the other one rubs up and down my thigh.

"Yes, little queen." His arm tightens and he lifts me farther up his lap until I'm comfortable, leaving me feeling secure, surprisingly.

"Tillie, don't call him Papi," Dalton says in a gruff tone and stares hard at the arm around my waist like he wants to rip off Dom's limbs.

Nicky huffs a sigh next to Logan, grabbing his gun to slip back into his jacket, and starts to walk around the table just as Tey does. Both of them coming at me from either side like sharks sniffing out for blood in the open ocean. Shit. I'm in trouble. I can see it in their gazes. Burning jealousy and their breaking point.

"Paris, leave," Logan orders, grinding his teeth and not bothering to look as Dalton grabs her elbow and shoves her at a guard who pushes her away like she has a disease.

She stumbles with her mouth hanging wide open, completely shocked. She blends in with the crowd and Dalton walks back over, dusting his cut off, as if she left a disease behind.

"If you don't want her, I'll gladly take her," Dom drawls out in a sexy rumble, as he climbs to his feet with me and keeps me close like he doesn't plan on letting go anytime soon.

"She's our property and no one touches what's mine," Logan says in a frightening tone that also sounds very fucking possessive.

"That's what I thought. Tell me, mama, do you want to stay with them?" Dom asks in my ear, loud enough for Tey and Nicky to hear, and making them freeze as they wait for my answer.

I suddenly feel trapped, the weight of their stares becoming too much for me. My gaze shifts left and right, stopping on the dance floor. I'm not sure what I'm seeing, maybe the flashing lights are playing tricks on me, but the man standing on the edge of the dance floor keeps glancing over here as he pretends to survey the crowd. Right at Dom. My body tightens, a pending doom feeling giving me chills. I watch as if in slow motion as the guy turns fully towards me, letting me see the gang tattoo on the right side of his neck. He reaches behind him, his arm coming back just as fast and starts to lift something metal that flashes in the strobe light. He's pointing it in this direction.

"Gun!" I'm moving as I shout, grabbing the glock in front of me off the table and aiming without thinking.

My finger pulls the trigger, making my body jerk backwards at the force and crash into Dom. The sound of the gun going off makes the crowd scream in panic and everyone starts running in every direction to escape. I gasp in a startled breath, it's been a long time since I even held a gun in my hands. When Uncle Rig was around still. Slowly blinking, I watch people trip over the body laying on the ground, not even pausing once to see if he needs help. But the bullet hole in his forehead says enough. Can't help the dead.

"You fucking set us up, Dom?" I've never seen Logan this angry as he pulls me out of Dom's muscular arms and shoves me at Tey, who easily grabs a hold of me.

It's like watching a standoff, any minute one of them is going to pull out their guns and fire, but too bad for Dom because I'm still holding his. Logan has his fist clenched on the front of Dom's shirt while his other hand places a gun to rest against his enemy's forehead. I crouch down between them, stretching my hand out to give Dom his gun back. Fair fight and all. I don't want Logan to die but maybe a shot to the thigh would make me feel better.

"Yes, I intentionally had some asshole come into my rave and point his gun at me." Dom's sexy lips curl in a sneer, sarcasm heavy in his tone.

"It's time to play, kitten. Buckle up," Tey announces and smacks a wet kiss on my cheek just as he pulls out his unicorn to tie the tail around his gun.

At first I'm confused as Logan flips the table in front of me and Dom drags me down behind it just as a gunshot blasts through the air, splattering wood pieces every-where. I watch, eyes wide, as Dalton and Nicky spring over the couches and start firing into the crowd.

"Stay down and don't move. You did good," Logan hesitantly says to me and stands up to fire his gun rapidly while looking hot as fuck.

Something about this man and the confidence he oozes is a big turn on, unfortunately. I'd rather he was butt ugly, so I wasn't attracted to him at least, but that's just my luck.

"Stick with the crazy blond over there. Don't worry,

mama, I'll be back in a flash. It's just a little gang rivalry," Dom smirks and leaves me speechless as he quickly places his perfectly, thick sculptured lips against mine, then he's gone.

"What in the..." I mutter to myself and shake my head in bewilderment.

I turn my head, seeing Tey laughing with his head thrown back as he fires his gun over and over again without looking. Jesus. I'm just going to stay in my safe little hideout, not worrying about anything as the gang war blazes around me.

"Shit!" Tey shouts suddenly, his gun making a clicking noise that lets me know the chamber is empty.

My whole body flinches as a gang member tackles him in a quarterback move. Both of them go down and roll until Tey shoves his boot against the guy's chest to send him flying. I watch as Tey sits up and quickly grabs his gun before I can blink... the gun with his unicorn on it. It's head is barely hanging by a thread, it must have ripped as he was tackled. I haven't seen that look on Tey's face before. It's sad, devastated, and that sends me into a rage at seeing him like that. While Tey's distracted, the same gang member strides up to him and places his gun on the back of my crazy psycho.

I don't fucking think so!

Grabbing the nearest object near me, which happens to be a beer bottle that rolled over here as everyone on the dance floor ran around in freaking circles. I don't think, I just act. I'm jumping out from behind the table and leaping onto to the couch to dive off the ledge, attaching myself onto the gang member's back like a fucking spider monkey. I bash the beer bottle over his head while screaming like a banshee even when he falls to his knees.

"How dare you touch his unicorn! Look what you did, you pencil dick!" I'm breathing hard by the time I climb to my feet and flip my hair out of my eyes only to freeze as Tey stares at me with a lost look in his eyes, heartache.

"I can fix it." I promise as I grab the unicorn out of his hand and examine the damage done to it.

The gunfire is starting to slow down, I can hear both Logan and Dom barking out orders behind me, but none of that matters right now. It's about never wanting to see that look in his eyes again, lost and hopeless, it's one that I know oh so well. I've had enough moments in my life where I question what else could happen to me. How much more can I handle? I'm not letting his psycho ass go through that.

"You're not allowed to leave, Tillie. It's too late." He actually says my name in a hard tone that makes the hair on the back of my neck stand up.

Usually, he's always using nicknames to drive me crazy, but I secretly like them.

"What's too late?" I cock my head to the side as I shove the stuffing back into the unicorn, not fully understanding what he's saying and why my heart is racing at his words.

"You'll find out soon enough." That's all he says, and I breathe easier as that wicked smile spreads across his lips.

I take the hair tie off my wrist, wrap it around the stuffed animal's head a few times, until it doesn't look like a decapitated unicorn. Good enough for now until I can sew it back for him.

He takes the unicorn back, carefully stuffing it in his pants back pocket and reaches over his head to grab the back of his black shirt in his fist. He pulls it off, leaving his hair messy, and helps me by placing his shirt over my head and down my body until it falls to my knees. Any normal woman couldn't help but stare at him, even with gunshots blasting around them, because hello, abs. Tight, chiseled abs that are meant to be touched.

"Are you kidding me? We don't have time for this right now. Tey, go with Nicky to the warehouse. He's over there sitting on the soon to be dead fucker, after you guys ask him some questions. I want to know why the west side gang is trying to start a war." Logan's jaw is clenched tight as he grabs my hand and starts leading us to the exit of the tunnel with Dalton close behind, while I try not to stumble over dead bodies littered on the dance floor.

"Until next time, mama." Dom looks just as pissed off as he kicks a body on the floor but he takes a second to wink at me as we walk past him.

"Not a word," Logan demands, I can practically feel the anger radiating off him.

"Did you have fun tonight, little bitch?" Dalton snickers behind me, grabbing my other hand and not letting go, even when I shoot him a nasty look.

"Not really. I really wanted to dance," I sigh in disappointment as we cross the dance floor, wishing it wasn't covered in blood and the DJ hadn't run off.

"You were dancing all right, and don't think we'll forget it for one second." I can hear the promise of retaliation in his gravelly voice.

Damn it. It was just one small, little itty bitty lap dance. So why does he care?

"Get over it! You don't get to talk about me, or to me, that way and get away with it." I poke at Logan's chest as we stand in his driveway, matching him glare for glare.

"Get over it? Get over it?!" he shouts at me with anger coloring his tone, his face flushed as his honey eyes darken.

This is the first time I've actually seen him use a real emotion, he always seems to hide from everyone else so he appears calm and collected. Anger is a good thing, it's what makes us human. It shows we actually are passionate about something, care enough that we release that pent up emotion just to feel better. Wait... why is he angry at me? I'm not the one who brought Paris along and tried to make a point by flaunting her in front of everyone.

"Yeah, I'm just going to, well, uh, go make us some food before we drive to the warehouse... how about you go get that paint off, princess?" Dalton rubs the back of his neck, watching as Logan and I just stand there glaring at each other. "Alright then."

Dalton whistles as he walks into the dark house, heading towards the kitchen, and disappears around the corner. I continue to stand here with my arms crossed, enjoying the way he actually looks uncomfortable as he shuffles and clears his throat. I'm waiting for any excuse for hurting me to come out of Logan's stupid mouth. I've had enough of his back and forth games. I should just tell him the truth, who my father is and why I'm here but I don't want that pity look to be directed at me. I'd rather he think I'm here to ruin his life, it makes it easier.

"Why are you so frustrating?" I grumble under my breath, shaking my head in annoyance, and head into the house without looking back because I'm done with his shit.

"We aren't done talking, baby girl," he growls as he follows behind me, matching me step for step up the stairs, right on my heels.

"Logan, I swear to God, I'm going to cut off your precious, big penis while you're sleeping and stuff it in your mouth if you don't leave me alone right now. I'm so tired of this. Go see your perfect Paris, and leave me alone." I'm at my breaking point, all I want to do is curl up in a ball and cry.

I want to cry for hours, days, maybe even years. To take back what's mine, to let it all out until I'm gasping for breath. My hands shake as I fling my bedroom door open and head towards the bathroom to wash off the itchy, cracking paint.

"Are you jealous?" I can hear the smile in his voice, the tone making my shoulders hunch in embarrassment.

He grabs my wrist and spins me around, into his arms, not letting go, even as I pound on his chest. He raises my chin with his index finger so I have no choice but to stare into his honey eyes that always seem to know what I'm thinking, what I'm feeling.

"You are," he says with a sigh and tugs me closer, his hand sliding to the back of my neck. "I had to check, Tillie. To see if he recognized you. I can't let Dom know that you're mine. But it's too late now. I couldn't have it both ways. I had no choice but to bring you, so I thought someone disposable would do as a stand in. Paris means nothing to me and she never will."

"What?" Even to my own ears, I hear the surprise in my voice, wondering if I'm hearing things... There's no way he really wants me without acting like I'm an object.

He runs a hand through his brown hair and steps back to start pacing, muttering to himself until he stops in front of me again as he comes to some sort of conclusion.

"I need to know why you're here. You just need to tell me... I'm losing my mind thinking about you all the time and I shouldn't when you could be my downfall," he rasps out, running a finger down my cheek as he stares intensely into my eyes.

"No. You don't get to say that. You're playing with my emotions and it's messing with my head!" I knock his hand away, my fingers tangle in my hair as I try not to scream in frustration, "What do you want, Logan? What?!" I've had enough, if he wants to keep playing this game then I'm done holding back because my body constantly gravitates towards him.

No more. I'll go full force at him until he's begging for forgiveness.

"I want you! Just you, but I can't trust-I don't know who to trust." He stares up at the ceiling in clear frustration as he takes a deep breath before he glances down at me. He reaches out to grab my wrist, but I knock his hand out of the way before he can touch me.

"You better figure your shit out then because I'm not a toy that you get to decide which way you want to bend me or control me anytime you want. Trust is earned, but I haven't done a damn thing to make you doubt me. This is who I am, take a good look." I hold my hands out to my sides, letting him look at me.

He stares at me as if he wants to sweep me off my feet and throw me on the bed. Hot, needy lust takes over his facial expression as he slowly drags his gaze starting at my feet and slowly moving up, taking his time until he's looking into my eyes again. I know what he sees. Me, drowning in his friend's shirt that hangs at my knees, as the rest of my body is covered in paint, but that doesn't stop his gaze from switching to anger and then going straight into lust. He tries to take a step towards me, but I move my hand in front to rest against his chest before he gets too close.

"No." He freezes before he can come any closer, hearing the way my voice croaks.

"Tillie-" He starts but I cut him off.

"I'm too tired to deal with this right now. If you come any closer, I'm going to cave and that just puts me right back at square one. Let me go." I stare at his chest, not wanting to see the pent up desire and longing in his gaze, knowing I'll break within seconds to give in to him.

He doesn't say a word, the only sound in my bedroom is our breathing that seems to be in sync. I slowly pull away, watching as he takes a small step backwards to give me space. I turn my back on him as I finally walk into the bathroom and shut the door quietly as my chest aches. When will it ever get easier? Will I ever be able to let anyone in without getting hurt? Tears form at the corner of my eyes as I stare into the mirror, hating the look on my face. One of hopelessness and defeat. Turning on the tap water, I splash my face until all the paint is gone and washing down the sink with the rest of my night. A loud thump comes on the other side of the door followed by a groan, making me wish he would just leave me alone. I can't tonight. I just can't deal with this right now.

With a sigh, I swing the door open, planning on ripping him a new one until he's storming out of my room but I'm only met with silence and the dark. Chills sweep up and down my body as I rub my arms. Walking towards the curtains where the moonlight is shining through, I'm about to open them when I trip over something on the floor. Crashing on my hands and knees, I swear under my breath and reach up to rip the curtains open and turn around to see what I fell over. My breath stalls in my chest as I see a pant leg sticking out from the other side of the bed. Crawling forward, I see Logan passed out and a pool of blood forming around his head. Scrambling towards him, I lean down and place my head against his chest. The steady thump under my ear makes it easier to breathe. What happened to him? I skim my fingers behind his neck as I lean back up and my fingers come away warm and wet at the base of his skull.

"Logan? Wake up!" I shake his shoulders roughly and feel relieved when he groans in pain but his eyes don't open.

"Tillie, come out, come out wherever you are." A voice so familiar, one that I could never forget, suddenly echoes almost like a whisper of the wind, taunting me from somewhere inside the house... Payne.

No. No. No. He's found me.

I quickly look around and my whole body shudders at how the walls seem to be closing in on me as my breathing comes faster and faster. There is no escaping this time, I'm going to die tonight. He's here inside the house. I glance down at Logan as his eyelashes flutter, noticing how quiet the room seems. I can't leave him out here like this, they'll put a bullet through his brain. This is all my fault, I shouldn't have come here. To keep Logan alive like this, for me to find him still breathing tells me enough. This is Payne's way of getting inside my mind to fuck with me, he's playing with his food, which just happens to be me. He's going to kill everyone who's ever helped me right in front of my very eyes and there's nothing I can do about it. He knows me well. I never was any good at my obedience lessons, and I rebelled with everything inside my body. He's provoking me to come out, to show myself. Logan can't stay here. Payne really will torture him in front of me before he kills him to make me suffer.

I stand on shaking legs and bend down to grab him under his armpits. I don't know how people do it in the movies, moving a heavy body around without breaking a sweat. I start dragging him across the room, a few feet towards my closet and his breathing picks up as if he's in pain the whole time I'm moving him. I pause and take a deep breath as sweat coats my skin even though I'm cold, beyond freezing. With one more pull, I let go of him and fall on my ass in the huge closet. His head thumps against the floor and his eyes snap open as he sucks in a sharp pained breath.

"Get out of here. Run," he whispers, his lashes fluttering as he tries to focus on me.

"There's no escaping, Logan," I reply back, my voice drained of any emotion because this is finally it... the end for me.

Everything I did was for nothing. That one small chance of freedom is already gone. At least I finally got to live for a little these last few weeks. I found a way to survive where I wasn't constantly hiding in fear. I made friends for the first time ever that made me laugh. I found pleasure that I never thought was possible for someone like me. I found a strength I didn't know I possessed, standing up for myself against these assholes who tried to bring me to my knees, but here I am. I'm still standing.

"Will you just listen for once! Run, Tillie," Logan says in a commanding, raspy voice just before he passes out.

Run? That's the thing...there isn't anywhere to run. All I have left is to face Payne head on. But, even if I die, I'm bringing him with me, straight into hell.

I search underneath Logan, feeling the gun tucked

into the back of the waistband of his pants, and pull it out from under him. I stare almost numbly down at it... it takes just one bullet to end it all. Glancing down at Logan, I regret that things couldn't have turned out a different way. He could have learned to trust me and I could have had him on his knees even just once as he learned I'm not his enemy but those things won't be happening. Leaning down, I rest my lips against his ear, only so he can hear my voice even though he's passed out.

"You asshole, I hate you for making me feel. You won't ever see me again and you won't ever know this but thank you." I stay like this for a second, trying to gather my courage to get up and face my father.

I reach into his pants pocket and grab his cellphone as I stand up. Placing his thumb on the screen, I scroll through his contacts and hit dial once I find who I'm looking for.

"Logan," Nicky's deep voice says through the phone, oddly calming me.

"It's me. I needed someone to know I'm going to disappear. Demon Jokers are in the house. Logan is in my bedroom closet knocked out and bleeding. I don't know where Dalton is..." I trail off, closing my eyes and praying he's not dead.

It takes a lot to take down my giant biker, but Payne doesn't do his business alone. I know he will have brought some of the club members with him.

"Stay right the fuck there. Don't leave the closet and, Tillie... if this is a trap, I'm going to have to kill you." His voice sounds strained and he curses in Japanese under his breath.

"Nicky," I choke out and stifle the sob trying to break free. "I need to make sure Dalton isn't... I can't leave him down there by himself. By the time you get here, I'll already be gone. Tell Tey I'm sorry I can't fix his unicorn. I'm sorry." The sob I've been trying to hold back breaks free as I hang up, cutting off whatever he was shouting.

Dropping the phone by Logan, I bite my lip to stay quiet as tears keep trailing down my face. I shouldn't ever have been born, this is an endless cycle of me going back right where I belong. I'll kill myself before they can drag me back to that hellhole. I take a deep, shuddering breath and walk quietly out of the closet, shutting the door behind me.

I'll say it again and again, I hate the dark. Every dark shadow looks like it's going to jump at me and drag me away until I'm just a memory, stuck in the darkness. Creeping out of my room, I don't hear anything but my own breathing and the sound of my teeth grinding to stop them from chattering. Glancing up and down the hallway, nothing moves and I step out, heading towards the stairs. Passing the doorways, I stick close to the walls and bring the gun up each time I look inside. At the top of the stairs, I freeze, feeling as if someone is staring at me. I pinch my eyes closed in dread, opening them a second later to confront my worst fear and slowly spin on my heels.

"You didn't think you could hide forever, did you?" Poe stands a foot away from me, his leather cut with the Demon Jokers patch mocking me.

Just hearing his voice causes me to flinch, almost dropping the gun as I aim it at his face. He grins when he sees my hand shaking, making the gun tremble, and steps closer.

I pull the trigger without thinking and only hear the clicking sound in return. Nothing happened. The blood drains from my face and it feels like I'm back in the basement, everything narrowing down to this moment.

"I'm very disappointed, Til. After all that training on how to use a gun, you don't check to see if the chamber is empty?" He shakes his head, clicking his tongue, and brings his own gun out faster than I can track it.

He whips it towards my face and slams it down on top of my head, making my knees buckle under the blow. Grabbing my head, my fingers come away wet as my stomach turns. I end up throwing up at his feet, everything a blur as he snarls in disgust and grabs a fist full of my hair. I whimper as he starts walking down the stairs, leaving me no choice but to follow. I scramble to my legs, almost falling again with how dizzy I am. He whistles, ignoring my weak attempts to swing at him but the angle he has my head leaves it impossible to reach him. I leave scratch marks on the walls as he drags me down, trying to slow him down. I'm not ready to face the devil.

He thrusts me down hard to the ground once we reach the first floor, and takes intimidating steps towards me as I crawl backwards on my hands and feet to get away from him. Each step he takes sounds loud to my ears, it's a noise that keeps jolting me into moving faster. I bump into a wall and he looms over me before bending down, clasping his hand around my throat like a collar locking in place. He lifts me off the ground by the neck, ignoring me as I gasp for breath and scratch at his forearms as my feet drag against the floor. Poe continues walking forward, leading us into the kitchen and slamming me backwards over the kitchen island. I claw at his hand, seeing spots dance in my vision and I know if my eyes close, I'll wake up to see myself living in my worst nightmare.

"Nice of you to join us, Tillie." Payne's voice skitters

down my spine, making me wish Poe would keep squeezing until he crushes my neck. "Release her, she doesn't get to escape that easily. I have many plans for her," Payne chuckles in the same gruff, sinister laugh he's always used just before he started his obedience lessons.

Fingers unwrap from my neck and I'm able to draw in a deep breath as I cough. I realize I'm always in this position where I can only ever see a ceiling as I'm placed on my back. Poe grabs the front of my shirt and makes me stand up while turning me to face the other side of the kitchen.

Dalton starts struggling in the chair he's tied to once our eyes make contact. His hands are bound behind his back and a piece of tape covers his mouth but he doesn't stop trying to shout. My lips tremble as I try not to cry when I notice his shirt is torn at his side, the material soaked with his blood and dripping onto the floor around him. Movement to his right finally has me glancing at the monster I call Father. I don't know what I expected, but it's not what I was imagining when I thought about seeing him again. Payne looks like the reaper is going to claim him any second now, his skin is sickly pale and heavy dark circles rests under his eyes.

"I went through a lot of trouble to find you." Payne toys with the knife in his bloody hands and clasps a hand on Dalton's shoulder in a threatening move that says he'll kill him without breaking a sweat, as he waits for me to speak. "Nothing to say to your dear old dad?"

I stay silent, my mind racing a mile a minute as I try to think of a way out of this, but I keep coming up blank. Footsteps to my right has me glancing at the mudroom, to see Whiskey striding towards me without planning to stop. I try to back up but Poe tightens his hold on the front of my shirt and lifts until I'm standing on my toes just as Whiskey grabs my arms to hold me still.

"Did you miss us? It's been a while since I've been between those creamy thighs. That night we all took a turn squeezing into that tight virgin hole of yours still plays in my head like it was just yesterday. I guess raping you never tamed your rebellious side, but we still have time to give it another try." Whiskey winks at me and lifts his hand to run down my cheek but I quickly whip my head away before he can touch me.

My stomach turns, feeling vomit climb up my throat again and sweat rolling down my spine, but I try to keep my face blank so he doesn't know how terrified I am. I can't seem to focus my gaze on anything, but the moment I glance at Dalton, my world seems to stop and all I can see is him. His eyes burn with fury, his jaw tight, and it looks like he's not breathing as he stares back at me.

"How did you find me?" I croak out, my voice sounding dead to my own ears.

"I paid a little visit to Hell's Devils and congratulations, boy, it seems you're the club's new President. I have to say, you're the spitting image of your old man. He had that same look on his face just before I killed him." He gestures to Dalton's face and I can't look away as Dalton bellows behind his gag in rage, reminding me of a caged animal, and his eyes widen with deep sorrow.

The chair groans under him as he struggles with the ties, his face turning pale as his blood keeps seeping out of his wound, soaking his shirt and the chair under him. Sweat rolls down his temple from his hairline and he gazes at me with violet eyes that promise chaos once he's free. I know he's imagining all sorts of ways to kill Payne, but I wouldn't blame him if I'm part of that plan, because it's all my fault that Dalton's dad is dead. I led the devil right to their doorstep.

It's all my fault.

"You fucking monster!" I scream at Payne with fury in my eyes, tears falling down my cheeks as I see the devastation in Dalton's eyes when I look back at him.

Payne just laughs and suddenly punches Dalton in the stomach, right over the area that's bleeding. I cry out, struggling between Poe and Whiskey, but they just tighten their holds on my arms. Locking me in place so no matter what I do, I can't escape.

"Bring her here, he'll get to watch. Tell me, boy, did you fuck her? Most of my club members already did, all but one." Payne taunts Dalton as Poe drags me by the shirt over to my father and shoves me face down over the counter so I have a clear view of Dalton.

Payne walks around the other side of Dalton's chair and comes to stand behind me. This is going to hurt, it always does. He's going to torture me right in front of my biker and there's nothing I can do to stop this. No one can. I can't see Payne but I feel something cold and wet rest against the top of my spine. The cutting of my shirt down the middle is like a gunshot going off and blood fills my mouth as I bite my tongue to hold in a whimper that desperately wants to escape. My shirt falls off to the sides, drifting off my shoulders to expose my back. Dressed only in my underwear and bra, my breathing picks up as the hairs on my arms stand on end.

"I've waited a long time to do this, you almost robbed me of this chance, but I'm going to claim this fucking cunt while your lover boy over here watches," Payne whispers in my ear, my whole body locking up tight as the air is sucked out of my lungs.

No! Not again. This can't be happening. Wake up, Tillie! Just a dream... it has to be.

I try to push up on my arms as I start to lose my mind, my legs kicking with everything I have, hoping to connect with any flesh but Poe and Whiskey hold my arms down as Payne kicks my legs apart with his boots.

"Why? How can you do th-this to your own daughter?" My teeth chatter, fear eating me alive as I ask a question I've never thought would come out of my mouth.

I feel everything, wishing I couldn't, and all I can do is stare at Dalton. His eyes are wild, going crazed as he keeps shouting behind his gag at me, but words don't matter. I know he's going to see everything and not be able to do anything, but for once I'm not alone. That might be selfish of me but I don't care. His gaze says he's here with me, to not look away as everything else fades away into the background.

"Don't you know?" Payne sneers behind me in mockery, his chuckle evil and haunting as he leans over my body with the sound of a zipper lowering. "I'm not your daddy."

To be continued...

THANK YOU

Thank you my amazing readers for following me along in this series! You okay? How's the cliffhanger going for you? Don't come at me with pitchforks because the story does continue in Part Three! There will be groveling in the next book and it won't be cute or sweet, so prepare yourselves.

I want to thank you guys for giving this series a shot, the first book was draining and difficult to write. Healing, too. Tillie has made it through a lot and I'm glad you guys are rooting for her. The characters will continue to take up space in my head until I'm done writing their stories. The support and encouragement with Dolls and Douchebags really has blown me away. I honestly didn't know it was going to get this much love. So thank you from the bottom of my dark heart.

Penn, my bestie from far away, you are amazing! You kept me going, telling me to keep writing when it felt like I couldn't. My endless worries and needing advice, never once did you tell me to stop bugging the crap out of you at midnight. Love you!

Beta team... Sam, Erica, Jess, and Amelie... I seriously

could not have finished this story without your amazing insight and keeping me laughing. Thank you for putting up with my crazy author ass, lol. Much love, ladies!

Polly. Girl. Cray cray woman in love with Cruz, I love your editing skills but those thirst comments kill me every time. Thank you for making me die with laughter and helping me give these punks a beautiful story.

Emma, I'm so glad you're part of my small little tribe and I'm going to keep you. Best proofreader out there!

If you love/hate this story, please consider leaving a review. Regarding spelling/grammar, feel free to reach out to me in one of the following links below or if you just want to talk about Vicious Punks. Thank you.

Please enjoy this epic drawing I did for the sex scene as I had to explain to Penn what was happening before edits. Lol

STALKING LINKS FOR MADELINE FAY

Facebook Group
Newsletter
Facebook like page
Instagram
TikTok

ABOUT MADELINE FAY

Madeline lives in rural Michigan in a castle with all her fur babies and husband. She loves to read, you'll find her in her tower with her kindle and drinking Boba tea. She has a few addictions, chocolate is her weakness and anything seventies related. She's a hippy at heart. She likes to pretend she's a main character in a Korean drama and listens to kpop, mainly BTS. She has an evil day job, but at night she watches over her city in the shadows and calls herself Batman. Not really but she keeps hoping it might come true one day. She's in her bat cave writing and plotting mad, evil genius stories while sipping some wine.

Printed in Great Britain
by Amazon